Just Shoot Me

The Cowboy Way, Book One

Dean's Story

BECKY McGRAW

This is a work of fiction. Names, characters, places and incidents are products of the author's imagination or are used fictitiously and are not to be construed as real. Any resemblance to actual events, locales, organizations, or persons, living or dead, is entirely coincidental.

JUST SHOOT ME (Cowboy Way, #1) Copyright © February 2014 by Becky McGraw

ISBN-13: 978-1495962202 ISBN-10: 1495962202

All rights reserved. No part of this publication may be reproduced, distributed, or transmitted in any form or by any means, including photocopying, recording, or other electronic or mechanical methods, without the prior written permission of the publisher, except in the case of brief quotations embodied in critical reviews and certain other noncommercial uses permitted by copyright law. For permission requests, write to the publisher, addressed "Attention: Permissions Coordinator," at the address below.

Becky McGraw Books

13057 SPID, Unit A, Box 189
Corpus Christi, TX 78418
www.beckymcgraw.com

Ordering Information:
Quantity sales. Special discounts are available on quantity purchases by corporations, associations, and others. For details, contact the publisher at the address above.

Printed in the United States of America

Be sure to check out all of the books in the
Texas Trouble Series by Becky McGraw:

Book #1 - My Kind of Trouble (Cassie & Luke)
Book #2 - The Trouble With Love (Sabrina & Cole)
Book #3 - Double the Trouble (Karlie & Gabe)
Book #4 - Looking for Trouble (Jess & Wade)
Book #5 - Trouble in Dixie (Katie & Tommy)
Book #6 - Asking for Trouble (Jazzie & Beau)
Book #7 - Chasing Trouble (Jenny & Chase)
Book #8 - Here Comes Trouble (Terri & Joel)
Book #9 - Worth the Trouble (Roxanne & Ethan)
Book #10 - Royal Trouble (Leigh Ann & Wes)
Book #11 - Trouble With the Law (Veronica & Trace)

Coming Soon! New Series
The Cowboy Way
Hope for Christmas
(Cord's Story – novella included in Santa Wore Spurs)
Just Shoot Me (#1, Cowboy Way, Dean's story)

Acknowledgements

Thank you to my Troublemaking friends for making Trouble everywhere you go! And thank you for nicknaming Mr. Cranky Pants! Glad he got his pipes fixed. Love you, ladies.

CHAPTER ONE

"Tina Montgomery," Tina announced, cradling the phone between her shoulder and chin to keep her hands free. She flipped through the pile of glossy photographs again, knowing it was useless. None of these men was her Texas Tomcat. Photographs of professional models pretending to be cowboys were scattered from one end of her desk to the other and none of them was right. They were handsome enough. What was missing though, was the attitude and life experience that would be in a real cowboy's eyes. Toughness.

Those men would never have that. It was what she knew Texas Tomcat needed to be different, to stand out from their biggest competitor, Laramie Western Wear. Even her friend Hope's new husband, Cord Dixon, former Mr. Laramie Jeans himself, was too pretty to fit the bill, in her opinion. All of the models at Laramie were too pretty. Hell, at this point if any of those men was close to what she was looking for, Tina wasn't above making them an offer they couldn't refuse to steal them away.

Maybe she needed to do like Tonya Laramie did to find Cord. Visit the rodeo. But then Tonya Laramie wasn't at those rodeos shopping for cowboys for the same reason as Tina was, if Cord Dixon was to be believed. Mostly, Tonya had been a fixture at the events to find lovers who might work as models in her catalogs. But if she got desperate enough, Tina might just have to buy a pair of boots and try that. If that took trying on a few cowboys for size too, she wouldn't mind that a bit if she found one as good looking as Cord Dixon.

Tina was hard up in more ways than one these days, thanks to her damned sister.

She huffed out a breath. Of the two hundred photographs she'd looked at so far, of all the men she had considered, Tina only had two weak possibilities, so she was almost there. Her time was running out. In two weeks she had to present her marketing plan to the board and her bosses. To convince them to launch this new men's line, she knew her presentation had to be irresistible. Finding the right face, the right marketing strategy for the new line would be the key to accomplish that. She was beginning to lose hope that she would find her Texas Tomcat in time.

Tina couldn't reschedule that meeting. It was her only chance to get into the production lineup for the season, maybe even the year. If she missed her window, the company may shelve the idea until next year, or for good. Her major selling tool, the momentum from the Christmas calendar sales, would be gone next year. The line might never happen then, and neither would her promotion. Tina was determined that wasn't going to happen. She wanted that promotion, needed it, had more than earned it in the six years she had worked at Texas Tomboy.

"Tina, this is Hope. You called?" her friend said. "Is everything okay with the calendar?"

"Oh yeah, the calendar is perfect," Tina replied absently, while reaching for the envelope of photos from yet another agency she had received that morning. "Sales are through the roof from the giveaways. Even the standalone calendar sales are amazing."

That was why she had this idea in the first place. It was also why her bosses were salivating to see her ideas on paper. Now, she had done research, talked to suppliers and designers, had gotten everyone worked up in her preliminary pitch. A lot of damned work for nothing if she didn't find her man soon. And she would look like an idiot.

She didn't know whether she was just being too picky, or if she was just afraid to move off the dime and pick someone. This was her baby. If it failed to walk, it would be all her fault. Instead of a promotion, she might end up jobless. Her perfect reward for sticking her neck out for a promotion instead of just going with the flow and doing the job she'd fought hard to get in the first place.

Six years of ladder climbing would be gone, and who knew if she could find another job if she lost this one. Unlike her younger co-workers who took their jobs lightly, even though nobody outside of Human Resources knew it, because it wasn't something she advertised, Tina hadn't had the opportunity to finish her college degree. Her education came from the school of hard work and hard knocks. If she got fired from Texas Tomboy, even with six years of experience, her job opportunities would be limited elsewhere.

On the other hand, if she got this promotion and was successful, her lack of a degree wouldn't matter anymore. Heading up the launch of a new line would mean companies would come to her begging her to work for them. Pulling out their pocketbooks to get her to jump ship. Maybe then she could give her niece the house and stable environment she and Lori had never had in their lives. Tina had been saving for five years for that day, and was still nowhere close to accomplishing that goal. And her sister was still nowhere close to settling down to be the mother that Laney needed.

Tina was still practically raising the child, but she was going to have a long overdue talk to her sister about that very soon. As soon as she found the time, and her sister wasn't on a date with a new flavor of the week. Tina hadn't even had a date herself in three years herself.

What was wrong with that picture?

Hope breathed what sounded to Tina like a sigh of relief. "What's up then?" Hope asked.

"I need some help." Tina needed a lot of help, and hoped her friend could provide it.

"You name it. I owe you," Hope replied with a laugh. "Want my firstborn? You'll have to wait a few months."

Shock rocked Tina and the photos slipped from her fingers to slither onto the desk. "You're pregnant?"

"Yeah." Hope's voice was all soft and dreamy, and jealousy punched Tina in the gut. She wondered if she would ever be as happy as her friend seemed to be since she married Cord Dixon.

But Tina would never begrudge her friend that happiness. Hope had been through a lot, was still going through a lot. She deserved every minute of her joy.

"Good Lord, girl. You work fast," Tina said shaking her head.

Hope had just married Cord Dixon at the end of last year. She could understand why her friend would be practicing making babies with her new husband though. That man was sex on legs. Very long legs. Tina had a crush on him since his face first appeared in the ads for Laramie Jeans. But even if he'd been interested in her, Tina wouldn't have gone there. She just didn't have time for a man in her life, hadn't had time in a long while thanks to her sister and her job.

Which was just too damned bad.

"Yeah, we're both thrilled…but that's not why you called. You sounded frazzled in your message. How can I help you?"

That's because she was frazzled, Tina thought, gripping the phone tighter to her ear. Still was frazzled. "I sold a new menswear line to Texas Tomboy. And if I can get things off the ground, I'm going to head it up."

Hope squealed and Tina flinched. She held the phone out from her ear then eased it back. "Don't get too excited yet."

"Why the hell not?" Hope asked, her tone still brimming with excitement.

"I need to find a Texas Tomcat and I'm at the bottom of the barrel."

Hope giggled. "Cord's done with modeling, but I'm sure he knows a few tomcats from his rodeo days. I've met a few of them that he calls friends."

"I would ask your smoking hot husband, but he's just too damned pretty."

"You're looking for an ugly cowboy?" Hope asked, with a snicker.

Tina snorted. "Hell no. But I want attitude, I don't want someone perfect. Like you said at Christmas, perfect has been done to death." And so had pretty cowboys. Tina wanted nice looking, but she also wanted interesting. Something about her man that would make people stop at their ads in magazines, instead of flipping the page to the next pretty face. "I don't want Texas Tomcat to just be a poor imitation of Laramie. The guys we used in the calendar are good, but they are too damned young and inexperienced. That Zack guy might have worked, he's a little older, but even he is too pretty."

Hope gave a disbelieving laugh. "You have access to every good looking man in Texas, and you can't find a man that fits?"

"Trust me, I've looked at every man in Texas.

I know what I want and I've looked at every model from every agency in town. Not one of them fits." Tina picked up the last packet and tossed it on top of the pile to her left.

"Go to the rodeo, like Tonya Laramie did," Hope suggested. "Maybe you'll find someone there. That's where she found Cord."

"I don't have time," Tina said and huffed a breath. "If I find the right guy, would you be on board with being my photographer?"

"Sure," Hope replied happily. "I just have to work around my doctor's appointments and probably sidestep my husband. He's gotten awfully protective lately. Could we do it out here?"

"That was going to be my next question," Tina replied with a laugh.

"You got it. Just let me know when."

"Tomorrow?"

"I thought you didn't have anyone in mind?"

Tina heaved another heavy sigh. "I have two maybes. I'd like to do some test shots. I'm probably spinning my wheels, but you never know how they'll look once I slap a cowboy hat and jeans on them."

"I'll help you cowboy them up," Hope assured her. "Don't worry, T—we'll work it out."

Her friend had a helluva lot more confidence in that than she did. "Whatever you say." Slapping a hat and boots on a man did not make him a cowboy. Both she and Hope knew that. Not the ideal cowboy to represent Texas Tomcat anyway.

"Keep your chin up, and get your ass out here tomorrow. Stay the weekend. I need some girl time. There's too much testosterone around here."

"I need to work this weekend," Tina replied flatly. Working was the last thing she needed, but it was what she had to do if she had any hope of getting this stuff together for her status meeting with her boss on Tuesday.

"It'll be there on Monday, I promise. And you sound awful. Stressing about it isn't going to get you anywhere. Trust me, I know that firsthand."

"Brittany Weston still on your two yard line?" Tina asked, knowing that was the source of Hope's stress. Being sued for five million dollars would up anyone's pucker factor. Having the fact broadcast in every paper in the city multiplied that tenfold.

"No she's at the goal line with inches to go." Hope huffed out a frustrated breath and Tina wanted to do the same. Her friend probably could use someone to talk to as much as Tina could right now. But she also promised to babysit her niece this weekend. Lori was going away for the weekend again. Her sister needed to stay home for a change to give Tina a break. And if she ever saw Lori, maybe she would tell her that.

"I have to keep Laney this weekend. I'll come out tomorrow for the shoot to make sure the models don't turn into divas, but I have to come back to Dallas tomorrow night."

"Bring Laney with you. She can play with my

nephew Jeremy," Hope suggested. "And bring your work, I'll help you. No excuses," she said firmly.

A weekend in the country did sound good. Even though she wasn't a country girl, hadn't ever spent much time out there, the slower pace would probably do both her and Laney some good. That kid needed a break. Her mother was going to drive both of them crazy before long. Tina gnawed her lip, glanced at the stack of envelopes and then said quickly, "Okay, I could use a second set of eyes. I've looked at so many photographs, I'm probably not seeing them anymore."

Maybe being away from the office would give her a clearer perspective on her vision for Texas Tomcat. And Tina also hoped in the quiet of the country, she could decide what she was going to do to help Laney. Lori needed to get her head screwed on straight, and it was time for Tina to have a serious talk with her about doing that.

"Good, I'll let Cord know you're coming. He'll be excited to finally meet you."

***

"Hope is pregnant," Cord said happily, looking down at his wife, the perky redhead sitting beside him who looked at him like the sun rose and set in his eyes. His brother's voice echoed through the living room of his mother's house, broken only by the crackling of the logs burning in the fireplace and his mother's excited gasp. The words ping-ponged around in Dean's skull to mold the shock inside of him into a tight band around his brain.

Hope. His brother's wife. He wasn't supposed to covet her, but he did. She was the kind of woman he needed for himself. A woman who cared more about other people than she cared about herself. Someone unlike the woman he had married. The woman who had given him a son then left him in the dust on her way to town to meet her lover.

His brother Cord, the man Dean thought was a flighty, irresponsible tumbleweed, was not only a husband now, he was going to be a father. In the space of five months, his brother had become the responsible one of the two of them. Of course his brother always found the pot of gold at the end of the rainbow. Hope was that pot of gold, and Dean was jealous.

Dean's claim to fame was being a single father, who had a failed marriage behind him, and a motherless son, who may not even be his son, that needed more of him than he had to give. And now he was playing second fiddle to his brother on a ranch where he'd invested every ounce of his blood, sweat and tears his entire life. More so the last three years, while his brother had been off finding his fame and fortune. Dean was starting to think that Cord had a horseshoe up his ass, he was so damned lucky. Not only had he been a famous model making fistfuls of cash in Dallas, he had been a successful rodeo bull rider before that.

And while he was off getting famous, Dean had stayed here keeping the home fires burning, trying to keep them all fed, and worrying about their daddy. It just wasn't right now that he was back, their parents seemed to think the second coming had happened.

"When's the baby due?" Barb Dixon asked with excitement.

Hope's green eyes lit up and she leaned forward. "The doctor says I'm due in August."

Dean's eyes fell to Hope's stomach which was concealed beneath the baggy sweater she wore. He could just see a small mound there. Four and a half months pregnant. In four and a half more she would be the mother of his brother's child. He'd bet Hope Car—Dixon wouldn't be leaving her child to go meet a lover she'd kept since before she married his brother. Jealousy hit Dean in the center of his chest and he couldn't catch a breath.

Dean shoved up to his feet, because he needed to get out of there. "I need to check on the mare," he said. The pregnant mare who was due to deliver any minute. It was as good an excuse as any to leave, even though he knew his daddy checked her not long ago.

"That can wait, son," Silas Dixon said with a reprimand in his tone. "She was fine when I checked on her an hour ago."

The warning tone fell on deaf ears. Dean knew if he didn't get out of there he was going to say something shitty and ruin his brother's moment. Then his daddy would really be on his ass. And he didn't want to hurt Hope. She didn't deserve his anger, even though his brother more than deserved it. "I'll be back in a few minutes—congratulations," he mumbled to no one in particular as he hustled through the room toward the front door.

Dean's chest finally loosened when he stepped out on the porch. He breathed in a deep lungful of the crisp night air. He didn't wait to see if anyone followed, he strode across the porch and down the steps. Halfway to the barn though, Cord called his name from the front porch. Dean didn't stop. He kept a steady pace toward the barn and his eyes on the light shining there. He hoped his damned brother would take a hint and leave him the hell alone. But his brother wasn't that smart. Cord called again from a lot closer just as Dean entered the barn.

"*Wait!*" Cord growled, catching up to him just as he reached the mare's stall. His hand dropped on Dean's shoulder.

Every muscle in his body tensed, as Dean fought the urge to turn around and plant his fist in his brother's too-handsome face. "What the fuck do you want?" He wished the bastard would just pack up his wife and move back to Dallas, model his fucking jeans and leave him and the ranch the hell alone. Dean couldn't take a piss these days without Cord in his back pocket.

"The best thing you can do is leave me alone right now," Dean warned in a low tone that should have told Cord to back off.

Instead his brother's hand tightened on his shoulder and he walked around to get in his face. "What the fuck is wrong with you, man?" Cord demanded.

Dean huffed out a breath trying to get control. He looked off at the mare who stared at him curiously over the stall. "Nothing," he ground out, brushing Cord's hand off of his shoulder. "I have work to do."

Dean walked over to flip the latch on the stall, but Cord still didn't leave. He walked up behind him again and leaned around him. "You always have work to do. You need to take a break and relax. Daddy's better, and I'm here now. Hope and I can watch Jeremy for you. You have no reason not to take a vacation."

"Yeah, everything is perfect now that you're back," Dean replied sourly, then turned and propped his arm on the stall door. "Wanna tell me where we're going to get the money to buy the spring stock if I don't stay here and figure that out?"

"Hope—"

"Has given enough. Don't you have any pride, man? You think I don't know, but I know your wife has given every penny she has to bail us out. To take care of Daddy."

Cord's eyebrows lifted and he looked a little shocked that Dean knew exactly where that money had come from. The only reason Dean knew the money hadn't come from Cord's modeling and savings like he told the family was because he had been present for Hope's meltdown when she was served the hefty lawsuit from Brittany Weston for screwing up her wedding. A woman with a trust fund the size of Hope's shouldn't have batted an eyelash, but she had fallen apart.

Right then Dean knew something was very wrong, so he point blank asked what he'd suspected all along. If all the money that had fallen from the sky when they needed it most was from her trust fund. She squirmed, danced for a while, tried to protect Cord, but when Dean pressed her she finally came clean. She was a good woman, and his brother had used her enough.

"I paid her back a lot of it," Cord replied indignantly.

"So you can borrow it from her again?" Dean accused. "She has her own problems with that lawsuit she's fighting with that woman in Dallas."

"Fuck!" Cord stepped back to shove a hand through his perfectly combed hair, evidently even more agitated that Dean knew about the suit too.

"My sentiments exactly," Dean replied with a dry laugh. "We're fucked," he said then turned away. He had work to do, and he was sure his brother had something else to do.

"The calendar sales—"

Dean spun around again and held up his hand. "Are going to finish paying her back. I don't want that damned money, and neither does daddy. Ask him how he feels about it," Dean challenged, knowing Cord didn't have the balls.

"Daddy thinks that money came from my modeling and investments. It did in a way since I've paid Hope back with it as it becomes liquid."

"Fine, and the calendar sales will make that completely true," Dean said. "Pay your wife back, and we're even with her." Dean wasn't taking another dime from Hope Dixon.

She'd paid off the mortgage on the ranch, paid for his daddy's treatments, and the repairs needed at the ranch before Christmas. Enough was enough. Even if what Cord said was true and he had paid her back a portion of it, they had to still owe her a lot more.

"We all need to talk about it," Cord said with frustration. "Me, you, Hope and Daddy need to talk. We'll figure something out."

"There's nothing to talk about. *I'll* figure it out," Dean said firmly. Dean had been in charge of figuring things out on his own at the ranch for a long time now. He'd figure this out too. Without his brother's input or his new sister-in-law's money. Decisions by committee never worked. The less people he had in the mix, the better. Cord needed to know that Dean was still going to make those decisions. His brother might be back, but Dean was still in charge.

The mare neighed loudly, and it wasn't a hello. It was time. This conversation was done. "Go get Daddy," Dean said gruffly as he opened the stall.

"But I need to talk about—" Cord protested.

"I'm done talking. Go get, Daddy, or get your ass in here and help me. She's tearing," Dean challenged. Cord's face blanched and Dean laughed as his brother turned on his heel and all but ran from the barn, because it looked like some things about his brother hadn't changed. Like Cord's aversion to blood.

CHAPTER TWO

Tina knew she was way too early, but she was too excited about taking a much needed break in the country to wait a second after five a.m. to hit the road. Laney had been just as excited. The kid had barely slept last night, and in turn neither had Tina. At least her niece was catching up on her sleep. Tina wished she was still in bed too now, but had been driving for over an hour.

Her eyes got heavy again, so Tina cracked her window, inhaling deeply of the sweet country air that rushed inside the car. The temperature dropped inside the car and a chill raced down her spine, so she quickly rolled it back up. She would sure be glad when it warmed up. Spring had arrived, because things had started to bloom, but there was still a definite chill to the morning air. And she had put up her sweaters and refused to bring them on this trip. She was going on a mini-vacation. Lord knew she and her niece could both use it too.

Lori was driving them both crazy. And Tina still hadn't had an opportunity to talk to her, but she was going to pin her down soon. Laney needed a mother, and Tina hadn't birthed her, so her sister needed to live up to her own responsibilities. She glanced at Laney sleeping peacefully in the seat beside her and her heart squeezed. The kid deserved so much better. Tina was going to make sure she got that. Like a home she could call her own, somewhere to put down roots, just as soon as she got this promotion. A kid needed that. Something she and her sister had never had. They had seen the country, too much of it. Tina had finally planted in Dallas after their parents divorced, but her younger sister was still a tumbleweed.

Narrowing her eyes, Tina watched the road closer. The trees broke and wide pastures covered by a thick blanket of fog appeared. Her turn should be coming up soon, according to the GPS on her dash. A few miles later, she saw the rutted gravel drive at the last minute. She made a quick right then gritted her teeth as her compact car bounced over a cattle guard. The front wheels cleared that to immediately take plunge into a deep pothole. She glanced at Laney, and her little body bounced and she moaned, but didn't wake up. The ground leveled out, and Tina sighed.

In the distance, she saw a big house at the end of the long driveway. As she neared, she also saw another thinner, longer building off to the left. That must be the bunkhouse where Hope and Cord were living. There weren't any lights on inside. Probably because it was just now six a.m. and Tina was four hours early. In the distance, an eerie yellow light cut through the thick fog and caught her attention. Tina squinted, the fog rolled, and she could see it was coming through the door of a huge barn. Someone must be up after all, she thought as she drove past the bunkhouse toward the barn. Maybe it was Cord. If it wasn't, Tina would just park there and take a cat nap for an hour or so until the residents at the ranch woke up.

The models she'd scheduled for the test shoot wouldn't be there until ten. Or at least she hoped they would. You never knew if they would show or not. Work ethic in the modelling industry was notoriously bad. Tina had encountered it many times from the female models she had worked with at Texas Tomboy. Often, if they weren't late, they didn't show at all. If they did show when they were running late, they were usually in a bad mood and turned into whiny divas.

She hoped working with male models would be easier, but she wasn't holding her breath. Good looking single men liked to go out on Friday nights. The two male models she was expecting today were definitely good looking. But if they showed up looking hungover or had bad attitudes, she would send them right back to Dallas. She wasn't paying them to take photos she couldn't use. And she wasn't going to coddle them. That had always been her mode of operation with models. She hired them to do a job, and they were going to do it or she would find someone else who would. She might cut them a little slack though, because she had incentive to get this shoot done today.

Stopping outside the wide barn door, she killed her engine. Laney didn't stir when Tina opened door and paused to slip on her high heels before she swung her legs outside. In hindsight, the stilettos probably weren't the best shoes she could have chosen for a trip to the country, but she didn't have much choice. She'd worn out her last pair of sneakers at the gym, when she actually had time to go to the gym. These days between taking care of Laney, and all the hours she put in at the office, Tina just didn't have time for anything anymore.

Besides she liked high heels. Vertically challenged at just a little over five feet, they added height and that boosted her confidence. Made her feel on more even footing with the world. When she wore them, people seemed to take her more seriously.

At least she had found a ruffled blue jean skirt in the back of her closet to wear. That was as close to casual as she could get. Nothing in her closet fit anymore, because she was a little curvier than she had been when she had time for the gym. And she didn't have time to shop for clothes that fit better either. It was a vicious cycle that wasn't likely to change soon. Her job as Assistant Marketing Director at Texas Tomboy was demanding. Once she got her new promotion, it would only get worse. Unless she made her sister step up and be a mother.

Tina stood and quietly closed the car door. The heels of her shoes immediately sank into the dewy earth. She moved her weight to the toes of her shoes to tiptoe toward the barn door. A horse whinnied loudly inside, then she heard a loud bang as if the animal kicked the stall. A throaty growl, followed by a loud curse told her someone was definitely awake and inside the barn.

When she finally stepped inside, she squinted against the bright lights until her eyes adjusted. Two horses swung their heads in her direction to look at her curiously over the top of their stalls. One of them nickered and tossed his head as if he was saying hello. Tina laughed then looked around. The rich earthy smells assaulted her nostrils and she wrinkled her nose. Other than the horses though, she didn't see a soul inside the barn. Walking a little further inside, she stopped on a concrete pad where she could ease onto her heels.

Cupping her hands around her mouth, Tina shouted, "Hello!"

The only reply she received were agitated snorts from the horses. She scanned along the walls from stall to stall hoping to see one open, but they were all closed tight. Noticing a light at the back of the building coming from a darkened hallway, she headed that way. The barn was so big, she knew yelling probably wasn't going to do anything except stir up the horses more. She held onto the rail and made her way toward the back.

At the end a narrow hallway, she noticed a door was opened a crack and a light was on inside the room. The person she heard must be in there, she thought as she walked there. At the door, she stopped, took a deep breath then pasted on a smile, before she pushed the door inward. Her smile turned to a surprised gasp when her eyes landed on a cowboy sitting in a chair beside a scarred wooden desk. The man wore nothing but tight, white underwear, a t-shirt and his black cowboy hat. His jeans were around his ankles, and he was massaging his thigh.

His stormy blue eyes swung to hers, but he didn't make a move to pull up his pants. His body tensed, and one dark eyebrow lifted beneath the brim of his hat. "Who the hell are you?" he demanded, and his deep, honeyed drawl crawled along her nerve endings, exciting each one.

The man looked somewhat like Cord Dixon, but he definitely wasn't. His face was squarer and more rugged, his jaw firmer, than Mr. Laramie. Cord's eyes were more of a sky blue, but this man's eyes almost looked like the sky when warning a summer thunderstorm was about to erupt. They perfectly matched his prickly attitude.

Those sexy, insolent eyes left fire behind as they made a quick pass down to her toes. They moved a little slower back up her body, before settling on hers again. He sat there staring at her when she didn't answer. Tina gathered her senses, licked her lips and found her voice. "Um, I thought Cord might be out here," she stuttered.

His eyes narrowed and his jaw tightened. "If you're here to pick up something with my brother, you're wasting your time. He's married now, and his wife is knocked up. Best thing you can do is get your pretty little ass out of here, before Hope sees you."

"I'm here to see Hope too," Tina clarified. When he flinched, her eyes fell to the hand on his thigh, he moved it and Tina saw a dark purple bruise beneath his fingers. Against her will, her eyes darted to the impressive goods those tight white underwear of his was trying to contain.

He cleared his throat, her eyes flew back to his and her cheeks heated. One side of his firm mouth kicked up into a cocky smile. "See something you like, buttercup?"

Tina saw a lot she liked, and that was the problem. She had to fight to keep her eyes from going back there for a second look. "Um, did you hurt yourself?" Tina asked, trying to cover the fact that she had been staring at his package. It was obvious from his widening grin that she hadn't fooled anyone.

He snorted and grabbed a rolled up Ace bandage off of the desk. "It's nothing," he grumbled as he wrapped it around his thigh. "Damned horse kicked me."

"It looks pretty bad," Tina said, moving in for a closer look.

He stopped wrapping and his eyes flew up to hers again. There was a warning there and Tina stopped in her tracks. "What the hell do you want here?" he demanded.

"I'm here for a photo shoot. I'm Tina

Montgomery with Texas Tomboy. Hope said I could do a photo shoot here today."

Blue fire sparked in his eyes. "Well, *Hope* failed to ask if that was okay with me."

The arrogance in his tone made Tina angry. As far as she knew, this was Hope's home now too. If she wanted to invite a friend here, who was this guy to say she had to ask his permission? Tina folded her arms over her chest, and snapped, "She lives here. Is married to one of the owners. Why would she have to ask you if she could have someone out here?"

"One of the owners, huh?" he said in a low lethal tone, as he clipped off the top of the bandage and leaned back in the chair to cross his arms over his broad chest.

"Yes, Cord Dixon is her husband. He's one of the owner's sons."

"Well I'm Dean Dixon, the owner's *other* son. The one who has been busting his ass here, taking care of this family, while my brother chased skirts like you all over Dallas. And unlike my brother, my name happens to be on the deed to this ranch."

Dean Dixon. Cord's brother. Hell, she didn't even know he had a brother, but then again she didn't know much about Cord Dixon other than he was Mr. Laramie and looked better than any man she'd ever seen in a pair of jeans. Her eyes dropped to the jeans around Dean's ankles and noticed they were Laramie jeans. She wondered how his muscular thighs would look in those jeans. Probably better than his brother's. Tina dragged her eyes away. "You think you could put your pants on so we can finish this conversation?"

"It's finished as far as I'm concerned," he said as he stood and bent to drag his jeans up his legs. His zipped them angrily, then shoved his belt through the loops. "You can get back in your car and get the hell out of here. I don't have time to deal with this shit. The only thing my brother and I are going to be doing today is getting these horses ready, so we can get them to the auction on Monday."

"I won't get in your way, and I'm not here to shoot with Cord. I have models coming," Tina informed him.

Dean finished buckling his belt, then put his hands on his hips. "I don't think so. Call them and tell them to stay in Dallas then head back there yourself. This ranch is not a photo studio." He limped past her to the door, and shoved it open, causing it to bounce off the wall. He put a hand on the wall and made his way down the hallway to the arena.

Tina strode behind him, but even injured the man's long-legged stride was hard for her to keep up with in heels. "But Hope said—" Tina started, but she made a step into the arena, her heel caught on the edge of the concrete pad and her ankle twisted painfully. With a yelp, she felt herself flying forward. She threw her hands out to catch herself, but her palms hit Dean Dixon in the middle of his back and he went flying too. They landed in a heap on the dusty floor with her on top of him. Dean immediately rolled to his back, and Tina scrambled up to straddle him.

Before she could stand, his hands gripped her hips in a steel hold. "The best thing you can do is leave," he ground out angrily. "There won't be anything shot here today, except you if you don't get the hell off my ranch."

As hard as his eyes were right then, Tina could almost believe he meant those words. The last thing she needed was a confrontation with Cord's brother, or to cause problems for Hope.

"I'll just stop by the bunk—"

"You're not going to shoot anyone, Dean," Cord interrupted angrily, as he stopped beside his brother to stare down at them with his hands on his hips. "I just talked to daddy and he's fine with it. Texas Tomboy is paying us to use the ranch for their shoot location, and we need that damned money."

Dean's eyes narrowed. "Well I run this place, and you didn't talk to me," Dean replied through tight lips. Tina tried to stand again, but his fingers tightened on her hips.

Cord didn't blink. He faced his brother's glare head on. "If you had let me talk last night, I would have told you. Maybe if you'd shut up long enough to listen now and again, you would know," he spat as he extended his hand to help her up.

Tina took his hand and tried to stand, but a sharp pain shot through her ankle and she moaned. Dean's arms closed around her waist, and it was like the brothers were having a tug-of-war with her. "Let her go," Dean grumbled. "She hurt her damned ankle in those stupid heels." His eyes moved to hers and Tina saw disgust there. "What woman in their right mind wears high heels into a barn?"

He was right, Tina decided. She was totally not in her right mind to be out here in the middle of this obvious battle of wills between the brothers. She would just have to find somewhere else to shoot.

"I'm leaving," she said, trying to pull away from Dean to stand again, but his fingers only tightened on her hips. Dean sat up with her on his lap, and Tina put her hands on his firm chest to push away. He muscled his way to his feet holding her against his hard body. Tina had no choice but to grab his neck, or end up on her ass in the dirt.

Dean Dixon carried her back down the hallway to the office. He kneed open the door and carried her to the chair where he'd been sitting earlier where he sat her down. Tina tried to stand, but he put his hand on her shoulder. "Stay," he growled as if she were a dog.

He stomped behind the desk and bent to open a drawer, pulled out a rolled bandage and slammed it down on the desk. Kneeling in front, he grabbed her calf and balanced her foot on his thigh. Dean gripped her calf tighter, and darts of tingly heat shot up her thigh as he carefully removed her shoe.

Cord came in and Dean glanced up to growl, "Make your damned self useful. There's a pair of Mama's rubber boots in the tack room. Go get 'em." It seemed like the man loved to growl, and issue orders. He wasn't very pleasant. Tina was going to steer clear of him while she was here. She had no idea how Cord worked with the man.

Cord shook his head as he disappeared through the office door. Dean took the bandage from the desk and unrolled it, then laid the end against her ankle.

"I don't need that," she protested, and tried to pull her foot away. His fingers became a hot vice on her ankle. The tingly heat turned into fire that shot up her leg to the top of her thigh, teasing the nerves there into a frenzy. Tina wiggled in the chair trying to settle them.

"Hold still," Dean growled, and Tina relaxed as much as she could. He made a round around her ankle with the stretchy bandage. "It's swelling, and if you don't put this on it, it will only get worse. Get some ice on it at the bunkhouse too."

It was damn tough, but Tina gritted her teeth and sat perfectly still. "Yes, sir," she replied sarcastically, and he looked up at her. Was that actually a fleeting smile she saw at the corner of his mouth? If so, that would shock the heck out of her. This man's personality, his whole demeanor, wasn't that of a man who found humor in much. Tina liked funny guys who could laugh at themselves, at life. This man wasn't her type at all. She didn't even like him. But dammit if he wasn't turning her on, even as impersonal and prickly as he was being.

It had to be because she hadn't had a man touch her in *any* way in nearly three years. Embarrassing to her, but understandable. Her sister was the one who had the luxury of getting laid every weekend. Because Tina stayed home and kept her daughter for her to do that.

Cord walked back into the office dangling a pair of ugly black rubber boots in his hand. He set them beside the chair, and Dean shot him a look, then wrapped the bandage around her ankle a final time as he mumbled, "Daddy says you can be here, so I guess that means you aren't leaving. But you will not wear those shoes here again, it's dangerous."

He stretched the bandage to the side of her foot then secured the end with a silver clip. He lowered her foot to the floor, then stood. Tina looked up into Dean Dixon's slightly weathered face, his haunted blue eyes that had a story to tell, and saw a person she never expected to find.

Her Texas Tomcat.

"I've got work to do," Dean said as he spun and walked out of the door.

What the heck was she going to do? Now that she had Dean Dixon as the bar in her mind for Texas

Tomcat, nobody else was going to do. Not the men who were showing up here in a few hours for the photo shoot, and not the hundreds of others she had considered. She would just have to figure out how to make Dean *want* to be the man to represent the line.

Somehow she didn't think money was going to do the trick. Dean Dixon seemed like a pretty down-to-earth—no earthy—kind of guy. Which is why he was perfect for the job. He was damned good looking, but there wasn't an ounce of flash to him. He was what he was and if anyone didn't like it, they could kiss his ass. Watching that ass in those jeans walking out that door made her want to bite it instead of kiss it. It was perfection.

Cord shot her a sympathetic glance, before he followed right behind his brother out of the door. Tina sat there stunned, wondering why it had to be him. The odds of her convincing Dean Dixon to be her model were about the same as the odds of her being made president of Texas Tomboy. She'd be better off buying a lottery ticket.

With a sigh, she reached for one of the rubber boots that Cord had sat beside the chair. She slid her uninjured foot down into the long neck of the boot and found out the boots were about one size too big for her. Not surprising really. Not many women had feet the size of a ten-year-old girl. She grabbed the other boot and slid her bandaged foot down into the throat, flinching as pain shot up her calf. She picked up her shoes, then went out to get Laney out of the car. As they walked to the bunkhouse, Tina thought about Dean Dixon again.

Maybe Hope could help her figure it out later. Give her some advice on how to approach the totally unapproachable man. Right now though, Tina needed to talk to her about the photo shoot. She limped toward the porch in the too big boots, picturing photos in her head, but none of them included the two men who would be here at ten o'clock.

CHAPTER THREE

At ten o'clock her assistant and stylist, Belinda, and Paulo, her hair guy, showed up together. The models didn't arrive until almost eleven o'clock. She helped Hope get her equipment out and sorted, but their organization went all to hell once Paulo and Belinda brought in their stuff in big duffle bags, and began laying things out.

"Get them their clothes so they can change," Tina said to Belinda, casting a sharp look at the two men standing beside Paulo shooting the breeze. They didn't have time for breezes. Those guys were late and she was not happy. "Paulo make the hair quick. We need to get started. Half the day is gone now."

"I'm sorry we're late," Brandon Sanchez said with an eye roll, as he took the jeans and t-shirt from Belinda. "He was late picking me up."

"Because you didn't answer the phone when I called," Joshua Gleason snapped.

"Because I was in the fucking shower," Brandon shot back.

"Because you were still in the bed," Joshua corrected with some neck action, taking a step toward Brandon. "You had to shower when I got to your apartment, dude. Don't you lay this off on me! Unlike you, I am a professional!"

All she needed were bruised and bloody models, and it looked like these two were about to go to fist city. "This isn't accomplishing anything! Get your asses dressed!" Tina yelled just as the front door flew inward and Dean Dixon walked inside. He didn't look happy.

"Where the hell is Cord?" he demanded.

Tina crossed her arms over her chest and asked, "How the hell would I know? It's not my day to watch him."

"Obviously it's not your day to watch your kid either," Dean shot back. "That girl has been bothering the crap out of me all morning!" He stepped to the side and pulled Laney inside the bunkhouse. Her lower lip trembled and it looked like the usually happy child might cry at any moment. Anger shot through Tina, as she unfolded her arms and walked over to Dean and pulled Laney away from him.

Tina stepped in front of her and pointed her finger at him. "For your information, *that girl* is my niece. She has a name and it's Laney."

"Well you need to keep *Laney* in here and out of the barn. She almost got stepped on by a horse. I don't have time to entertain her, or make sure that doesn't happen."

Fear replaced her anger, and Tina guessed she shouldn't have let her go out there alone when she asked if it was okay. Tina didn't know a damned thing about ranches or areas that might be dangerous here.

"Fine. I'll watch her closer. I'm sorry she bothered you." Tina turned away from the man she was fast seeing was a big bully. But not really in this situation. He was right, there were large animals out there, and Laney was only six. She could have gotten hurt. Tina felt like the incompetent guardian he had all but accused her of being.

She took two steps but his gruff growly voice stopped her. "I'm not done." Tina turned back toward him and raised a brow. "Who the hell is driving that piece of shit black convertible?"

"My assistant," Tina replied haughtily, crossing her arms over her chest.

"It's blocking my truck and I need to go to the feed store."

"Daddy can I go to the feed store with you?" a little red-haired boy about the same age as Laney asked as he nudged his way past Dean into the doorway.

"No. Jeremy. Go find your grandma and tell her I'm leaving for a little while," he said with frustration in every line of his big body. "I don't have time to deal with you right now either."

The little boy's face fell, and his eyes dropped to the toes of his scuffed up boots. "I'm sorry, Daddy."

"He can stay here with us," Tina offered, feeling damned sorry for the little boy. It seemed like nobody was given a pass from Dean Dixon's surly attitude. Not even his own son. "He'll keep Laney entertained."

"Like you watched Laney this morning?" Dean

asked nastily. "I don't think so. Jeremy, go find your grandma, and stay up at the house until I get back." The kid nodded, and walked past his father onto the porch. Dean looked back at her. "I need that car moved now."

Tina shook her head, and turned to go find Belinda who was in the bedroom laying out clothes for the shoot. "I'll get the keys."

Dean Dixon might be one of the best looking men that Tina had seen in a long time, but he was also the most snarly and sour. It was no wonder his wife had left him. According to Hope, that had happened three years ago and Dean had been bitter ever since. Well Mr. Dixon needed to focus that bitterness on the person who caused his pain, not the world in general, definitely not his son. Just like Laney deserved better from her mother, that kid deserved better from his father.

Working with him on this project became less and less appealing.

Maybe he wasn't her Texas Tomcat. That imaginary man would never be rude to his kid like that. He was a genuine cowboy and cowboys just didn't do that. They were good-hearted men who loved kids and animals. And they treated women with respect.

Her eyes traveled over Dean Dixon's firm body, his square jaw with the beard scruff. But he sure looked like a real cowboy, and he was the best bet she had for getting that promotion. In the photos nobody would be able to tell that he was an asshole of the first order. They would just see an alpha male with experience who looked good in a pair of blue jeans. Hope was a damned good photographer, and she knew this man. She could find his good side. If he had one. Tina was starting to doubt that.

If she could even convince him to do it. Hope didn't think so, but Tina wasn't giving up yet. The best thing Tina could do was keep her mouth shut, and let Hope work her magic. Try not to antagonize Dean until Hope had a chance to talk to him. Telling him right now what she thought of him, like she wanted to do, wouldn't accomplish that. Tina didn't see Belinda in the bedroom, but she saw her keys on the dresser, so she jerked them up and went to move the car for Mr. Cranky Pants.

Dean sat in the truck staring at the dusty black convertible in the rearview as Tina Montgomery ground the gears on the manual transmission, but still didn't find reverse. He needed to get out of here before the feed store closed at one o'clock. Cord was supposed to restock the feed room yesterday, but he'd been too busy, according to him. What he'd been busy doing, Dean had yet to figure out.

The gears ground again and the little car bucked, but didn't move. Dean had enough, so he threw the truck into park and opened the door to go move the damned thing himself. Stopping beside the driver's door he tapped on the window. "Get out," he ground out.

Tina held up a finger to him, then pushed the hair on her forehead back with her wrist, before she tried to crank the car again.

Dean flung the door open. "Just get out!" he shouted, and her head rocked back on her shoulders, and her gray eyes widened. "I don't have all fucking day!" Her left eyebrow lifted and she shot him a glare with her angry blue eyes, before she swung her legs out of car. He noticed she was still wearing the rubber boots. At least the woman had a little sense. But not enough to get the hell out of his way evidently. She just sat there staring up at him. Dean pulled the door wider and shouted, "I said get out!"

Tina Montgomery stood, put her fists on her hips then met his eyes directly. "Fuck you," she said, so primly Dean almost laughed. He thought he might be hearing things. Surely this prissy little woman didn't just say what he thought she had.

"Excuse me?" he asked with a disbelieving laugh.

She lifted her eyebrow higher, put her fists on her deliciously curvy hips then repeated very clearly, "I *said* go fuck yourself."

Dean chuckled, and it looked like she got angrier.

She was so small, her neck was laid back on her shoulders like she was staring at the sky, so she could glare up at him. Unfamiliar laughter tickled his belly. If her eyes were a laser beam, Dean would be melted in a puddle at her feet. That's how hot her eyes were when she got a little neck action going and said, "You aren't the boss of me, and your attitude sucks!"

You aren't the boss of me? How old was this woman?

She was the size of a child, but from her word choices, and her full breasts which were heaving with every agitated breath she took, he didn't think she was that young. Until that moment though, Dean hadn't realized just how beautiful his sister-in-law's friend actually was. In the barn this morning, the dim lighting hadn't done her justice. Standing here under the tree with shafts of late morning sun setting the auburn streaks in her dark hair on fire, the soft light painting her skin a golden glow, and her anger making her cheeks rosy, Dean decided she was *amazingly* beautiful. As beautiful as one of the china dolls in his mother's collection, which he realized she resembled.

And that damned full pink mouth of hers was calling to him. He'd like to kiss the sassy right out of it. Dean would bet it tasted just as good as it looked. Like moist, ripe cherries. She licked those lips and his dick stirred in a big way, which pissed him off. He didn't have time for this. The feed store was closing soon.

Besides he should be pissed at her, not standing here daydreaming about kissing her. This tiny little woman with a mouth the size of Texas had just told him off. That was pretty ballsy, since she was the one getting in *his* way here. "Where did you learn to drive, sugar? Wal-mart special driver's ed course?" Dean asked with a nasty snicker.

"I've never driven a stick before," she answered defensively.

He huffed out a frustrated breath. "Give me the keys, and I'll move it," he said holding out his hand for them. She gnawed her lower lip, and he had the sudden urge to do the same thing. Dean jerked the keys out of her hand and opened the door.

"You're not going to fit in there," She screeched. "That car is a mini."

Dean leaned down to gauge the odds of fitting himself inside, and realized she was probably right. He cursed and handed her the keys back. "Get your assistant to move it."

"She's busy. I'll do it. I think part of the problem is these damned boots," she informed, with a wave of her small hand toward the boots. "They're too big, and I can't get the clutch in far enough." She sat back on the seat, and tried to toe off one of the boots.

After a minute, when she couldn't remove them, Dean bent to grab the boot. He put his hand behind her knee to get leverage and she gasped. His eyes met hers, and he saw a look there he hadn't seen in a woman's eyes for him in a long time. Interest. Desire. His heart kicked in his chest, and she looked away.

Dean swallowed hard, got a grip on his suddenly active libido and the boot then pulled it. He held her leg a moment longer than necessary, because he couldn't resist taking the opportunity to stroke the smooth, soft skin of her inner thigh with his thumb. His dick got harder. With a growl he dropped her leg, then picked up her other foot to remove the boot. When it slid off, he noticed the size of her feet. His mother's feet were small, because she was petite too, but this woman's foot was even smaller. She was smaller.

And that's when it hit him, right between the eyes. Tina Montgomery looked a lot like his mother. Acted like her too. Even though she wasn't young anymore, his mother was still beautiful. She was the most amazing woman he'd ever known. The only woman in the world he trusted. She didn't get mad often, but when she did you better find a place to hide. One thing he could count on with her is she would always tell him how it was without holding punches.

Dean didn't have a mommy complex or anything. He usually preferred taller, leggier women too. But maybe that's what this strange attraction he was feeling toward Tina Montgomery was about. Whatever it was, he didn't have time for it. The feed store was going to close.

Dean knelt beside her and leaned inside the car to study the gear shift. "Reverse looks to be down and over to the left," he informed her.

He inhaled and her soft, flowery scent surrounded him. It wasn't overwhelming, it was subtle, but called to something inside of him. The scent fit this woman perfectly. Soft and feminine. Everything about Tina Montgomery screamed girl, except her salty attitude. Cindy had the same attitude, only coarser, and she had been tall and lanky. A country girl to the core. This woman was her complete opposite. Maybe *that* was the attraction.

Dean leaned back out of the car so he could get some fresh air. "Make sure it's in neutral. That's the center position. Push in the clutch, hold the brake and start it. To put it in reverse, push in on the stick with your palm, then move it down and to the left. Ease your foot off the clutch at the same time you release the brake."

"Yes, *sir*," she said sarcastically. His eyes flew to hers, and he was about to blast her, but he saw hers held teasing laughter.

Dean ignored the tug in his gut and stood to hold the door open. "Give it a try."

She wiggled the gear shift to make sure it was in neutral. He closed the door and stepped back to watch her fiddle with the controls. The engine cranked smoothly, and she smiled out the window at him. Dean's lips automatically curved up too, and the pull of his skin felt strange.

After a few grinding tries, she finally found

reverse, and her smile widened. A light feeling developed in his chest, and the skin on his cheeks stretched more. The car lurched backwards a few feet, before it died. A laugh bubbled in his chest when she frowned and pounded her tiny fist on the steering wheel.

Dean picked up the rubber boots and walked to the door to tap on the window. She rolled it down, but he opened the door. "That's fine. I can get out now," he said, dropping the boots beside the car. "Put those boots on, because there are stickers out here."

She growled, then jerked the keys from the ignition then pivoted on the seat to swing her legs outside. "Yes sir, anything *else* sir?" she asked in a snarky tone.

Damn she was cute when she was mad.

"Yeah…have a nice day," he said with a wink. She growled at his back as he walked off, feeling lighter than he had in a long time. Dean didn't hold back, he did laugh.

It was almost sundown when he got back to the ranch. After the feed store, Dean had to stop at the hardware store to pick up some wire and a few posts. Big mistake. Walter Sims, the owner, decided he wanted to catch up.

Dean didn't want to be rude to the old-timer who had been good to his family. Before he could escape though, he had to talk about his daddy's condition, Cord's coming back home with a new wife, and beef cattle prices. They talked about that so long Dean could probably quote the current prices of every breed by memory. That was useless information to him though, since he couldn't buy any beef cattle at the moment.

And now it was dark. Another day pissed away.

But something good did come out of his conversation with Walter. The old man gave him a lead on a good breeder bull a neighbor had for sale. As if he could afford to buy the bull right now either. Dean knew by the time he got that much money again that bull would probably have third-generation calves old enough to breed.

Huffing a breath, he picked up his hat from the seat and slapped it on his head. He got out and walked to the house. Wishing things were better for them wasn't going to make it happen. He just needed to be thankful that his daddy was healed. Whatever it took to make that happen was worth it. Even losing the ranch would be worth it. But hopefully it didn't come to that.

There had to be something he could do to buy new stock.

If his brother would stop trying to convince his daddy to go with some get-rich-quick scheme, maybe they could figure it out. Recovery was going to be a slow and steady race here, not a sprint. Dean had faced the fact that they weren't going to make the ranch successful again overnight, and he wished his brother and father would too.

Dean's hand was on the doorknob of the front door when he heard giggling and then a soft curse from around the corner of the wraparound porch. Curiosity set his feet on a path in that direction. He rounded the corner and rocked back on his heels. Tina Montgomery, Laney and Jeremy were engrossed in a heated board game.

None of them noticed him, but he noticed her. She sat cross-legged in a pair of soft, grey sweat pants that were a size too small. The cropped football-type jersey shirt she wore stopped right under her full breasts, leaving a lot of smooth. bare skin visible. Her dark hair was pulled back in a ponytail, and her feet were bare.

She looked fresh, and about sixteen years old. His body reacted instantly, and it pissed him off. Dean dragged his eyes away, and cleared his throat. He pinned his son with a stern look then said, "Jeremy you need to get ready for supper."

"But daddy we were playing a game," Jeremy whined as he glanced slyly at Tina Montgomery for support.

Her full lips pinched, and there was a challenge in her eyes, like she was daring him to argue, when she said, "We're almost finished here."

"Yeah, please let him finish," Laney piped in. Dean's eyes swung to the tiny blonde girl with the big blue eyes just like her aunt's. He realized he was outnumbered. If he met the challenge the girls were issuing, insisted that Jeremy leave the game, he was going to have a fight on his hands. It just wasn't worth it. And it was Saturday.

"Fifteen minutes," he said gruffly as he walked off.

Excited giggles followed him around the corner, then he heard Tina say, "You're not sorry, squirt. You're just too good at this game for me."

"Yes, ma'am!" Jeremy shouted gleefully.

Dean shook his head, but couldn't help smiling as he made his way inside the house. Voices in the kitchen told him his mother was getting dinner ready. He walked into the kitchen, and saw Cord and Hope sitting at the table with his father. His mother was leaning against the counter with her arms folded over her chest. Whatever they were discussing must not be pleasant, because none of them were smiling.

"What's wrong?" Dean asked.

His mother forced a smile and pushed away from the counter, and turned her back to him to flip biscuits from the baking sheet to a plate. "Nothing, honey. We were just talking."

"About what?" Dean asked, taking a seat at the table with a funny feeling settling in his chest. That his entry into the room seemed to halt the conversation meant he was probably the topic of their discussion. He looked at Cord, whose face he could usually read like a book. Not this time. "What were ya'll discussing," he asked again.

His daddy cleared his throat and looked away. "Mama found out from a friend in town that Cindy is remarried and living at a ranch on the outskirts of town. I guess her husband got a job there," Cord informed, looking away too.

Dean's heart took a dive in his chest, but he mentally dragged it back where it belonged. "To what unlucky bastard?" he asked gruffly.

"Last one she took up with, I think," his daddy said with disgust. "What was his name?"

"Bobby Jones," Dean supplied. It was a name he wasn't likely to forget anytime soon. The cowhand he hired, because he was Cindy's old high school friend. Dean found out later what Bobby Jones had been was her old high school *boy*friend. A man she'd kept as lover behind his back almost the whole time they were married, when he wasn't out on the rodeo circuit. A fucking bronco rider. The man who Cindy claimed was Jeremy's biological father.

She'd dropped that little nugget of sunshine on her way off the ranch the day Dean caught them out in the barn and told her to leave. What Bobby Jones probably didn't know was when he wasn't around, she cheated on both of them. Faithless bitch. Dean had only married her because she was pregnant, and told him it was his. Doing the right thing had bought him three years of misery, and a son who probably wasn't his to raise.

"I'm so sorry, Dean," Hope said, and the sympathy in her voice was his undoing.

He scraped his chair back and stood. "I'm not hungry, since I didn't get a chance to do any work today with that photo shoot going on. I'll see ya'll in the morning."

Dean left his family at the table and walked down the hall to his bedroom. It was way too early to sleep, but staying at that table a minute longer, seeing his family feeling sorry for him wasn't an option. What happened to him was his own damned fault. The person they should be feeling sorry for was that sorry bastard Bobby Jones who was stupid enough to marry her knowing she was a cheater. Dean just hoped the conversation ended before Tina Montgomery joined them in the kitchen. Wouldn't that be humiliating for his dirty laundry to be aired in front of her?

The best thing Dean could do right now was stay away from all of them.

Two hours later, his mind had just settled enough for him to get to that relaxed state between wakefulness and sleep when someone knocked at his bedroom door. Dean wasn't in the mood to talk to anyone, so he ignored it, until his visitor knocked the third time just shy of banging. With a sigh, he tossed back the light cover he had over his legs and got up to walk to the door. He pulled it open and didn't see anyone. Leaning outside, he saw Tina Montgomery headed back down the hall.

"Did you need something?" he asked gruffly.

She stopped then turned back toward him. In one hand she held a plate with a sandwich and the other held a glass of iced tea. She walked back to him and shoved the plate into his stomach. "Your Mama asked me to bring you this. I told her you should starve if you were too good to come eat with us, but she insisted."

Dean took the plate, then reached for the tea, but she held it out of his reach. "Why didn't you come to supper?"

"I'm not good company right now," Dean warned, reaching for the glass again, but she took another step back.

"When the hell are you good company?" she asked with a short laugh. "Your attitude sucks. You could have at least made an appearance. Your mother and your son were worried about you."

Dean's eyes tracked down to her perfect belly button, which was on prime display between the hem of her shirt and the waistband of the pants. His dick jerked and he dragged his eyes back to her angry eyes. "Thank you for bringing the sandwich, but I don't want it with a side of your opinion. Mind your own damned business!"

He stepped into the hall and grabbed the iced tea from her hand, then moved back to lean on the door to shut it. Dean was surprised when Tina

Montgomery pushed against it to keep it open.

"You're right, it's not my business. But I care about kids, and I have a problem with how you treat yours. That kid cares about you and all you do is either yell at him or ignore him."

With a growl, Dean let go of the door to walk across the room. He set the sandwich and glass on the bedside table then rounded on the nosy, irritating woman who thought she had a right to judge him. "My son is well taken care of. He has a roof over his head, food on his plate and a family who cares about him. That's a helluva lot more than a lot of kids have."

"He deserves your time…and love. You're his father."

Maybe he was and maybe he wasn't, Dean thought. "I love him, and I give him as much time as I have to give. Ranching requires a lot of work."

"That's not enough," Tina Montgomery said, crossing her arms under her full breasts, which pushed over the V in her shirt. Dean had to force his eyes up to meet hers, because they seemed to be glued there.

"You've been here all of twelve hours, and you've come to that conclusion? Lady, you've got a helluva lot of nerve, you know that?" More nerve than any woman he'd ever met.

"Someone needed to say it. Hope knows it. She said the same thing to me, but I guess she's afraid of you. I'm not afraid." No, she definitely didn't look afraid of him. All hundred pounds of her looked ready for battle.

"So you got voted to be the one to tell me this?"

"I *chose* to tell you. Your family is afraid to hurt your feelings. I think they need to be hurt. You're an asshole, and need a wake-up call. If someone doesn't point it out to you, how will you know? From the looks of it, you're too stupid to realize it on your own."

With that parting shot, she spun toward the door, leaving Dean speechless. At the door she stopped. "It's Saturday night, and your family is playing a game of Monopoly. I don't know why, but they would like you to join them, if that's not too much trouble." Dean's eyes fell to her perfectly formed ass as she walked out of his room.

Monopoly? Dean couldn't remember the last time his family had played a board game together. He definitely wasn't in the mood, but couldn't resist a challenge. And that is what Miss Priss Montgomery had just issued him. He would play her damned game to show her what a good daddy he was. Prove to her he wasn't the one with a bad attitude. He could do that for one night. She was leaving tomorrow. Thank the Good Lord. He didn't need her or her aggravation in his life.

In fact, if he never saw the nervy, curvy brunette again, it would be too soon.

CHAPTER FOUR

"No, I'm not doing it," Dean said, throwing the hoof pick into the tool kit sitting beside the arena rail. He owed Hope Dixon a lot, loved her a lot, but her request wasn't even in the same arena as the debt he owed her. He'd rather she ask to peel every inch of his skin off then douse him in alcohol than ask him to be a model. That was his brother's speed, not his.

Dean was curious what went on during those shoots, exactly what his brother had been doing in Dallas while he was gone, so he watched some of the circus they called a photo shoot at the ranch on Saturday. Tina Montgomery and her entourage ran roughshod over those two men who looked as plucked and shaved as any men he'd ever seen.

A chill skated down Dean's spine.

Those two weren't men. They were mannequins in cowboy hats. Tina Montgomery had posed, poked and prodded them until she got them into the position she wanted them, so Hope could take their picture. Sort of like the poseable Toy Story action figures his son had.

Well Dean wasn't an action figure, and he wasn't a model. He was a real-life cowboy, with real ranch chores to do. If he didn't get those chores done, he wasn't going to be a cowboy much longer though. He'd be a broke, unemployed and *homeless* ex-cowboy.

And the woman he was arguing with would be

homeless with him, so he just wished she'd drop it and leave him alone. But it didn't look like she was going to do that. He unclipped the roan mare he'd been grooming from the cross-ties and clipped a lead rope onto her halter then lead the mare toward her stall, and Hope followed behind him.

She put her hand on his arm. "But Dean, Tina needs you—*I* need you to do this."

"No way, Hope." he said firmly for the fifth time, as he flipped the latch on the stall and opened it wide.

"Get Cord to do it. He's the one with the looks in the family." Dean looked back at her for a second. "I'm just the workhorse, and I've got work to do." He led the mare inside, and unclipped the lead rope. He turned around and Hope was still there, standing in the doorway so he couldn't pass.

"Please, Dean," she begged with a plea in her gorgeous green eyes.

After having to play Monopoly with them until almost midnight on Saturday night, Dean was in family overload. Cord told him the game had been Tina's brilliant idea. Dean decided he didn't want to see what her next idea of family fun involved, so he had hidden out in his room until he saw the taillights of her white compact car heading down the driveway Sunday night.

Dean had a feeling Tina Montgomery was good at games. She'd won at Monopoly, but she wasn't winning this game. Even using Hope, a woman he owed his father's life to, as her mouthpiece wasn't going to convince Dean to shave his ass and get in front of a camera.

There was nothing that would convince him to do that.

"That's it Hope," he said with finality. She sighed then stepped aside so he could walk out and closed the stall. "Ask Cord. I'll cover his slack here." Dean always did that anyway, like right now when his brother was supposed to be helping him, he had gone to town with their daddy to look at fucking tractors they couldn't afford.

Somehow Cord had convinced Silas Dixon, who had been a rancher all his life, that they could subsidize the cattle operation with farming. And according to his brother, they needed a new tractor to do that. Fixing the old tractor they had was on Dean's to-do list so they could cut hay, but that list was so long these days he had no idea when he would get to it.

At least that offer might get Hope off of his back, and keep Cord occupied so he didn't have time to cook up new schemes.

Hope surprised him though, when she said, "Tina doesn't want Cord. She wants you."

"Well Tina can want in one hand and shit—" Dean started then cleared his throat when Hope's amber brows shot up. He brushed past her to go to the next stall in the line. "I'm not doing it—end of discussion," Dean said, but it evidently wasn't over yet he realized when Hope followed him again.

"That little girl that was with her out here is her niece. Tina is all but raising her, since her sister runs around and leaves Laney with her all the time. The kid has nobody but Tina to look out for her. If she's successful with this new line, Tina's company is offering her a big promotion and raise. Tina needs that raise and promotion to support Laney."

Dean huffed out a breath, and hardened his heart against the compassion trying to take root there. He definitely knew what that felt like. Cindy had dumped Jeremy with him all the time to go out too. "That's not my problem," he grumbled, reminding himself he had enough of his own without taking on someone else's. "This family is what I'm concerned with."

"This will help us too, Dean. You ought to at least listen to Tina's offer, before you turn her down," Hope volleyed.

"If she wrote me a blank check, I wouldn't do it," Dean said throwing up his hands.

Hope's eyes watered, and she covered the small mound of her stomach. Dean swallowed down the emotion that shot up to his own throat. Her eyes were determined, but her voice quavered when she told him, "Then I need every penny of the money I loaned you paid back. She wants to buy a house for herself and Laney and I'm going to help her do that, since she won't get her promotion now."

"God, you sure know how to put the screws to me, don't you? Why would you care?"

"Because that's what friends do, Dean. She helped Cord and I when we needed her and I'm going to return the favor. Maybe if you stopped letting what Cindy did to you make you hard as nails, you would have a friend. Then you might understand." Hope dragged her eyes away. "Maybe your son wouldn't think you hate him."

Anger the likes of which he hadn't felt in a long time engulfed him. He clenched his fists and grated, "Don't you say that woman's name again. You *and* your friend just need to mind your own fucking business. I don't know how I'll do it, but I will get you that money back. Every fucking cent."

Hope's lips pinched like she was holding back a scream. She turned away from him and he heard her whimper as she stiffened her spine to storm down the aisle toward the barn door. Rage built inside of him with every step she got closer to the door.

Dean needed to scream too.

He needed to get away from civilization for a minute. Visit the place he hadn't been to in a year to do just that. Scream. Until he found peace again. Dean's hand shook as he unlocked the door to the stall that housed his stallion, Blaze. His daddy and Cord wanted to run the ranch? Well they could go to the auction on their own too.

It was nearly six o'clock when Dean finally

rode Blaze back into the barn. He was still frustrated as hell, as he swung out of the saddle. The solitude he always found out at the lake at the back of their property wasn't there this time. Neither were the answers he needed.

No matter how he sliced and diced it, Hope's demand had backed him into a corner he couldn't escape. He had no chance of paying her money back without doing that damned photo shoot. Taking out another mortgage wasn't the answer. The reason he owed her the money in the first place was because she used her inheritance to pay off a mortgage that almost took the ranch from them. Taking out another one would defeat the purpose of the loan. And they couldn't afford a note right now. Besides, they needed the ranch free and clear for collateral in case his daddy got sick again. He was in remission, but now he *couldn't* get the insurance Dean had been after him to get for years.

The money from the auction today was going to buy cattle. Last fall, Dean had to sell off the entire herd to help pay the last mortgage note, before Hope came along and paid it off. They were starting over now.

He was just going to have to keep thinking about it, and come up with another solution.

Dean dropped the reins, and reached to unbuckle the cinch under Blaze's belly. He heard someone come into the barn behind him and glanced up. His brother stopped in front of him with fire in his eyes and his fists balled at his sides. The look on his face said he was ready for a fight. Well Dean was ready too. A good fight with Cord would probably go a long way to making some of the anger and frustration inside him go away.

"What the fuck did you say to Hope?" Cord demanded, giving him a push when Dean stood to face him. "And why the hell weren't you here to go to the auction with us?"

"I needed a break," Dean said defensively. He shoved Cord with his shoulder as he bent to jerk up the reins.

"*Break*?!?" Cord yelled crowding him.

"Yeah, you know all about taking breaks, don't you? Your three-year break almost broke this ranch and your family. I think I deserve a small one for keeping this shit together for so long by myself, don't you?" Dean knew that would get Cord going. He pushed past him to lead Blaze to the cross-ties where he removed his bridle to slip on a halter.

"I'm sick and damned tired of you throwing that in my face." Cord said crowding even closer to him.

Too close. If Cord knew what was good for him, he would back off. Dean pushed him away and spat, "And I'm sick and tired of carrying the load around here. You haven't pulled your weight around here in a long time. Going to the fucking auction is the *least* you could do."

"Your pity party is getting old, Dean. I'm back now, and I'm working as hard, *harder,* than you are. It's time you quit taking out your frustrations on the people who love you, or pretty soon there won't be anyone left. I'm beginning to wonder why I do."

"Well you might want to work a little harder. Your *wife* told me earlier she wants her money back right now, and I have no idea where it's gonna come from," Dean said nastily.

"Hope wouldn't say that. She doesn't even want the money back. I had to force her to take my check from the calendar payment."

"Well she wants it from me, and I don't have it," Dean informed. His brother needed to feel some of the stress he was feeling, so he added, "I guess we'll just have to get another mortgage on the ranch to pay her off." Dean leaned back under Blaze's belly to loosen the cinch on the saddle. Dean thought he might up the pucker factor for his brother a little. He was enjoying himself. "I'll probably need you to co-sign. I don't want to be the only one putting my balls on the chopping block this time."

Cord huffed out a breath, then said, "Hope is at the bunkhouse locked in the bedroom, and I think she's crying. What the hell did you say to her?"

"I just told her I wasn't doing that damned photo shoot for that woman Tina. I'm not a model, I'm a rancher. You got the looks in the family. I have a ranch to run. You do the damned photo shoot."

"Tina wants you to represent Texas Tomcat?" Cord asked with a laugh.

"You think that's funny?" Dean replied, a little insulted as he pinned Cord with a glare.

"Hell yeah I do. Why would Tina want a grumpy *old* bastard like you to be her guy? What happened to the two guys she shot with on Saturday?"

Old. His brother was thirty, and Dean was thirty-four. Considering the ages of those men Tina had at that photo shoot with her on Saturday, Dean guessed he was old. Those guys didn't have to worry about shaving their bodies. They probably weren't old enough to grow hair. With all that Cindy had put him through, it was a wonder Dean didn't have a headful of gray hair and look ninety-five. That's how he felt sometimes. But Tina Montgomery had asked him to model for her, so he must not look that bad. As bad as his brother seemed to think he did.

"Hope didn't say why they didn't work, but she did say Tina wants me to do it now. Those guys did seem pretty damned prissy for pretend cowboys. Let 'em actually work out here for a day or two, and that'll toughen them up." Dean knew all the hard work and problems at the ranch had toughened him up over the last few years, that was for damned sure. Hell, according to his family, he was practically tough as an old boot now. He felt that way too. Worn out and used up.

What the hell was Tina Montgomery thinking asking him to model for her? Why him?

Dean slid the saddle off of Blaze's back to drop it on the ground. But he had other things to worry about than what that woman thought of him. He bent and hefted the saddle over his shoulder. "How did the auction go?"

"Not good. Daddy was pretty upset. Four of the horses didn't even sell. They're in the trailer outside."

"Well, he's going to be even more upset when he finds out that Hope demanded her money back," Dean said as he walked past Cord toward the tack room.

"Just do the damned photo shoot, Dean," Cord said following behind him.

"I'd rather be shot. I'll even load the shotgun for you," Dean offered tossing the saddle onto the saddle rack. "I'm not going to shave all the damned hair off my body, and coat myself in oil so I can prance around in my underwear. I'll leave that to you, baby brother."

"I did *not* prance around in my underwear," Cord corrected indignantly.

"But you did shave your ass, so you looked like a ten-year-old boy. I saw the proof in those magazines."

"You saw my pictures?" Cord asked with surprise.

To Dean's own surprise his brother's face heated, and he looked a little embarrassed. Embarrassed wouldn't begin to describe how Dean would feel if he were in his brother's shoes. And that is exactly where Tina Montgomery wanted to put him. So she could get a promotion. What the fuck did he get out of it, other than getting the money to pay back a loan he hadn't even taken out? Cord and Hope had decided on that plan of action themselves, without his permission or knowledge even. But that loan had saved the ranch, and saved his Daddy's life. It also resulted in his brother settling down. Dean did owe her a lot.

"Yeah, I saw 'em," Dean said, remembering his brother in those jeans ads. Shaved and shirtless looking like a greased pig, showing off his gym generated muscles.

How could he have not seen them? Those ads were in every fucking magazine and newspaper he picked up, and on television too. His brother had been famous, and Dean was sure Cord got laid every time he blinked at a women who saw him in those ads. They didn't impress him, though. Why women would want to see a man like that, Dean didn't know. It might sell jeans, but it just wasn't reality. It sure as hell wasn't how he wanted the world, his family or his son to see him. Regardless of whether it got him laid.

"Is shaving the only thing you have against doing it?" Cord asked, following him out of the tack room, then back down the aisle toward Blaze.

"Hell no, it's not the only thing," Dean grated.

"What else then?" Cord asked impatiently, but Dean could almost hear the wheels in his brother's head spinning.

Well, he could just shut them down, because Dean wasn't doing that damned shoot no matter what he came up with. He had too much work to do. His brother seemed to have forgotten in the last three years how much work this ranch took to keep going.

"Who is going to manage this ranch while I'm off prissing in front of a camera? And I have a son to raise. Did you forget that small, but important, fact?" Dean replied shortly, as he grabbed the towel off of his shoulder and rubbed at the sweat on Blaze's black coat.

"I'll do the work, just tell me what you want done. I'll make sure it gets done. Mama and I will help with Jeremy, while you're shooting. Besides, you'll be here too."

"She wants to take the pictures out here?" Dean asked with surprise.

"That's what Tina told Hope on Saturday. I agreed, because we need the money. I didn't know the shoot would be with you though," Cord said with a snicker.

It wasn't going to be with him, and his brother sure agreed to a lot on his own these days. But Cord was right this time, they did need the damned money. Dean couldn't help but wonder how much his dignity was worth. "Did she mention how much?"

"She offered five grand to use the ranch for the location. Probably a grand an hour for your time. That was my rate when I was modeling."

Dean's heart shot to his throat, and his knees went weak. "Holy fuck!" he shouted as the towel slipped from his hand to the dirt floor.

A cocky smile eased up his brother's mouth. The same smile Dean had seen on his face in those magazines, the same one that women all over the country seemed to go weak-kneed over. "A lot more than ranching or rodeoing, huh?" Cord asked smugly.

"That's just stupid. Those companies have more money than sense," Dean said, trying to regulate his breathing.

"Understand now why I shaved my ass and moved to Dallas?"

Dean picked up the towel, then met his brother's eyes. "No, I'll never understand why you abandoned your family for money."

Dean thought about it while he made one more pass over Blaze's back with the towel. He didn't have much choice really. Hope was forcing his hand. Dean hated being cornered, but that damned money was too tempting to resist even if she hadn't pressured him.

"I'll do it, but I'm not shaving my ass," he said firmly.

"You got it. No ass shaving," Cord agreed with a chuckle. "I'll let Hope know, so she can call Tina.

They'll both be happy."

Tina Montgomery had outmaneuvered him after all, and she'd won. Dean was sure she would be ecstatic. He was going to do the damned shoot, but he wasn't going to make it easy for her. She was going to do things on his terms.

CHAPTER FIVE

Friday morning, Tina and her crew of rodeo clowns invaded the ranch. By then Dean was having second, third and fourth thoughts about agreeing to this crap. He sat on a stool in the bunkhouse where they set up what they called a staging area, while a man who looked as feminine as the women in the group cut his damned hair. He needed a haircut yeah, but what this guy was doing to him was way beyond that.

Gel? Hairspray? Definitely not him. And Dean had about had enough of his flitting around. When the guy named Paulo reached for the hairspray again, Dean clamped his fingers over his wrist and gave him a glare. "That's enough," he said, standing but not releasing the hairdresser's wrist.

"Daddy, can Paulo cut my hair now too?" Jeremy asked with excitement as he skidded to a stop beside the hairdresser. "He said he would cut my hair too."

"Not now. Go find Grandma," Dean said gruffly, still not releasing his hold on Paulo's wrist. "Paulo is finished with the hair for now."

"But, Daddy—" Jeremy started, but Dean gave him a hot glare. Jeremy's eyes dropped to the toes of his dusty boots, and he turned and walked off. Dean swung his gaze back to Paulo. "Where is Tina?" he asked darkly.

She needed to get this show on the road, or he

was going to do what he should be doing. Helping unload the stock his father and brother bought at the auction. He wanted to see the stock anyway. He trusted his dad, but Cord had a way of talking Silas Dixon into things that Dean didn't agree with. Dean wouldn't put it past him to have talked their daddy into buying peacocks to stock the ranch, instead of cattle.

Paulo jerked his wrist from Dean's hold and folded his arms over his chest. "I haven't put the wax in your hair yet to separate it," he complained. "And I did tell your son I would cut his hair too."

Tina Montgomery scheduling this shoot right away, now when Jeremy was on spring break from school for two weeks, was just stupid. But according to Hope, it had to be now. She had some kind of big meeting she needed the photos for. With his son, and her niece, who must be on break too, under their feet it would be damned tough for Dean to focus on anything.

This was a shit show waiting to happen, and Dean didn't have time for the delays that was going to cause. He had to get back to his real job. Ranching. And his fricking brother needed to watch Jeremy like he said he would. And Tina Montgomery needed to get this shit show on the road. Now. "Where is Tina?" Dean repeated with a growl this time.

The small man took a step back, and his perfectly arched eyebrows shot to the edge of his slicked back, black hair. Paulo tilted his chin to say indignantly, "Don't get huffy with me, cowboy. She went out with Hope to scout out locations."

"Well, I need to talk to—" Dean grated through his teeth, but stopped when a tall, thin woman dressed all in black slid her hand through his arm and pulled him back.

"Time for wardrobe, Tomcat," she said evenly.

Dean pulled his arm from her grasp, and clenched his fists. "My fucking name is Dean, and I want to talk to Tina first!" he shouted. Texas Tomcat. What a stupid name, Dean thought. And he was the pussy who was going to have his face attached to that stupid name.

The woman's brown eyes narrowed, and anger sparked there. "Don't you curse at me, mister," she said with a haughty tilt of her chin similar to Paulo's. "They are getting the equipment set up, and expect you to be ready when they are. Time is money here, and if you don't want your paycheck docked, you'll cooperate." A thousand dollars an hour. Dean kept repeating that to himself since they arrived there this morning. Since he agreed to this insanity.

"Fine," Dean replied, storming past her to go stand beside the clothing rack at the back wall. When the woman got there she yanked a pink and green shirt with pearl buttons off the rack, and a pair of creased dark blue jeans. She handed the hangers to him, then knelt to dig in a box under the rack. Her black leather pants creaked as she stood back up to hand him a rhinestone-studded black leather belt. Dean stared at the sparkly, girly belt like it was made of snakeskin and the snake was still in residence.

"I'm not wearing that," he said firmly. He had to draw the line somewhere, or he had a feeling this woman might have him looking as prissy as Paulo.

"Yes, you are," she said folding her arms over her chest.

"No, I'm not. That's a woman's belt."

The woman huffed out a breath. "It will work. I left the other ones at home."

"That's your problem," Dean replied smugly.

"Just take the damned belt," she said with frustration. When he didn't move, she sat back on the floor and glared up at him. "Are you always this difficult?"

Dean heard a hoot from behind him, and spun around. "No most of the time he's much worse. This is his best behavior, Belinda. Be thankful," Cord said with a smile for the woman, and a sideways glare at him. "C'mon man, just take the damned belt." Cord took the belt from Belinda and laid it over the clothes on his arm.

"What the hell are you doing in here? You're supposed to be working," Dean reminded gruffly. It sure didn't take his brother long to shuck off the responsibilities Dean had given him this morning. So much for him doing what Dean asked him to do, while he did this. Not only had Jeremy been in here this morning bugging the crap out of all of them, now Cord was doing the same.

"And so are you," Cord reprimanded. "Sounds like the only thing you're working at is being an abrasive asshole. Oh yeah, that's not work for you. It comes naturally."

"Pssht—this isn't work either. But it is frustrating as hell." Dean shoved a hand through his hair, and heard dual gasps from Belinda and Paulo. He patted the top of his hair then let his hand fall to his side.

Paulo grabbed the can of hairspray and a pick off of the coffee table and headed his way with a determined look on his face. Dean turned and almost ran down the hallway toward the bathroom. He felt Paulo hot on his heels, but he shut the bathroom door in his face and locked it for good measure. Dean needed some breathing room for a minute to get his head right.

He'd told his brother this wasn't work, and compared to being a rancher it wasn't. But Dean was fast seeing that the frustration factor alone made it worth every penny of the money they were paying him to do it. Even a thousand bucks an hour almost didn't seem like enough. All those people buzzing around him like he was some kind of project they had to complete for a grade made him nervous.

Dean laid the clothes on the vanity, and pulled the jeans off the hanger then unbelted the robe he was wearing and let it drop to the floor. He inspected the jeans and decided they were a little heavy on the fancy stitching on the back pockets, but might be something he wore for special occasions. He surely wouldn't be working outside in them.

At least they were bootcut and not those damned skinny leg jeans that men were wearing these days. He had no idea how men wore those damned jeans. He'd feel like he was in a sausage casing. One thing was for sure, the men that wore those type of jeans like Paulo, didn't wear cowboy boots with them. Boots would never fit under the tight legs.

Dean put his legs in the jeans then pulled them up. To get them buttoned he had to suck in and lean back against the vanity. Before he zipped them he had to rearrange things to make sure the zipper didn't catch anything important. God, if a man got excited in these jeans, there would definitely be trouble, he thought, as he finally got the zipper up and looked down at himself.

They were too tight, he decided, patting his ass and not feeling an inch of give in the material. He ran his thumb along the waistband and there was no room there either. Surely, that woman Belinda had brought more than one pair. Tina had sent a tailor out Wednesday to take his measurements, but the guy must've gotten the numbers wrong. Dean shoved his undershirt into the waistband of the jeans, put on his boots then opened the door. He walked back down the hall to the living room of the bunkhouse. Belinda was talking to Hope and Tina, so he just walked over there.

"These pants are too tight," Dean complained and all three women swung around to face him. He figured they must've realized it too, because as a group they gasped and put their hands to their chests. He even heard a whimper from over by the sofa that had to come from Paulo. "I'm gonna bust out of these if I breathe too deeply. Get me another pair," Dean said shortly.

Tina broke from the others to walk over and slowly circle him, inspecting him like she would a side of beef. That's exactly what he felt like right then with the petite brunette's hot eyes on his body. Uncomfortable, Dean shifted his weight from foot to foot.

"They're perfect," she said softly, as she stopped to face him.

Her gray eyes made it up as far as his mouth and lingered a second, before her gaze tracked back down his throat, moved slowly over his chest down his legs to his toes. "Perfect," she repeated. On the return trip up his body, her eyes lingered for a moment at his crotch. That look he'd seen in her eyes the other day when she was moving the car came back. Interest. Desire.

Dean quickly found out that he was right about the lack of stretch in those jeans. Tina might as well have actually touched him there considering his reaction. That thought made him harder. "Get me another pair of damned jeans!" he demanded as he turned away quickly before anyone noticed his problem.

He strode back down the hallway, and slammed the bathroom door behind him. Leaning back against it, he shut his eyes. He'd had a fucking hard on since he met that woman. Her staring at him like that when he hadn't had sex in three fucking years wasn't helping his problem. He hadn't taken the edge off in a long time either.

Why did his damned sex drive have to come out of hibernation now? And why because of a woman he did nothing but argue with? Because even though his mind might resist the idea of being attracted to the tiny spitfire, his body was definitely there.

Big time, he thought, looking down at the straining zipper on the jeans.

He kept feeling her soft skin against his palm when he took off her boots, and wondering if the rest of her shapely body was just as warm and silky. Wondered if the tips of her perky breasts were dusky pink or coral colored. And how they would taste. The tip of his tongue tingled, and Dean got so hard, he really did think he might break the zipper out of those jeans.

And there wasn't a damned thing he could do about it. This photo shoot was about to go to hell in a handbasket. Dean was about to be humiliated too. He knew someone would probably be knocking on that door soon, expecting him to come back out there. When he did, the whole crew was in for a surprise. Unless he did something to fix the situation himself.

Dean unzipped the jeans, and shoved them down his legs, grabbed the hand towel off the rack beside the sink, then shuffled over to sit on edge of the tub. He jerked his underwear down and fisted himself. Sitting sideways he leaned back against the wall, straddled the tub edge and closed his eyes. He gripped his painful erection, and stroked himself, as he pictured Tina Montgomery using that beautiful mouth of hers on him. Dean held back a moan, his breathing hitched, and his heart beat an unsteady rhythm in his chest.

With each stroke, each fantasy he indulged, the tension inside him ratcheted up. Pleasure built, his balls tightened and he moaned, damned close to coming when the bathroom door opened. A soft gasp followed, and his eyes flew open to see the woman he was fantasizing about standing there, looking as embarrassed as he felt right then.

God, he wished someone would just shoot him. Put him out of his misery. His face felt like it was on fire as he threw the hand towel over his lap and sat up.

"Um, I was just coming to see what was taking so long," she said, her voice barely above a whisper. She waved her hand, put it to her cheek, then shook her head and dragged her eyes toward the toilet. "You just, ah…finish up…and I'll be out there," she said without looking at him. Tina crawfished back out of the door and pulled it shut. Dean just sat there with his heart pounding in his ears, more embarrassed than he'd ever been in his life.

His chin dropped to his chest, and he took slow even breaths trying to get himself together.

How in the hell was he going to face that woman now? Dean didn't know, but he knew he couldn't hang out in the bathroom all day. His eyes slid to the wall and up to the small window near the ceiling, gauging his odds of fitting through it. Not good. With a heavy sigh, he stood and grabbed the hand towel before it fell on the floor. He looked down at himself and realized his problem had resolved itself now.

Odds were he would never have to worry about that problem again. Every time he looked at Tina Montgomery from now on, he'd probably shrivel up. She definitely wouldn't be giving him that look again. Her walking in and catching him, a thirty-four-year-old man, jerking off like a teenager had to have been a shocker. A teenager would have been smarter than he had been. At least a teenager would remember to lock the damned door first.

Dean shook his head, and situated his underwear, then pulled the jeans up and zipped them. He tucked in his undershirt, then grabbed the shirt off of the vanity and slid into it. How the hell was he going to explain this and not look like the fool he was?

There was no explaining it. But she was a grown woman, and she knew he was divorced. Out here in the country there wasn't an overabundance of available women. He was a man. With needs. But damn.

Dean felt his face heat up again, as he worked the buttons on the shirt, and tucked it into the jeans. The sparkly belt on the vanity mocked him. He stared it a minute, then decided that the best thing he could do was keep his mouth shut and do as he was told. He needed the money he made from this shoot. So maybe he could run away to Tahiti where nobody knew about what had just happened. The most he could hope for was that Tina Montgomery knew how to keep her mouth shut. Dean sucked in a deep breath and let it out slowly, then slid the belt through the belt loops on the jeans and buckled it.

Stiffening his shoulders, Dean grabbed the knob and opened the bathroom door. He walked down the hallway to the living room, and saw her entourage standing in a circle on the other side of the room talking and laughing loudly. Paulo stepped to the side, holding his flat stomach while he laughed uproariously. Tina was standing right in the middle of the group holding court. Her eyes met his, a small knowing grin kicked up the side of her mouth. The conversation stopped, and all eyes swung his way.

Just Shoot Me

The entire group grinned from ear-to-ear, including Tina, whose grin was wider than the rest. Tina Montgomery had told them. They were laughing at him. A feeling of betrayal momentarily displaced his embarrassment, but then turned into full blown anger.

If he felt like a teenager jerking off in the bathroom, then they were acting like teenagers gossiping about it. And it looked like Tina Montgomery was the head cheerleader. Dean was done with this shit. And he was done with her. He had work to do. They could enjoy their laugh, because they wouldn't be taking any pictures, since their model had just quit.

"I'm outta here," he said as he stomped across the room past them to the door.

He flung it open, and Cord stood there looking surprised. Dean gave him a heated glare, as he brushed past him. He was almost to the driveway when Tina yelled behind him. Dean didn't stop. He needed to go for a ride. Maybe he'd just keep riding and never come back. That's how he felt about his life these days. It sucked. The situation sucked. Tina called him again, and Dean increased his pace toward the barn. As short as her legs were, he could probably have Blaze saddled and be out of the barn before she caught up to him.

When he walked inside, the familiar smells comforted him, and he took a deep breath. This was what made him happy. Hope said he needed friends? The animals in this barn were his friends. They understood him, he could talk to them and not worry about them telling tales and laughing behind his back. These were the only friends he needed.

At least he could trust them.

Dean walked to the tack room, and pulled his saddle off the rack. He grabbed a striped blanket from the stack on a shelf, then took his bridle down from the peg by the door. When he walked out the door of the tack room, he went straight to Blaze's stall, where he angrily unlatched the door. Blaze nudged his shoulder with his nose, but stepped back when he walked inside. Dean didn't waste time with cross-ties today, he tossed the saddle blanket over the horse's back, then haphazardly sat the saddle on top and secured it. He needed to get out of here fast.

The stall door creaked and swung wide. Even as small as she was, Tina Montgomery filled the space with all five feet of her angry body. "What the hell are you doing? We have a photo shoot to do."

"We don't have anything. I'm done with this shit," Dean replied just as angrily, moving around in front of Blaze to slide the bit between his teeth. He pulled the straps over his ears, then scratched his jaw before grabbing the reins to move him out of the stall. Tina didn't move. She stood there with her tiny fists perched on her hips, and her eyes burning him.

"Move," he grated through his teeth.

"Not until you tell me what the hell is wrong with you."

Dean laughed dryly. "You have to ask me that?"

"Are you upset because I walked in on you choking your chicken?" she asked and her lips twitched. "Because if so, trust me, I wanted you to finish. It might improve your disposition."

"My disposition?" Dean repeated with a snort.

"Yeah. I think I finally figured out why you're such an asshole."

"Oh yeah? Do tell," Dean invited sarcastically. "I can't wait to hear this."

To Dean's mind, the only thing wrong with him was the woman standing in front of him being at the ranch. Ever since he met her, his life had been one trial after another. His peace was shattered, and his life disrupted. She just needed to take herself and her entourage right back wherever they came from and he would be just fine.

"I think you need to get laid," she announced bluntly.

Shock shot through him, then anger. "Is that what you and your friends concluded after your discussion?" he asked gruffly, taking a step forward, leading Blaze with him. She had no choice but to move. Dean tied Blaze to the rail, then closed the stall door.

"Me and my friends?" Was that confusion he heard in her voice? He took a sideways glance at her, and saw it in her face too. No, he heard what he heard, saw what he saw. They had been laughing at him.

Dean shook his head, and untied the reins. "Playing dumb doesn't work for you, buttercup. You're too smart to pull it off."

Her brows pinched tighter between her gray eyes, then suddenly her face lit up and her eyebrows shot toward her hairline. "You think I told them what you were doing in the bathroom?" she asked with an incredulous laugh.

Dean didn't laugh. He didn't find a damned thing funny about the situation. "Ya'll were sure enjoying something when I walked into the room. Everyone shut up real fast to stare."

"We weren't laughing at you, and I didn't tell them. I wouldn't embarrass you like that. Paulo was telling us about his date from hell on Saturday night. That's what we were laughing about," she said, coming to stand in front of him.

Dean looked deeply into her eyes, gauged the sincerity in her tone and almost believed her. Almost. His chest loosened a little.

Tina took a step forward to put her hand on his chest and his heart did a funny little hop. "The reason we shut up was because we were all in awe of how handsome you looked. How perfect you are for the Texas Tomcat." She moved her hand up to his face, and her thumb stroked his cheekbone. "Thank you for agreeing to do the shoot. It means everything to me."

Silence settled between them, as their eyes held. The air between them sizzled, and tasting her lips became a driving need inside of him. Dean's head gravitated toward hers as if pulled there by a magnetic force. Tina slid her hand to the back of his neck and pulled him toward her. The reins slithered from his fingers, and he put his hands at her hips to pull her closer. His lips met hers, and she sighed.

Her plump lips tasted like water to him, a dying man who had been marooned in a desert of loneliness far too long. Sweet desire ripped through his veins, and Dean lapped it up. Her tongue traced the seam of his lips, and his heart kicked in his chest. Opening his mouth, he deepened the kiss and lifted her against his body.

Tina moaned, leaning in to press her breasts against his chest, and he held her tighter. She said he needed to get laid. Well at that moment, she couldn't be more right. And Dean was definitely on board with the sexy woman in his arms being the layer. Her enthusiasm for the kiss told him she was offering, and he was not about to refuse.

At least he might get something out of this damned situation.

"Daddy why were you choking the chickens? Grandma gets mad at me for chasing them. She's *really* gonna be mad at you," Jeremy informed and his laughter mixed with feminine giggles.

Shock broke the sensual dream world Dean

had been caught in and he moaned, as he eased Tina back to her feet, and took a step back. She stumbled and put a hand on his arm to steady herself. His eyes flew to the stall adjacent to Blaze's stall then back to his son. "Were you eavesdropping?" he asked sharply.

Jeremy cast his eyes down at the toes of his boots. "No, sir, we were just playing a game of marbles in there and heard ya'll talking."

The little blonde girl beside Jeremy folded her arms over her chest, and her eyes took on a look very similar to her aunt when she was pissed. "Aunt T, why were you kissing him? He's mean to Jeremy!"

Tina groaned and slapped a hand to her forehead, then cast him a mischievous sideways glance at him. "He's not mean, sweetie. He's just frustrated from having to choke the chickens. Me, I just prefer a nice sharp knife to take care of them."

A cold chill passed through Dean's body, and he slid his hand up between her shoulder blades to grab a hank of Tina's silky black hair and jerk.

She squealed then laughed. Both kids said, "Ewwww." Tina's laughter mixed with Jeremy and Laney's. The joyful sound danced around inside of Dean's skull, and carried a happy feeling through his body. At that moment, the last thing he wanted to do was work, either on a photo shoot or ranch chores. What he wanted to do was get this woman alone and kiss her again.

"Do you ride?" Dean asked when Tina's

laughter subsided.

"As in horses?" she replied and her eyes shot to Blaze.

"Unless you want me to saddle up a chicken for you?" he teased and Tina's eyes widened. "That could definitely be arranged." Dean winked at her then threw his head back and laughed like he hadn't laughed in three years now.

It felt damned good.

Still smiling, because he couldn't seem to flatten out the curve, he said, "Jeremy you and Laney go up to the house and hang out with Grandma until we get back. I think she made brownies." Jeremy looked a little surprised, but then whooped and grabbed Laney's hand to drag her toward the barn door.

CHAPTER SIX

Tina watched as Dean positioned the huge black horse at the rail and fear squeezed her heart. Large animals weren't her thing. She was so small they scared the crap out of her.

"I don't think this is a good idea," she said, taking a step back, then another. "We, ah, need to get some work done." Tina took another step back, then improvised, "It's supposed to rain tomorrow, so we need to get what we can done today."

The weather had been good, would probably be good tomorrow too. She had no idea if it would rain or not, but it seemed as good an excuse as any. It was the best she could come up with on the spot to get out of riding, without admitting her fear to this cowboy who had probably ridden since he could walk.

Dean turned toward her. "Have you found a place where you want to take photos?"

Tina huffed out a breath. She and Hope had only been out as far as they could walk. Tina didn't ride, and Hope couldn't because she was pregnant. The golf cart would've been much too bumpy for Hope too, according to her overprotective husband. Tina found some places on the ranch that might work, but none that excited her. "Not really. We couldn't get everywhere. I thought we'd do some test shots and see what we get."

"Well, we'll be working then. Tell your crew

we're going to scout locations. I know the perfect place," Dean told her with excitement in his tone, as he gave her the second smile she'd seen on his face since she met him. It was fleeting and disappeared, but she had seen it. And liked it. When he smiled, Dean Dixon looked younger, softer around the mouth. And a helluva lot more handsome, if that was possible.

He and his famous brother weren't so different after all. The panties of the women who saw the Texas Tomcat catalog would melt just as fast as they had with the Laramie Jeans publication featuring his brother. Faster probably, considering Dean Dixon's dark edge. Women loved edgy men. Those who were a little less than friendly and approachable. Dark and brooding types were a challenge, and Dean was definitely that.

There was nothing Tina loved more than a challenge.

Another kiss from those hot lips of his was the prize for overcoming that challenge. That unexpected, magical kiss evidently had powers other than making her want more from him. His attitude toward her had obviously changed too. If it took kissing Dean Dixon between frames to drag out that smile, get him to relax for the photos, it certainly wouldn't be a hardship for her. It would be an excuse to get more of those magical kisses and see where that might lead.

I think you need to get laid. The same could be said of her. It had been a long damned time since Tina had sex, and the last time hadn't even been good. Her eyes traveled over Dean Dixon's muscular thighs, and delicious ass as he bent over to fiddle underneath his horse.

She had a feeling with him she wouldn't worry about him being good, she'd have to worry about keeping up with him. As stoic and surly as he usually was, there was some serious heat inside that man. If that heat was captured in the photos for Texas Tomcat, the pages of the magazine would probably spontaneously combust. The women who saw the photos would for sure. She knew she almost had. A lovely tingle flitted through her to settle between her legs.

Texas Tomcat jeans would fly off the shelves. Tina would get her promotion, and probably a huge bonus at the end of the year to use for the down payment on the house she wanted for herself and Laney. Her sister could live there too, if she got her act together. Maybe she'd use part of her bonus to see about getting custody of Laney. Becoming the real mother to Laney that her sister wasn't. Maybe just the threat of that would be enough to motivate her sister to get her head out of her ass.

"Daylight's wastin', buttercup. You want to go or not?" Dean asked, and Tina realized she had drifted off into dreamland and he was standing there waiting for an answer from her.

Wherever he must be wanting to take her must be special to him for some reason. She suddenly also realized he was about to go riding in her custom-made Texas Tomcat jeans and shirt. "I'll go tell them, but you have to change out of those clothes. Those are the only samples I have."

"Yes, ma'am. I have a change of clothes in the tack room," he drawled, giving her a broad smile that did funny things to her insides. "I'd be more than happy to take these clothes off."

His fingers went to the button of the jeans, and Tina spun around. "Um, make sure you're dressed and the chickens are in the coop when I get back," she said as she walked quickly toward the barn door. She heard the uncommon sound of his hearty laughter follow her out into the yard and smiled herself.

"I'll pick you up at the bunkhouse!" Dean yelled.

Pick her up? On that huge horse of his. Fear shot through her, and Tina stumbled before getting her balance to make her way up the steps to the front porch. Her hand landed on the doorknob, but the door flew inward. Paulo, Belinda and Cord stood there in the doorway. Hope stood behind Cord fiddling with her camera. "Did you talk some sense into him?" Belinda asked with agitation. "Was it the belt?" she asked with a puff of breath.

"Belt?" Tina asked pushing between them to get inside.

"I forgot to bring the right belt, and made him wear one that one of the models left behind on

Saturday. It was a little girly, and macho man had a problem with that."

Tina laughed. She hadn't even noticed the belt. She was too busy looking at other things. Like that man's spectacular ass in those jeans. "No, it wasn't the belt. He thought the jeans were, um, too tight, and felt uncomfortable. It's all good now. But we're delaying the shoot until tomorrow, because he wants to show me a location."

"Really?" Cord and Hope said, looking at each other with disbelief.

"Yeah, he said he knew of a perfect place to shoot, and he's going to show it to me."

Cord guffawed, and a small smile eased up the corner of Hope's mouth. "I'll bet he has a lot to show you," Cord said sarcastically. "I'd be careful going out with my brother alone. We might find you tied to a tree."

The thought of being tied up by Dean Dixon did have its appeal. It sent all the moisture in her body flooding south. "He's good now. I promise." More than good. Spectacular. Delicious. And a damned good kisser. Another feather of desire floated through her tickling all the way down. "We had a meeting of the minds, and he's going to cooperate."

"That must've been a helluva meeting," Cord said with a shake of his head.

"She kissed him," Laney tattled around the huge bite of brownie in her mouth. Heat rushed up to

Tina's face and she shot a glare at her niece, who she hadn't even seen come inside.

"Yeah," Jeremy confirmed, with a smile that showed the brownie stuck in his teeth. He shoved another bite in his mouth, then added, "And he was choking chickens. I told Grandma and she was mad. He's in big trouble."

Right that minute, Tina wanted to wring both kids' necks like that chicken.

Tina groaned and her face felt like it was on fire. Dean was going to be mortified. And Jeremy was the one who was going to be in big trouble, if she didn't get him out of there. "I thought your daddy told you to stay up at the house with your Grandma?"

"Paulo is gonna cut my hair like daddy's," Jeremy said, glancing at her hairdresser.

Dean walked through the doorway just then and all eyes swung in his direction. Jaws dropped as they studied him, and Dean just scanned the group curiously. Tina couldn't even take time to appreciate how delicious he looked in his black cowboy hat, faded Wranglers and tight white t-shirt. She knew if she didn't do something fast, disaster was about to land right on her head. Even riding with him on that big black beast didn't seem so bad right then.

"Um, you ready to go?" she said walking over to grab his arm. Dean looked down at her and his lips curved just a bit. Tina yanked on his arm and turned him toward the door. "We need to get going." Tina pulled him onto the porch, hoping she could get him out of there before someone made a comment.

Her heart skidded to a stop in her chest, as she stopped beside the horse and looked up, way up, to the seat of the saddle. Swallowing her fear she asked, "Okay, how do I do this?"

The bags behind the saddle were stuffed so full they bled over into the seat of the saddle. It made the seat look even smaller. Tina wondered how they would both fit in it.

Dean Dixon was not a small man.

"Up you go," Dean said as he clamped his hands at her waist. Before she knew what he was doing, she was flying through the air like she weighed nothing. Tina's butt hit the leather with a jarring impact, the horse shifted his weight, and Tina felt herself sliding off the other side of the saddle. She yelped and her heart shot to her throat, but Dean's fingers dug into her thigh and he caught her.

"Whoa, buttercup," he said with a laugh, pulling her upright again. "No riding side saddle." He reached over her to grab the saddle horn, put his foot in the stirrup and in one fluid motion swung into the saddle behind her. His hips rocked forward against her, and Tina fought the urge to push back. "Scoot up, you're crowding me."

Crowding hell. There wasn't an inch of spare room between them, and she didn't really have anywhere to go. Tina scooted a few inches forward,

Just Shoot Me

the horse took one step and she felt herself sliding sideways again. Dean's hands gripped her hips, and the heat of his fingers seemed to burn through her jeans.

"You're gonna have to hold on better than that, or this is going to be a long ride. Hold onto the horn," Dean suggested. He covered her hand with his, and put it on the horn, then patted it. He grabbed the reins, clicked to the horse and she felt his thighs flex under her legs. The horse started moving forward and she gasped, as her body rocked from side to side and she felt as if she was falling again. Tina's other hand found the horn, and she held on for dear life, praying where he was taking her wasn't too far.

The sooner this ride was over, the better, in her opinion. She was not, and probably never would be, a country girl. She might work for a western wear company, have on brand spanking new jeans, boots, and a cute western shirt, but that did not make her a cowgirl. Just like her samples for the Texas Tomcat apparel hadn't made Dean Dixon a model. He was a cowboy, a country man. That had never been her type of man before, cowboys were her sister's flavor. But damned if it didn't seem to be hers with him.

The horse took a stutter-step and Tina wobbled, even though she was holding on. Dean's left arm wrapped around her waist, and he pulled her back against him. She wiggled trying to get comfortable, and he leaned near her ear and growled, "Sit still."

"How the hell do you figure I'm going to do

that on a moving mountain of a horse?" she asked with a huff.

"Moving?" Dean laughed. "This ain't moving, sweetheart." Dean walked the horse to the gate behind the barn, then dismounted and opened it to lead the horse through into the pasture. He shut it, then got back on the horse. "Hold onto your bloomers, Priscilla, it's about to get bumpy. I don't want this to take all night."

Neither did Tina, but they were going fast enough for her. Dean's arm clamped around her waist, he leaned over her back pushing her forward, and his legs flexed. The horse shot forward and she squealed, almost tempted to throw her arms around the horse's neck. She gritted her teeth against the jarring, as she was bounced willy-nilly in the saddle and against Dean Dixon. Dean groaned, then pulled the horse to a stop suddenly. Tina grabbed the horn to keep from pitching over the horse's head.

"Okay this isn't going to work," he said gruffly near her ear. His hot breath tickled her there, sending chills snaking down her spine. "You're going to have to move with me and the horse, or we're both gonna wind up on our asses."

"I'm doing the best I can," Tina said with frustration.

"First thing you need to do is relax," he instructed. Tina nodded and tried to force some elasticity into her body. "That's better. Now feel how the horse moves under you and roll your body with him…with me." Dean clicked his tongue, flexed his legs and the horse started walking. Tina focused on the roll in the horse's movement and tried to match her body movements with his. Dean's hips rolled behind hers and they seemed to be in perfect rhythm after a while.

The fact that the slow gentle roll was very akin to the slow gentle roll of making love was not missed by her body. With each forward motion, the seam on her too tight jeans pressed against the bundle of nerves at the top of her thighs, and sent delicious tingles floating through her body. Tina bit her lip to stifle a moan and took short even breaths. She tried to shift her position a little, but that made things worse.

She decided the best thing she could do was be still and focus on keeping the rhythm. If she came on the back of this horse with Dean Dixon behind her, so be it. Tension inched up inside of her, her heart fluttered in her chest. Her breath got shorter, and she leaned back against Dean's solid chest trying to ease the pressure. His arm tightened around her under her breasts.

"You okay?" he asked with concern.

There was no way she was going to tell him what was going on. It was just too embarrassing. She couldn't talk anyway, so Tina just shook her head from side to side, and fought the orgasm that was so damned close she could taste it.

"You still scared?" he guessed, then commented, "Your heart is beating like a time bomb, and you're not breathing right."

His arm was around her, so he would notice that, Tina realized and held her breath.

"Relax, you were doing fine," he said and his legs flexed again.

The horse picked up speed. The seam of the jeans raked her clit harder, and Tina flew apart. Her body vibrated, her inner muscles clenched and she couldn't hold back the moan that forced past her lips with the unexpected orgasm that racked her body. Delicious waves of pleasure floated through her. She dropped her chin to her chest and sucked in a breath. Letting go of the horn, she gripped Dean's thigh near his knee and threw her head back. He pulled the reins back, and the horse stopped, slamming her back against him.

"What the hell is wrong with you?" he asked gruffly. "You're shaking like a leaf!"

Tina waited until the last tremor ceased, then she sucked in a deep gulping breath and let it out slowly. "I'm sorry."

Dean swung down off of the horse, then reached up to grab her. He pulled her down and sat her on her feet in front of him and her legs felt like jelly. Her knees wouldn't lock so she all but crumpled at his feet. Dean pulled her back up and held her to him.

"Tina, what's wrong with you?" he demanded.

Scorching heat pushed up her throat to her cheeks, and she looked off at the trees in the distance. "I'm fine now," she replied, hoping he'd just let it drop.

No such luck. He put a finger under her chin and tilted her face up, so she had no choice but to look at him. "Tell me now, or we're not getting back on that damned horse. I'll carry you back to the barn if I have to."

Her face had to be glowing it was so hot. "I had an orgasm."

Dean's mouth dropped open and he stepped back. "You *what?!?*"

Tina tilted her chin up to meet his eyes. "I had an orgasm from all that rocking and rolling that horse was doing."

His face flushed and he shook his head. "You're shitting me, right?"

"Afraid not."

"Good Lord almighty, and here I was thinking you were terrified of Blaze," he said incredulously. "I guess I don't need to be embarrassed about what happened earlier then. This is much better." Tina Montgomery had an orgasm from riding a horse. It was amazing to him, and the funniest thing he'd heard in forever. Laughter bubbled and built inside his chest. Dean couldn't help himself, he started laughing. Once he gave it free rein, the laughter was all encompassing. He laughed so hard he had to grab his stomach as cramps started in his muscles there. He laughed so hard his legs went weak, and he had to sit down and hold his stomach. Bent forward, he laughed until he thought he might pass out from it.

Until a tiny booted foot kicked him in the shin. Hard.

His eyes flew upward and met angry gray eyes, set in the cutest damned face he'd ever seen. But her cheeks were practically on fire. Dean didn't know if it was anger or embarrassment making her cheeks so red, but he knew one thing. It made her damned beautiful. His laughter stuttered then stopped when her brow lifted. "You done yet?" she asked shortly.

Dean chuckled and felt it starting again, but roped the fresh round of laughter that was tickling his insides. "Yeah, I think so, but can't guarantee it," he replied weakly.

Her lips wobbled and tears built in her eyes like thunderclouds building for a storm. Guilt shot through him. He guessed she didn't like being laughed at any more than he had earlier. If there was one thing he couldn't take, it was a woman crying. Or making a woman cry. Except for Cindy. That was one woman he'd love to make cry. This woman wasn't Cindy though.

"Aww, don't cry, sweetheart," he said softly putting his hand on her calf. "I'm sorry."

She just nodded then folded her arms under her breasts and dragged her eyes from his. Dean reached up and put his hands on her hips, then pulled her down onto his lap. She struggled, but he held her still.

"Look at me," he said seriously. When she refused, he grabbed her chin and turned her face to him. "Look at me, buttercup." Finally her gray eyes met his, and he saw sadness there. Her lower lip was swollen and red from biting it. Dean ran his thumb over it, then leaned in and kissed her forehead. He wrapped his arms around her and hugged her.

"I'm sorry. I didn't mean to embarrass you."

He kissed her hair, and she leaned her head on his chest, to mumble, "It was worth it to see you smile." Dean's heart wiggled in his chest. "You're always so damned grumpy, this is a definite improvement."

"I have a lot on my plate," Dean replied defensively. He knew he was not the nicest person in the world. Considering what he'd been through, this was as nice as it got. And good as it was likely ever to get again. Nice hadn't gotten him a damned place except broke in more ways than one. "Besides I don't do nice."

"You should do nice with your son. He loves you, and sometimes you're outright mean to him. I know your ex-wife is a bitch, but don't take it out on him."

Dean loosened his hold on her as anger replaced the laughter in his soul. "That's the second time you've challenged me about my son. You've been here a total of three days, and you make assumptions you have no business making," Dean replied shortly. He pushed her off of his lap, then stood, leaving her sitting on the ground staring up at him. "When you've walked in my shoes, make all the assumptions you want to make. Until then, keep your damned opinions to yourself. I don't want 'em."

"I am walking in your shoes," Tina said as she scrambled up to her feet. "I have a six-year-old niece whose mother decided she doesn't want to be a mother, so she leaves her with me to raise so she can chase cowboys. I don't treat Laney like she's an inconvenience. The kid deserves better. It's not her fault," she said. Taking a step back from him, she put her hands on her hips and looked up at him with a challenge in her eyes. "I love her like a daughter, because she doesn't understand why her mother doesn't."

"My shoes are a little bigger than that," Dean replied, and it was his turn to look off at the trees. This wasn't a discussion he was going to have with this woman who he barely knew.

"How big then? There's really no reason I can think of for you not to be more open and loving with your son."

Dean's gaze swung back to her. His fists clenched, along with his teeth. "I have my reasons, and they are none of your business."

"Knowing you're loved is important to a kid," Tina persisted.

"Saying you love someone isn't nearly as important as showing them," Dean countered. "Words are cheap. Working your ass off to provide for someone shows them you love them. Making sure they know right from wrong."

"Words *are* cheap. Why does it have to be one way or the other?" Tina volleyed back. "Why can't you show him *and* tell him?"

This woman was smart and quick. And this conversation was over. "We need to get to the pond, so we can get back to the house before dark," he said gruffly.

"Avoiding the issue isn't going to solve it," Tina replied.

"Neither will beating a dead horse. I need to get back to the ranch soon. If you want to see the location, just drop it and let's get this done."

That's what this subject was to him. A dead horse. Dean put his hands at her small waist and hefted her up into the saddle, then picked up Blaze's reins and mounted behind her. The picnic lunch in the saddlebags wasn't going to be eaten out by the lake today. His mood was now as black as the clouds he saw gathering in the distance. He didn't know what he'd been thinking anyway when he asked his mother to pack it for them.

The best thing he could do would be show her

this location and take the damned pictures. The longer Tina Montgomery stayed at the ranch, the more unsettled he would become.

She was nosy, intrusive and she asked too many damned questions.

Dean had worked damned hard to find some shred of peace in his soul these last three years, and he thought he was getting close. He was not going to let this little bundle of questions upset that apple cart. She could take her damned pictures, then get the hell away from him.

CHAPTER SEVEN

Dean led Blaze onto the narrow, muddy path that someone might miss if they weren't paying attention. He was definitely paying attention, because he was determined to get this trip over with as soon as possible. Riding double with this woman had not been a good idea at all. As if her unwanted questions weren't bad enough, the entire ride her firm round ass had been pressed against his fly, sliding up and down as the horse moved.

The friction had caused his *problem* to crop up again. He felt like a damned teenager, and was afraid he would come in his jeans like one if he didn't keep Blaze at a walk. Not only had that made the trip to the back of the property twice as long as usual, it had been slow, agonizing torture. Tina Montgomery was right, he did need to get laid. He couldn't wait to get out of the saddle for a few minutes to walk off the stiffness in his muscles and behind his fly.

Under the thick canopy of trees, the temperature dropped and he felt a shiver pass through the woman riding in front of him. The same kind of shiver he'd felt move through her body earlier when she'd gotten turned on. That she'd had an orgasm on this horse was totally amazing to him and still damned funny. He'd laugh about it later though, because right now he had other issues of his own to deal with.

Then another thought smacked him in the

head. He'd like to watch her beautiful face as she came. The soft dreamy look that women got when they found their pleasure always did it for him too. Knowing he had put that look there was a complete turn on. Then the realization dawned that all he seemed to think about when she was within fifteen feet of him was sex.

For a man who had been a sexual camel for three years now, a man who avoided even thinking about it because he didn't want to torture himself, that fact was astonishing. And it had to stop. Dean had priorities and having a woman in his life was not one of them. He was doing this shoot for money, pure and simple. She would give him that money, he would buy the stock or pay off Hope, and she'd take her pretty little ass back to Dallas.

Maybe then his life would get back to normal.

"How would the crew get back here with all their equipment?" Tina asked softly, interrupting his thoughts.

"There's an access road on the other side of the lake. It's rough going, but you can get back there by truck."

"Good, because I don't think we'd be able to get Paulo on a horse," she said with a laugh and the light tinkling sound lifted his mood a notch. The image of the prissy hairdresser on a horse lifted it another notch. "And the photographer is pregnant, so she can't get on a horse. Cord would run me out of town if I even suggested it."

"Yeah, my brother is a mite protective of his wife." If Dean suggested it his brother wouldn't just run him out of town, he would probably beat the crap out of him.

Tina snorted, and the sound was so damned cute, Dean couldn't help but smile. Tina's stomach rumbled under his palm, and he didn't think it was laughter. "You hungry?" he asked.

"Starving. It was stupid, but I skipped breakfast this morning. I was excited about the shoot," she admitted.

It looked like they'd be having that picnic after all. It had taken over an hour to ride back there, and it would be an hour back to the house. By the time they got back, she would be gnawing her arm off. Or his. And he had brought lunch for a reason. If she went back to the ranch hungry and his Mama found out they hadn't eaten the lunch she took the time to pack, she was going to be mad. "Yeah, that was stupid. You're lucky I had Mama pack us lunch."

Dean wasn't going to call it a picnic, because that made this sound too much like a date. Picnics by the lake on a beautiful sunny day like today were his idea of the perfect date. They hadn't been Cindy's idea of one though. She had liked to party and dragged him down to the Electric Cowboy. That is where he'd met her in the first place.

He thought he'd probably never go back there again. He hadn't even gone there for his brother's wedding reception because of the bad memories associated with the place. Those days were over for him.

Tina gasped, and Dean thought she might have stopped breathing when he walked Blaze off of the horse path into the clearing by the lake. He pulled to a stop and waited while she took it all in. Evidently this place affected her the same way it did him.

The sun sparkling on the water was almost too bright to look at. The browns of the cattails on the other side of the pond in contrast to the blanket of bluebonnets behind them looked like they'd been painted by God's paintbrush. Even though he'd lived on this ranch his entire life, been to this spot frequently, the sight did the same thing to him every time he came here.

It was that beautiful. And peaceful.

Until the other day, he hadn't been out here in over a year though. He hadn't been out here with a woman since he was a teenager. This was a good necking spot. He brought girls out here a lot then. The romantic spot was guaranteed to get him what he was looking for. He hadn't thought about more than it being a pretty spot when he suggested riding back here. But now he realized maybe that's why he suddenly decided to bring Tina out here today.

He glanced down at the top of Tina Montgomery's head. The bright sun on her dark hair made it appear like she was wearing a halo. He could just catch the faint hint of her shampoo. Something fruity. He inhaled, and Dean knew he was in deep trouble.

"It's absolutely perfect," she said on a breathless whisper.

Dean kneed Blaze to lead him around toward the end of the lake. The bluebonnet field would be as good a place as any for a picnic. For lunch, he corrected in his mind. No picnics, and no kissing. Kissing her again would make promises his bankrupt soul couldn't fulfill. Dean had nothing left to give a woman. Cindy had sucked him dry emotionally.

Tina Montgomery was one of those soft, flowery women who would expect hearts and flowers. Dean's hearts and flowers days were long behind him.

"I thought it would be a good place for pictures," he said gruffly, as he rounded the row of cattails and walked Blaze into the field. It would probably be too damp closer to the lake, so he moved a little further into the field before he stopped. He swung out of the saddle, then reached up to lift Tina down. He stepped away from her quickly. As soon as her feet touched the ground. She looked up at him curiously. Dean turned his back on her to remove the saddle bags from behind the saddle.

"Thanks for bringing me out here. It will be perfect for the photos."

It was perfect for a helluva lot more than that and that seemed to be all he could think about. He felt her eyes on his back, but he didn't look at her.

"No problem," he said as he brushed past her to kneel down and unload the bags.

He unpacked the blanket first, spread it over the ground then laid the sandwiches and fruit out. He yanked two bottles of water out then tossed the bags to the side.

"Eat," he said brusquely as he sat on the corner of the blanket. She sat on the opposite corner and Dean realized that the blanket that fit in his saddle bag was entirely too small. He could still smell that damned shampoo, because she wasn't two feet from him.

Maybe if he pissed her off she wouldn't have that soft look in her eyes that wonder in her voice and he could think straight. He knew it was more a reminder to himself than a warning to her when he said, "Um, don't get any ideas from me doing this."

"Ideas?" Tina repeated dumbly as she unwrapped her sandwich.

"You know. I'm not interested in a relationship with you. This is not a date. I'm just trying to help you with the photo shoot, so we can get this over with."

"God forbid you should consider dating a woman, right? That wouldn't fit in with your tortured, wronged cowboy persona, now would it? What excuse would you have for being mad at the world then?" she asked in a sing-song voice.

His eyes flew to hers. "What the hell are you

talking about?"

"I don't think you want to be happy again. You're hiding behind your anger. Being so nasty keeps people from getting too close. That way you don't get hurt again."

"Thanks for the analysis, Dr. Phil," he said sarcastically. "Where did you get your psychology degree? Latest prize in your box of Cracker Jacks? Or was it a two-for-one special with your driver's ed course?" Dean shook his head, hoping that would shut her up. He gnawed a bite off of his sandwich, chewed then took a long drink of his water, before he said, "Again, mind your own fucking business."

"You're hurting your son," she said softly and his sandwich stuck in his throat. He glanced over at her and noticed she wasn't eating. She was too busy judging him evidently. Analyzing him. And getting entirely too close to the mark.

"Well, you are hurting me with all your bullshit," he growled. This woman had some gall that was for sure. "You don't know me or my situation from Adam, and you have no right to judge me. If you want to do this photo shoot you won't bring up this shit again." Dean shoved his sandwich back in the bag and tossed it onto the blanket. He wasn't hungry now, he had a knot in his gut. Because of her. "Now eat your sandwich, I'm ready to get the hell out of here."

"You're scared...a coward," Tina Montgomery challenged. She leaned forward to pick up the baggie with her sandwich. "And you're a bully."

"Any other virtues you want to list?" Dean asked with anger building inside him like lava inside a volcano. If she didn't stop he was definitely going to erupt soon. "I don't give a damn what you think about me."

"Well you should at least care what your son thinks," she said evenly, removing the plastic from the sandwich. "You want him to grow up being like that? Because that is what's going to happen."

Dean shoved up to his feet. "Goddamn, you have a lot of nerve, lady!" he shouted, staring down at her with his hands on his hips. "Since I'm your only ride back to the house. I suggest you just drop it."

"And I suggest you sit back down and finish your sandwich. I'm just saying what someone should have said to you a long time ago. It's time for you to man up and stop feeling sorry for yourself." She calmly ate another bite off the corner of her sandwich and chewed.

Well one good thing came of her continuing to run her mouth. Dean was not thinking about sex now. He was too busy thinking about strangling her. His eyes fell on his half-eaten sandwich, and his stomach growled. He wasn't sure if it was because he was still hungry, or because of the acid swirling there. It sure didn't look like she was in any hurry to finish her sandwich. He thought about leaving her ass there to walk home, but he sat down on the blanket instead.

His mother would probably kill him if he did that, if there was anything left after Hope finished with him. "What it's time for is for you to shut the hell up," Dean said shortly, as he jerked his sandwich up from the blanket.

Her face swung toward him, and her eyebrow lifted. His eyes fell to the dot of peanut butter at the corner of her full lips. A chill skated along his spine when her pink tongue darted out to swipe it away. "Make me," she invited with a small cocky smile. Dean watched her lips move, but didn't hear the words over the pounding of his heart in his ears.

Make her? Is that what she said? There she went with her childish taunts again. Well, Dean was about to teach her a lesson about being cute with him. He was going to shut up the aggravating woman the only way that seemed effective. She had pushed him far enough today. Right past the limit on his control. Dean tossed his sandwich over his shoulder onto the grass and wiped the crumbs off of his hands.

In a flash of movement he pounced, shoving her shoulders back onto the blanket, as he slammed his mouth over hers stifling her surprised shriek. Tina struggled under him for a moment, but then stilled. Her hand slid around his neck and a thrill shot straight down his spine to his dick. Dean held her down while he devoured her smart mouth in a punishing kiss. She moaned and shoved her other hand into his hair, knocking his hat off.

The birds sang in the trees, a slight breeze rustled through the leaves, and the sun beat down on his back, but Dean just kept kissing her like none of that existed. In his mind it didn't. All he could focus on was how good her body felt under him, how incredible her mouth tasted. Dean loved peanut butter and jelly, and with her lips in the flavor mix, he loved it even more. With another strangled moan, she wrapped her calf around the back of his thigh, and Dean knew it was time for him to slow down. If he didn't, he wasn't going to stop at kissing.

The kiss meant as punishment for her quickly became an erotic lesson to him. Don't kiss Tina Montgomery again, because it would just make him want more. She wiggled her hips against him suggestively and Dean groaned then shifted off of her onto the blanket. And he had to quit kissing her, but he couldn't make himself do it just yet. The kiss went on forever, took on a new dimension, and Dean was about at his snapping point when her small hand stroked over his erection. His whole body felt electrified as he groaned and jerked his mouth from hers.

"I can help you improve your attitude," she offered with a tight squeeze.

Dean squeezed his eyes shut, took heaving breaths then put his hand over hers to brush it aside. "No thank you. My attitude is just fine," he said, rolling to his back to cover his eyes with his forearm.

When he finally caught his breath and felt under control again he looked at her. "The best thing you can do is mind your own damned business and take your photos. Or you'll be finding yourself another model. Don't mention my son to me again."

She held his gaze a moment, then must've figured out he was serious. Her lips pinched, and she nodded. Tina sat up and gathered up the lunch trash, then rose and found the saddle bag to stuff it inside. "I've seen enough. Let's go back."

Dean could practically feel her anger like a force field around her. That she was angry wasn't a bad thing though. Perhaps if he was lucky she would stay mad until she left and he had a chance of keeping his sanity. Dean licked his lips and he could still taste her salty sweet flavor there. The nerves on his tongue sizzled, and he had a moment of regret that he'd never find out if she tasted like that all over her curvy body.

But then some things he was just better off not knowing.

Like whether his son was really his son. And whether Tina Montgomery's tasted like sweet honey between her legs. Getting addicted to another woman was not in Dean's life plan.

She walked away from him then stopped to dig in the pocket of her jeans. "What are you doing?" he asked.

"Calling Hope to have Cord come pick me up," she informed shortly.

Anger shot through him, because his brother was busy holding down the ranch so he could be out here with her. Or he should be busy. Odds were he was hanging out at the bunkhouse with his wife. "Cord is busy. You can ride back with me," Dean growled as he stood.

"You just head on back," Tina said, folding her free arm around herself while she cradled the phone to her ear. "I'll be fine waiting here alone."

"I'm not leaving you out here by yourself," Dean said firmly.

Tina Montgomery was a city girl. If a frog came out of the lake, they'd probably hear her screaming in Amarillo. And there had been an overabundance of bobcats out here recently. Lord knew what would happen if she saw one of those. Probably climb a tree, because he had a feeling the city girl was just that dumb when it came to taking care of herself out here.

"Hey, Hope. I'm out by the lake at the back of the ranch. Dean says there's a road that leads back here. Can you get Cord to come pick me up? I don't want to get back on that horse." She disconnected the call then pocketed the phone. Turning toward him with a glare, Tina demanded, "Where's the road?"

Dean tilted his chin toward the west tree line, and she spun on her heel to stomp off in that direction. He watched her for a second, then with a sigh, he walked over and picked up his hat and slammed it down on his head, before he hefted the saddle bags over his shoulder. Blaze was busy munching grass at the edge of the lake, so he went over and tossed the bags behind the saddle. After he swung up into the saddle, Dean followed Tina Montgomery, because there was no way in good conscience he could leave her out here and head back to the ranch until he knew she was safe. The damned rattlesnakes were out in full force now too. If she got bitten, before Cord got there she could be half dead.

She didn't seem to notice him behind her though. Either that or she refused to acknowledge he was following her, because she was ignoring him. "I could give you a ride to the end of the road to meet him," Dean offered.

Her back stiffened. "No thank you."

"It's a long walk to the main road," he informed.

"I need the exercise," she replied stubbornly.

Dean didn't turn back, he just followed behind her for the twenty minutes it took his brother to meet them on the road. By the time she walked around the truck to get in, she was limping a little. He imagined those new boots were giving her blisters. She needed to soak her feet tonight or tomorrow she was going to be in a world of hurt.

If she wouldn't have been so damned stubborn, she wouldn't have those blisters, he reminded himself. What the hell did he care anyway?

He had accomplished his goal of getting her to back off. Letting her know he cared would just invite her back into his business, which he had no intention of doing. Cord waved at him, and Dean notched his chin at him. He watched as Cord made a series of front and back motions with the truck until he got it turned back toward the road. Dean turned Blaze back the way he'd come and kicked him into a gallop. He hoped by the time he got back to the ranch, the run would get rid of the tension inside of him.

When he rode back into the barn nobody was around. He glanced out the front door and saw his pickup parked in front of the bunkhouse, which meant they were back. His brother was messing around at the bunkhouse instead of working, just as Dean suspected he'd been doing all day. Dean quickly unsaddled Blaze and rubbed him down. He stashed the saddle and bridle in the tack room, then headed to the bunkhouse. He'd had enough of his brother's laziness. There were things that needed doing around here, a long list of things, as his brother well knew from the list he'd given him this morning.

Dean stomped across the yard, up the steps and had his hand on the doorknob when it opened. His brother stood in the doorway, but he looked back over his shoulder to say, "Okay let me finish the chores, and I'll be back to clean up. Zack said he'd be here at seven."

"Be here for what?" Dean demanded with his

fists clenched at his sides. With as much work as they had to do, it could be eight before they finished. And yes, it would be they, because he was going to make sure things got done.

Cord turned toward him. "He's coming out and we're having a bonfire, why?" Cord asked and Dean heard the defensiveness in his tone.

"We have work to do."

"I'm well aware of what needs to be done," Cord shot back. "You might work twenty-four seven around here, but I don't. Besides Zack and Ryan have an idea for the ranch, and I want to hear it."

"What kind of fucking idea?" Dean grated then took a threatening step forward, so that he was nose to nose with Cord. "I've heard about enough of your hair-brained ideas lately. Did you talk Daddy into buying that new tractor? If so, you better figure out how to pay for it."

Cord pushed him and Dean staggered back. When he regained his balance, Dean charged back at him and they locked up in the doorway. Cord pushed him backwards and Dean stumbled down the steps landing on his ass in the dirt. With a growl, he scrambled to his feet and grabbed his brother's arm then threw his weight to sling him away from the steps. Cord fell and Dean landed on top of him then they rolled across the dusty yard as they fought for position. Adrenaline surged through him as they rolled, and Dean realized this is exactly what he needed to get rid of his anger and frustration.

A good old fistfight with his fucking brother.

It had been brewing since Cord came back, but they had both kept themselves in check. Until now. Not upsetting Hope was the only thing that kept Dean in check so long. Now he didn't really give a shit. His brother needed a reality check, and Dean needed the release of giving him that. Cord's fist landed a glancing blow on his cheek, and Dean welcomed the stinging pain. He returned the favor by landing a solid punch to his brother's jaw.

"Boys, stop it now!" Barb Dixon shouted, as she stopped near the steps of the bunkhouse. Cord landed a blow to Dean's stomach and he grunted. Their mother put her hands on her hips and yelled again, "I'm going to take a switch to your asses if you don't stop this stupidity now! You're brothers and you need to start acting like it, before I call your daddy!"

Dean had gained position. He sat on top of Cord with his fist cocked back ready to deliver a blow to his brother's perfect nose, when his mother's words cut through the adrenaline and anger shooting like lava through his veins. Silas Dixon had just gotten well. If his mother bothered him with this he would get upset. Stress could make him sick again.

Dean rolled off of Cord onto his back heaving for breaths, while he swiped the back of his arm over his mouth to wipe away the blood he could taste in his mouth. "I'm sorry, mama," he said without a helluva lot of remorse in his tone. Dean glanced at his brother, who was rolling to get to his feet. Cord had a long scratch on his jaw, and a bruise starting at the corner of his eye. Dean looked at his knuckles and saw they were pretty banged up too.

"You are both grown men, and you have a son who sees you doing this stuff, Dean Dixon. You want him to think fighting is the way to solve problems?"

Who the hell did she sound like right then? She sounded a lot like fucking Tina Montgomery. Dean was tired of being preached to by women today. "I'm going up to the house," he said rolling to his feet. He shot his brother a hot glare, as he passed him.

Hope was fussing over Cord like a mother hen. He'd had worse. Dean had given him worse, and gotten worse from him too. They were brothers. That's just how they settled things. And they knew when to stop. Before they did serious damage to each other.

"Dean wait!" Cord yelled behind him, but Dean kept walking toward the ranch house. His brother caught up to him at the front porch. He grabbed his arm and Dean tensed up, getting ready for round two. "What the hell is wrong with you today?"

"Same thing that's wrong with me every day. I'm tired of carrying the entire load around here alone." Dean took the three steps and was at the door when Cord stopped him again.

"Zack and Ryan are coming out here tonight

with some of the guys and their girlfriends. They have a business idea I think you should listen to. It could really be the answer to our problems. After looking at the tractor, and running the numbers on planting a crop with Daddy, you're right, it's not a good idea, but this is."

Fucking fantastic. Another hair-brained idea of his brother's to fix things. If he'd work half as hard as he thought about working, the ranch would be in high cotton. And now he had his damned rodeo buddies on the bandwagon. Like they knew their ass from a hole in the ground when it came to ranching.

"I need to be alone," Dean replied shortly as he twisted the doorknob. He was halfway into the foyer when Cord caught him again. Before Cord started again, Dean growled, "The mood I'm in isn't fit for company, polite or otherwise."

"So get rid of it. You need some stress relief. We both know that's what that fight in the yard was about. Mama's watching Jeremy and Laney. We're going to build a bonfire out back, and have some beer."

"I said I need some space," Dean growled, jerking his arm from Cord's grasp as he headed for the living room.

"Goddammit, Dean. Don't make me beat your ass again," Cord threatened from the foyer.

Dean spun around to glare at him. "Beat my ass *again*?"

Cord huffed out a breath and had the audacity

to smile at him. "Just get your ass cleaned up, and stop being a hard ass. Meet us in the field at seven-thirty. I'm driving the golf cart, so you can have as many beers as you want."

Damn, a beer did sound good. Several beers. He could have those here at the house, but drinking alone just sounded so…pathetic. "Just don't give me shit tonight. I don't want to end up in jail, because I had to kill your ugly ass."

"Promise," Cord replied with a wider grin, marking an X over his chest with his finger. "The guys are bringing women with them, so who the hell knows, maybe you'll even get lucky tonight. Lord knows you need to. Maybe it would improve your mood."

Another person telling him he needed to get laid. They just all needed to mind their own fucking business. He was fine. What Dean needed was every one of them to get off his back.

CHAPTER EIGHT

After he showered, Dean decided he might as well go to the damned bonfire and drink. He didn't have anything else to do, other than lay in his bed and stare at the ceiling thinking about the damned woman he couldn't seem to get off his mind. And with Cord's rodeo buddies coming, if he wasn't out there, those saddle tramps would probably be all over her, while he laid in his room thinking about her.

He walked into the kitchen and opened the fridge to get a pre-beer to settle his nerves. Pulling open the drawer, he found the opener and popped off the cap. It had been a helluva long time since he'd been around people in a social setting, and that's exactly what a bonfire in the country was. As close to a party as country folk got. Even though this was a spur-of-the-moment gathering, by the time all was said and done, they could have half the county at the ranch. Word usually spread like wildfire through town, and invitations weren't needed. Anyone who wanted to come showed up.

Dean had liked them when he was younger, but he was a different man now. Groups of people made him itchy and nervous since his divorce. Cindy used to drag him down to the Electric Cowboy often, and other than the dancing all he had to look forward to was a fight. He could always count on her doing something with someone that made him angry. So, toward the end of their marriage he figured out he was best to avoid crowds.

Thank God his brother hadn't suggested going to the only bar within fifty miles.

This would be a lot more laid back than the Cowboy and maybe he could reinitiate himself into polite company since his ex-wife wouldn't be in the mix. But there would still be people out there. People who he no longer had a damned thing in common with. Young freewheeling guys who were just looking for their next good time. Dean had responsibilities now, including a kid. They had women to chase.

"Oh, honey, you look nice," his mother said with a wide smile as she walked into the room. She stopped in front of him to study his face. With a frown she reached up and touched his cheek, and he flinched at the sting. "You have a bruise," she said, with a click of her tongue and a frown. "You and Cord don't need to be fighting." Dean pulled his face away and after a shake of her head, she turned to walk to the oven. "Do you want dinner before you leave?"

"No, ma'am. I ate a sandwich. And I think they're roasting hot dogs out there too."

Dean glanced at the clock above the wall phone. Six fifteen. Maybe he should head back to the field, or walk over to the bunkhouse now. The sooner they got this show on the road, the sooner it would be over and he could come home. Dean took a long drink of his beer, then another to finish it off, before he threw the bottle in the trash.

"I'm just gonna go over to the bunkhouse, Mama. You need anything before I go?"

She was keeping two six-year-olds tonight alone, and he was sure she had forgotten how trying keeping even one that age could be. Dean was usually around to take care of Jeremy. Even though she helped out a lot going it alone at her age could be nerve-wracking. "Mama, if they give you any trouble, call me and I'll come home."

Dean was almost thinking about changing his mind.

"Don't be silly, Dean. I raised you two boys, and if I can do that, I can take care of Jeremy and Laney. Ya'll broke me in well," Barb Dixon said with a snort. "Almost broke me."

It was a wonder they hadn't broken their mother. He and Cord were hellions of the first order. He was surprised his mother's hair wasn't gray by the time she was thirty years old. She was right, she could handle the kids. He kissed her cheek then gave her shoulders a squeeze. "Thank you for babysitting."

"I'll do it more, if you'll start going out and enjoying yourself again," she said seriously. "You're getting too old too fast, son. You're a young man and you need to start acting like one again."

"Mama, I wouldn't want to be young again." Dean laughed dryly, then reminded, "Think about what you're saying there. I was a hell-raiser from the seventh ring of hell." His father had bailed him out of jail enough to know, even though he hadn't always told his mother. Thank God.

Barb Dixon narrowed her blue eyes. "You still are, just in a different way. Not a good one either. Son, lose your attitude, and get your head right tonight." She tilted her head then winked at him. A small smile eased up the corner of her mouth. "Whatever *that* takes. I have the kids *all* night."

Oh, good Lord—did his *mother* actually just tell him to get laid too?!?

Heat rushed to his face. "Good night, Mama!" he said with disgust, then turned on his heel and headed for the front door. Dean was getting out of there, before his father chimed in with the same opinion.

It looked like his whole damned family thought he was a crazy, sex-starved idiot.

Who knew, maybe he was. Dean really hadn't realized what a grumpy asshole he must've become, but it looked like everyone was calling him on it. Some in nicer ways than others.

On his walk to the bunkhouse, the beer he'd drank started working its magic. By the time he opened the front door, he was feeling a lot more relaxed than he had been. Dean had no idea what he would find out there. Paulo and Belinda were still at the ranch, even though they hadn't done the photo shoot today. It looked like even though it was only a little over an hour back to Dallas, they were staying at the bunkhouse until the photos were done.

And Tina Montgomery was still there too. Would probably be there until next weekend. They would all probably be at the bonfire tonight. Thank God there would most likely be a lot of people at the party, so he could avoid her. He certainly didn't want any more of her advice or questions. And he sure didn't want to give in to the temptation to have her be the one to clean the pipes his family thought needed cleaning.

That temptation would be there until she left the ranch. But he had a feeling Tina wasn't the pipe cleaning, head out the next morning kind of woman. She'd want a side of relationship with her sex, and that wasn't something Dean was willing to give her.

It was only Tuesday. If Dean planned on avoiding her, he had a long row to hoe until next weekend when she and Laney would leave. If he could just last that long though, after that he'd probably never see her again, except for the occasional visit she might make to see Hope.

His heart did a strange little twist in his chest, but he untwisted it fast. The thought of never seeing her again did make him think more though. Maybe he was thinking wrong and she was a clean-the-pipes-and-head-out-town type of woman.

This afternoon, if he had been agreeable, they would have had sex out there in that bluebonnet field by the lake, and Tina Montgomery knew she was leaving in a few days. Maybe she was the perfect solution to his problem. Or what everyone thought was his problem, including her. They could have sex, then she would leave. Go back to her big job in Dallas. He'd never have to see her again. Problem solved, and no hard feelings or hassle.

His pool of potential candidates out here in the country was as dry as the creek bed in a drought. It was now or never, and her or no one. If she came back for a visit with Hope, he could just make himself scarce. Dean had become good at that.

Instead of going into the bunkhouse, Dean did an about face and made a beeline for his truck. He opened the door and climbed up inside to dig around in the glove box. He was damned rusty at this thing, but he'd had sex enough times in his life to write a book on it probably. Kinky, straight up, vanilla. You name it, he'd tried it in his younger years. It had been a helluva long time for him, but whatever Miss Montgomery's flavor was, Dean was sure he could more than accommodate her. He was definitely primed for it. Because of her.

Dean found the box of condoms he'd put in there a couple of years ago when the thought of going to town hit him, but he chickened out. He pulled out a couple then put them back into the box, and took out a whole string of them instead. If he was going to have one night with her, he was going to make it a long night, and make sure they both remembered it. Folding them up, he pulled his wallet out and tucked them inside then closed the glove box.

"Hurry up, Paulo...we're going to be late!" Tina said, squirming in the chair while the hairdresser teased her hair up even higher on top. He reached around her and sprayed it more than thoroughly, until she inhaled a lungful and coughed.

"It's just a bonfire. That's enough!" she said firmly. "You keep going and my hair is gonna be bigger than Dolly Parton's—" Their eyes met in the mirror and Paulo lifted a perfectly arched brow to give her 'that' look. They had been co-workers and friends for a long time, and he had the darndest way of saying things without uttering a single word. And she read him right now. He'd worked hard on her hair and makeup, and she was being critical. "Thank you for doing my hair and makeup, Paulo. I love it," she said, standing to kiss his cheek.

"Well I'll say it..." Belinda leaned toward the mirror to separate her bangs. "My hair is stiffer than Dean Dixon's—" The door opened and Belinda's thin lips pinched off her words as her eyes darted toward the doorway. Tina spun around and saw Dean standing there.

"Finish it, Belinda. As stiff as Dean Dixon's?" he repeated walking over to stare down at her darkly. "I know you weren't talking about my upper lip."

Her assistant and Dean Dixon faced off, and Tina knew if she didn't do something the night would go downhill before it even started. Tina stepped between them and put her hand in the center of Dean's chest. "Spine…as stiff as your spine," she inserted quickly.

A crisp, woodsy scent wafted down to her and it was so heady, she was stunned for a second. He didn't have a lot of cologne on, but whatever he was wearing was as good as guaranteed sex in a bottle. All she could do was inhale deeply and hold back a moan. Clearing her throat, she said, "You have to admit, you're a little uptight."

"Is that so?" he asked evenly, but Tina felt his pounding heart under her palm, and saw the anger in his stormy blue eyes. Thank God, Hope walked in right then, or Tina had a bad feeling she was going to say something that would end their evening before it even started.

"Hey good looking," Hope said with a wide smile for Dean. Cord walked up behind her and she reached back to pat his thigh. "Cord, bring your stick, baby. You're gonna have to beat the women off of your brother."

Cord snorted. "I'll save my beatings for the men he pisses off. Look at that frown. One look and they're all gonna want to punch him in the face." Cord walked around his wife and took her hand in his then looked at Dean. "Lighten up, man. This is supposed to be fun," he reminded his brother then glanced at Tina and his grin spread from ear to ear. "I think I might need that stick for you though, darlin."

Hope elbowed her husband in the ribs and he grunted. "You keep your stick right where it is cowboy," she growled, but smiled up at him. "My friend can take care of herself."

"This was a great idea, huh?" he asked with that smile that had melted a million panties, but was now reserved for his beautiful pregnant wife. Hope smiled wider, and Tina sighed.

One day she wanted a man who would look at her just like that. One day when she took some time for herself to find that man. One day when she wasn't struggling to keep her head above water, and could actually focus on something other than her job. One day, one man, she thought and sighed again as her gaze wandered to Dean.

After today, Tina knew that man wouldn't be Dean Dixon. He'd made it clear, even though he'd kissed the stuffing out of her twice now, he wasn't interested in her. He was just too damaged for her to be interested in him either. Maybe he'd find someone tonight too, someone who had more patience for his black moods than she did. Tina sure hoped so.

They both had a rare free night to let their hair down, and she hoped he took advantage of that just like she planned on doing. On their way back from the bluebonnet field, Tina had unloaded to Cord about the situation with Dean. She told him that she thought Dean needed to loosen up and have a little fun. Do something other than work the ranch and take care of Jeremy.

Then as if it were providence, his friend Zack called to say he needed to discuss a business proposition with him. Cord suggested he come down to the ranch for a bonfire. Zack let out a whoop that Tina could hear on the other side of the truck. He said the rodeo was on hiatus for a week so he'd round up the boys and barrel ladies, whoever they were, and they'd be down tonight. Supposedly all of them were staying at the bunkhouse tonight with them. It should be interesting. Tina was a little excited to do something new and to meet Cord's friends. She'd never been to a bonfire, and wondered what all it entailed.

His friends had gotten there an hour ago, but she hadn't met them yet. Cord met them outside, and directed them where the bonfire would be. When Tina glanced out the window she saw five or six trucks stuffed with people, including several women. Her eyes darted back to Dean.

If Dean Dixon didn't get lucky tonight, the women at the bonfire must be blind. If he looked any sexier right now in his striped western shirt and perfect fitting jeans, Tina was afraid she would melt into a puddle at the toes of his well-worn eelskin boots.

She licked her lips and his eyes met hers and held. Shock rocked her when she realized he was inspecting her just as closely as she had him. When a small smile played around his lips, and his eyes met hers again, there was heat there. What game was this man playing?

Tina had all but offered to have sex with him that afternoon, and he turned her down flat. Now he wanted to look at her *that* way? *Too little, too late cowboy.* She turned back toward the hall to go get her purse out of the bedroom. The living room was empty when she walked back into the room, so she went to the front door.

She stopped there to tug at the hem of her short, ruffled blue jean skirt that she'd paired with the pink rhinestone studded tank top Hope had loaned her. Hope wasn't nearly as full-busted as she was, so she tugged up the scooped neckline of the shirt to make sure the twins were sufficiently covered. She'd probably be tugging at the damned thing all night. She'd only worn it because it matched her new black and pink cowgirl boots.

When Tina finally thought she was reasonably together, she opened the door and walked out onto the front porch. The truck was cranked and idling in the yard. It looked like everyone was waiting on her. That was confirmed when Cord honked the horn impatiently.

She quickly shut the front door, and walked to the truck. "I thought we were taking the golf cart?" she asked as she opened the back door.

"There were too many of us, so I decided to take the truck. The ride won't be as bumpy for Hope either." Cord looked at his wife sweetly, and she rolled her eyes.

Tina pulled the back door wider and saw door-to-door bodies inside the back seat. Paulo sat by the other door, Belinda was in the middle beside Dean, and with his wide shoulders, Tina realized there wasn't another inch of space to be had on the seat of the truck.

"Where the hell am I going to sit?" Tina asked.

"I guess you'll have to sit on my lap," Dean informed with a smug smile, as he extended his hand to her. Tina didn't take it. She was seriously thinking of walking back to the field.

"C'mon, get in the damned truck," Dean grumbled, leaning down to grab her hand. "We're gonna be late! Cord said the guys are already out there setting up."

Electricity zapped up her arm to her chest, and her nipples hardened. Dean's eyes fixed there, as he yanked her onto his lap and shut the door. "Eyes are up here, cowboy," she mumbled, folding her arms over her breasts. "And next time ask me before you jerk me around."

She was small, so this man seemed to take that as permission to jerk her around like a ragdoll, just because he could.

His arms closed around her and his hot breath tickled her ear, as he leaned forward to drawl, "Why?

You've been jerking me around since you got here."

"When you're a jerk you get jerked," Tina replied grumpily, leaning forward to put her hand on the back of the front seat, trying to put as much space as she could between her and the aggravating, intoxicating man. She was almost tempted to scoot over and sit on Belinda's lap to get away from him, and probably would have if his arm wasn't around her lower back. His hot touch sent unwanted messages to all kinds of places in her body. Tina pressed her knees together, and scooted farther forward on his knees.

"Sit still or you're about to wind up on your ass on the floorboard," Dean warned as his fingers tightened on her hip.

"How far is this drive anyway?" Tina asked loudly, as Cord put the truck in drive and started up the driveway toward the barn.

The sooner she could get off of Dean Dixon's lap, the better.

"Not far," was Cord's vague reply.

Tina huffed out a breath and stiffened her spine. A few minutes later, Dean's fingers loosened on her hip. Tina relaxed a little, thinking maybe he would finally take his hand off of her. Instead his fingers trailed upward and he shoved his hand under the hem of her tank top then his thumb rasped against her skin in slow, irritating circles. She glared back at him, and saw his stormy blue eyes held an invitation she couldn't miss. He gave her a wink, and a soft, sexy smile, and heat rushed to her face.

"You wish, cowboy. You had your chance," she hissed under her breath. Tina dragged her gaze out the side widow and fought the unwanted tingles that buzzed along her nerve endings, all converging in one place. Tina shifted to face forward, hoping he'd move his hand. His thumb just shifted position to stroke along her spine now, as he cupped her waist with his hot fingers.

They finally made it to the center of a pasture off to the left of the barn where the trucks she'd seen earlier were parked. As soon as Cord put the truck in park, Tina threw open the door. She could almost use a parachute to reach the ground, but she didn't care if she broke an ankle if it resulted in her getting away from Dean Dixon. Because her ankle was still weak from twisting it the other day, her knees buckled when her boots hit the gravel, but she fought back to her feet.

Once she had her balance, she immediately started toward the huge pile of wood in the middle of the field. Several cowboys were there placing logs around the pile to circle it. Three of those cowboys turned toward her as she approached. She smiled tightly at them, but made herself add a wave to be friendly. She felt a little uncomfortable, since it was blatantly obvious they were checking her out.

These were real country men, and they probably could see she was a fraud in her brand new clothes. Clothes she definitely didn't normally wear.

Her boots got a little tighter, and her skirt a little shorter in her mind, and she rethought her wardrobe choices. Maybe she should have worn the new jeans she'd bought from work. The ones she'd worn to go riding with Dean earlier today. But they had smelled like horse when she took them off, and she didn't have time to wash them.

Tina's shoulders relaxed a little when they smiled back, more than that, they tipped their hats back and grinned at her, then waved back enthusiastically. One of the cowgirls that had been helping them carry logs, a tall, lanky woman with long white blonde hair didn't smile. She stopped in her tracks, and brushed her hands on her jeans, then tapped one of the guys on the shoulder. With the smile still on his face, the good looking cowboy turned toward her, listened a moment then nodded. They walked off toward the green truck at the end of the row.

Probably his girlfriend, Tina thought, as she continued her hike toward the fire site. It was just getting to be dusk, so she imagined they would light the fire soon. She should probably ask them if there was anything she could help with.

"What can I do?" she asked the first cowboy she saw.

"Sit your pretty little self down over there on that log," he said, pointing toward a log positioned on the right side of the fire. "That's where I'll be sitting." His smile was engaging with the small chip out of his right front tooth. It didn't make him unattractive, it added character to his friendly boyish appeal.

Tina smiled back. "Now, I have to know a cowboy better before I sit on his log," she said and immediately realized what she'd just said without meaning to. Her face baked as she slapped a hand over her mouth, wishing the ground to open up and swallow her.

His eyes widened, then a slow smile almost took over his whole face. She heard a rumble, his lips twitched, then he threw his head back and deep laughter exploded from him. He laughed so hard, Tina thought he might drop to the ground and roll there. Instead he took a few gulping breaths, then stood upright again.

He shook his head, and was still grinning when he said, "Darlin, you just made my night. My name is Lucky, and I think I've earned it, since you just showed up. C'mon help me get the hot dog buns out of the truck, so I can get to know you better. I damn sure would love you sitting on my log tonight."

CHAPTER NINE

Dropping an arm over her shoulders, Lucky led her toward a black truck that was the second one in the row. They passed Dean on the way. He was standing in a group with Cord and a couple of other men, but she felt his hot eyes on her back. She and Lucky stopped at the tailgate, and he lowered it.

"I think Twyla went overboard at the grocery store. She bought enough buns and dogs to feed an army," he said with a laugh as he leaned inside and grabbed a box of buns.

Tina saw bags and bags of marshmallows too. She loved marshmallows, and had only had them toasted one time, during the week she was a girl scout, but she could still remember their gooey crispness on her tongue. That was the week before her father got re-stationed from Arizona to Iowa. After that she hadn't gotten involved in anything, because it was just too heartbreaking to have to give it up on a moment's notice to move again. They moved two more times, before their final move to Texas and her parent's divorce. That was why she was determined Laney was going to have a home. So she could make memories that weren't packed away in boxes to be moved around every few months her whole life.

They had stayed in Texas, but to date had moved three times in her niece's young life. Once when Tina's lease ran out on her apartment, because she'd forgotten to renew it because she'd been so busy at work. The second time was when the owners of the small house she had rented for them decided they wanted to move back in, so they didn't renew her lease. Now they were in a temporary apartment. It was a one-bedroom to make sure they didn't get too comfortable there, and she could save up money for a down payment.

Tina wanted a house. For all of them. Her new job would give her the funds to pay for a house. If she could just get the photos she needed to convince the owners of Texas Tomboy to see her vision and approve the menswear line. She had one week left to get the presentation together. One week with a stubborn cowboy model who she knew would be perfect to convince them.

She'd wasted a full day today messing around out at the lake with that man. Tomorrow was a new day though. She was going to get her pictures, then she was going to put together the best presentation her bosses and their bosses had ever seen. She was going to blow them away, and she was going to get her promotion and her house.

But tonight, she was going to have fun and forget about all that. "Hand me some of those marshmallows. I want to make sure I get some," she said. Lucky leaned back into the truck and dragged three bags toward him. He handed them to her, then picked up the buns again. "You like marshmallows?"

he asked with a laugh.

"Hell, yeah," she replied stepping back. "They get all gooey when you toast them."

"Good, I like 'em too. I look forward to licking them off of your lips tonight."

A little something shifted inside her chest, but it was nothing compared to the rockslide of desire that Dean Dixon caused earlier today. She grinned and shook her head. "Damn, cowboy you sure cut to the chase, don't you?"

"I don't let any grass grow under my feet, beautiful, if that's what you mean," he replied with a bodacious wink. "If I don't get first dibs on you, my friends will. Now, let's finish getting this stuff set up, so we can get to those marshmallows."

"Rodeo bulls?" Dean repeated, eyeballing his brother like he'd lost his mind. "I hear those don't eat too well," he said sarcastically.

The Dixons were beef cattle ranchers. Beef cattle was always in demand. They could always rely on their cows and calves selling to keep the family fed and the ranch going. Even though things had been rocky in the last couple of years due to their daddy's health problems, they had been able to sell their herd with no problem to help pay for his treatments. Or get them started at least.

"We're not going to eat them, dumbass," Cord shot back with a shake of his head. "We're going to

Just Shoot Me

lease them to the Pro Rodeo associations. And I'm not only talking about bulls. There's broncs and even sheep for the mutton busting the kids do."

"The feed and vet bills alone would break us," Dean said like his brother was an idiot. Because that's exactly what he was. The people who raised livestock for the rodeos were wealthy men who played at ranching. Those men could afford to drop a hundred grand on a good breeding bull. This ranch was so far in the red, their books looked like they were bleeding to death.

"The circuits pay well for their stock leases," Zack chimed in. "And they pay for the vet bills while they're leased. Ryan and I have a lead on a retired bull that was damned good bucking stock. And a few cows who threw some good bulls too. The rancher selling the bull hasn't advertised him yet, but he needs the money fast. He's agreed to give me and Ryan first shot at him, but we have to hurry."

"What's in this for us? "If we're doing all the work, providing the upkeep on the stock, what kind of cut do you expect from the stock leases?" Dean asked pinning the tall, blonde cowboy with a hard look.

"That's what we need to negotiate. Ryan and I want to invest in the herd, and help with the training and breeding in our off time. We have to do something when we retire, and we know rodeo rough stock. We could get the stock contracts."

"Why don't you just do it yourselves?" Dean

asked shortly.

"Because we're rodeo riders right now. Damn good riders who make a good living riding. We don't have time to manage a herd, and we're not ready to hang up our spurs just yet." He huffed out a breath. "Besides we don't have a ranch to hold a herd or enough money to buy one."

"Okay, I'll ask again. What's in this for us? The answer to that question will determine our answer." Dean looked at Cord again. "We can't just make a decision on a pie in the sky deal without some specifics."

"This isn't a pie in the sky, Dean. It's a good idea, dammit!" Cord threw up his hands. "You are so damned hardheaded and unbendable sometimes I think you're made of stone. Or that's what your brain has turned to from being so set in your ways."

Dean sucked in a deep breath. He was not going to put his fist in his brother's face right now, he was just not going to do it. But that is what he wanted to do. The best thing he could do to preserve the party mood was remove himself from this discussion and get another beer.

"Let me think about it. Talk to daddy and see what he says."

Now, that wasn't inflexible was it? He had listened to his brother's stupid idea, said he'd think about it. Now, he was going to purge it from his brain, and have another beer. Dean turned and walked toward the fire that was just now starting to smolder. He'd been so engrossed in the conversation with his brother and his brother's friends he hadn't even noticed it had gotten darker, or how many damned trucks were here now. There must be thirty or more parked out in the field. Everywhere he looked there were people. Dean's collar got a little tighter around his throat, and he ran his finger underneath. He'd have a few beers, then he was going back to the house.

This was not his idea of a good time.

He walked over to the ice chest beside a table set up on the far side of the fire, and flipped open the lid. Pulling out a beer, he used the opener on the side of the chest to remove the cap then stood back up. A radio from one of the trucks suddenly blared country music across the field and several other trucks joined in. At least they were all tuned to the same station, he thought as he lifted his beer toward his lips. His eyes snagged on Tina Montgomery sitting on a log beside one of Cord's rodeo friends and the beer stopped halfway to his mouth.

The guy was showing her how to skewer a weenie on a coat hanger. The way she watched him you'd think he was showing her something her life depended on her knowing. The cowboy couldn't be more than twenty-one, but Tina didn't seem to notice or care. She was almost sitting on his lap. He said something and her dark hair danced around her shoulders as she threw her head back and laughed.

All of a sudden the fire caught hold with a loud whoosh. The heat blasted him, but was nothing like the heat that surged through his veins. His heart beat ninety to nothing in his chest, as old instinct kicked in. He wanted to go over there and snatch her away from the man, and put his fist in the bastard's grinning face. But Tina Montgomery wasn't his ex-wife. She wasn't his anything, he reminded himself as he turned his back and walked around to the other side of the fire. He found an empty log, grabbed a hanger from the stack near the fire, and a got a hot dog out of the pack. He sat down on the log and shoved the dog on the end of the hanger.

"Hi cowboy, wanna cook me one too?" a soft voice asked.

Dean looked up and his eyes met grass green eyes that had to be from colored contacts, because he'd never seen natural eyes so green. They were rimmed by mascara so thick the blonde woman's eyelashes resembled spider legs. Her lashes nearly touched her arched eyebrows. She had to be at least ten years younger than he was too. Like most everyone else at this party. He felt like a used up old man in comparison. And this woman was definitely not his type.

He dragged his eyes away, and stuck his hanger into the fire hoping she'd take his cue to take a hike. Instead, she sat down beside him, slid a hot dog onto a hanger then stuck it into the fire beside his. "What's your name?" Chatty Cathy who couldn't take a clue asked.

"Dean," he replied gruffly.

He heard her sniff a couple of times, then she leaned closer to his neck and sniffed again. "Damn, boy, you smell delicious. Good enough to lick all over."

"Not interested, honey. I'm not in a good mood." That was about as blatant as he could be without insulting her.

"Bet I could improve your mood…if you'd let me," she drawled suggestively.

Not likely, he thought. Dean picked up his beer from beside his leg and took a long drink, followed by another until he'd emptied the bottle. He pushed it at her. "Get me another beer will you, sugar?" He could only hope she would get distracted and find some other man to bother on the way to the cooler. If she made it back at least he didn't have to go over there again and see Tina Montgomery with that cowboy to get another beer.

"Hold my hot dog and I will," she said sweetly and passed her hanger to him.

Damn, that meant she was coming back.

Dean held both hangers in the fire, and watched the edges of the meat blacken. When they were done a few minutes later the girl still wasn't back with his beer. He lifted the hangers out of the fire and blew on the hot dogs. He'd forgotten to grab buns off the table by the beer. Since Blondie wasn't back he'd have to get a beer himself anyway. With a sigh Dean got up and walked around the fire to the table behind the cooler.

Against his will, while he slid the hotdogs off into buns, his eyes drifted over to the log where he'd seen Tina sitting before. His heart jerked in his chest and the old betrayal he was ever so familiar with when he was with Cindy tried to take root inside of him. Jealousy all but grabbed him by the balls and brought him to his knees. She was sitting on the man's lap now, while he wiped marshmallow goo off of her cheek. The cowboy laughed as he leaned in to lick what was left, and she swatted him away with a giggle.

"Here's your beer, honey. Sorry, I got hung up talking," the blonde said.

He took it from her and drank a long, slow swallow to wash away the bitterness inside of him. When he lowered the bottle, he motioned to the other hot dog on the table. "That's your hot dog, baby. It's a little burnt, but if you put enough ketchup on it you can't tell."

"Oh, thank you for cooking my weenie," she said then giggled like she was about sixteen. "I'm weird, because I like 'em burnt." She slathered ketchup over the dog, then looked up at him as she took a slow bite. A dollop of ketchup sat the corner of her mouth, and without thinking, he thumbed it off. She stopped chewing, heat filled her eyes and her eyebrows lifted.

Just Shoot Me

Someone bumped into him and Dean stumbled forward into her. His arms went around her to keep them both from falling. He looked behind him and saw some of the partygoers had begun dancing in the firelight to the music blaring from the trucks.

He looked back at the blonde, glanced at Tina, then back at the blonde. In the dark they all felt the same. He wasn't particular right about now. He wasn't looking for Miss Right, he was looking for Miss Tonight. This woman wasn't his cup of tea, but she would work if they took a walk in the woods. And she looked easy enough in her shirt that was unbuttoned so low her black lace bra was showing, and the shorts that were so short he could see the curve of her ass cheeks. Dean finished his beer while she ate her hot dog, then tossed his bottle in the trash can. "You wanna dance, sugar?"

Her face perked up and she smiled, then slid her arm through his. "See, I told you I could make you feel better! I'd love to dance."

Tina wiped her face with a napkin as she watched Dean and the young blonde walk off into the dark where everyone was dancing. Her heart did a little flip in her chest. It sure didn't take him long, she thought. In the truck he'd been hitting on her. Now he found someone who was evidently more to his liking than she was. That girl was young enough. Maybe she would be too naive to see past Dean

Dixon's good looking exterior to see what a project he was. And that was just mean, but it was the truth. A woman would have to be either stupid, or have the patience of a saint to deal with the man. Tina wasn't either. The woman was welcome to him.

Lucky evidently saw her staring, because he looked over his shoulder, then back at her. "Everything okay, darlin?" he asked with a smile.

Tina forced her lips up at the corners. She was having a good time, and she wasn't going to let Dean Dixon ruin that. "Everything is just perfect."

"You want to dance?" he asked looking back at the dancers.

"I don't know how to do that kind of dancing," she admitted. Tina had never country danced before in her life, and the songs the radio station was playing weren't slow.

"Well you can just stand on my boots, and I'll do the dancing until you get the steps down. How about that?" he asked with a laugh.

"I'd probably be on your feet anyway, why not?" she said with a chuckle.

"Honey, you can step on my toes any time you want," he said leaning in to hug her.

There wasn't a darned thing dark or tortured about this cowboy. He was all light and happiness. She was glad she'd met him tonight. After her run-in with Dean today, she needed some of that tonight. It was refreshing.

Lucky stood and grabbed her hand then pulled her toward the group of dancers. Once they stepped outside of the firelight, the temperature dropped a little since it was completely dark now, and she shivered. He must've noticed. "You cold, honey?" he asked.

"A little." He stopped and slid off his blue jean jacket and helped her into it. The darned thing was about three sizes too big, and she probably looked like she was a little girl playing dress up, but at least it was warm. "Thank you," she said smiling up at him.

"I'd put my hat on you too, but that sends a message out here in the country. I'm not sure you're ready for that."

"Oh yeah? What kind of message?" Tina had to ask, because she had no clue but was damned curious.

He wrapped his arms around her and pulled her close to kiss the top of her head. "That you're my girl, and only I get to kiss you tonight." Tina wondered if she'd see the blonde wearing Dean's sexy black hat tonight, and her heart squeezed in her chest. That wasn't her business. If that happened, it would be a good thing for him.

"Um, let's wait on the hat. The night's still young, and we're still getting to know each other. Thank you for the jacket though."

He laughed, and put his arm around her shoulders to walk her into the crowd. He lifted her and set her back down on his feet, and Tina put her hands on his shoulders. They made several circuits around the group, and Lucky, true to his word, danced like she was dancing with him. Out here in the dark, nobody could tell anyway. She hadn't seen Dean or the blonde yet, and dammit she'd been looking, even though she didn't want to. Lucky made another pass around the circle then she saw them standing just outside the light of the fire kissing. Tina's lips twitched in remembrance of his hot kisses. The man knew how to kiss.

"That's Cord's brother isn't it?" Lucky asked and his dance steps slowed a little.

Tina hadn't realized how hard she'd been staring, or that the man she was dancing with would notice. He seemed to know exactly who she had been staring at. "Yeah, that's Dean," she replied dragging her eyes away to focus on him.

"Something going on between you two?" he asked and his voice wasn't light like it had been all night.

Dean Dixon had kissed her twice now. Once just a few hours ago out in a bluebonnet field that had to be the most romantic place on earth. The man who had been doing the kissing didn't have an ounce of romance in him, but he appreciated the beautiful setting. Tina couldn't tell Lucky that though. "Um, no there's nothing there."

"Good," he said and his voice returned to normal as his steps picked up again. They danced a little while longer then Tina decided she needed a drink. She wasn't a big beer fan, but that looked like her only choice if she wanted something alcoholic and she definitely did.

"Hey can we go get a beer?" she asked.

Lucky danced them to the edge of the crowd. Tina stepped off of his feet and he dropped an arm over her shoulders. They walked over to the cooler, Lucky bent to take out two beers then opened them and handed her one. Tina heard raised voices, and at first thought it was the radio until her ears zeroed in on the tone of one of those voices. It was Dean Dixon's. The other was a female voice. And they weren't just yelling to hear each other over the music. She walked toward the end of the fire pit. When she rounded the corner she saw him arguing with a tall redhead, who looked almost like a she-devil with the firelight flickering over her angry face.

"Cindy, you need to get the fuck off this ranch. You lost the right to be here three years ago and you lost the right to see your son."

"We never finalized the custody agreement, or property settlement," she said, throwing her chin up. The other guy standing behind her tensed up, but he didn't say a word. Tina hoped he didn't jump in, because she could see the rage in Dean's tortured face in the firelight too.

He looked mad enough to kill someone.

"There wasn't anything to settle. You fucking left me and you left your son. We didn't have a pot to piss in then, so there was nothing to settle."

"My attorney says differently. And I want to see my son. I'm remarried now and Bobby wants his son."

A roar erupted from Dean, and his hands flew up toward her throat. She jumped back and Dean's hands flexed in midair then he dropped them to his side. "I wanted a fucking son too. Thought I had one. But you made sure you told me I didn't have one when you left didn't you? But you sure didn't mind leaving him for me to raise!"

"I couldn't take him with me," she said in a whiny voice that went through Tina.

"Because you fucking hit the road with Bobby. That's not an excuse, Cindy. That's abandonment. No court in the country would give you custody after you abandoned your son for three years."

"We'll see," she said smugly. "My attorney—"

Dean's growl was feral. It was obvious the man had just reached his breaking point. Cindy stopped talking. Dean took an aggressive step forward, hesitated, then spun on his heel and walked off into the darkness.

Cord came up behind Cindy. "You're trespassing here. Get the fuck off this ranch, and don't come back," he grated cutting his eyes to the man with her.

"My son—"

"You don't have a son. The kid doesn't even

know you. Haven't you hurt my brother and that kid enough? Just leave and don't come back, or you won't like what happens."

She snorted. "Are you threatening me, pretty boy?"

"No, ma'am. I'm making a promise to personally toss your ass off this ranch if you come back here and cause problems. Now get your *husband*, and haul your ass out of here, before I do it now." Cindy folded her arms around herself, and lifted an eyebrow.

She and Cord had a whole conversation without saying a word, and she evidently figured out Dean's brother was dead serious. She looked at the man with her and said, "C'mon Bobby—we'll let my attorney handle this."

"You better break out your checkbook bitch, because I have a lot more money than you do and you're not getting him without a fight," Hope yelled loudly at her back. Cord jerked her to his side.

A crowd had gathered, Tina suddenly noticed. The music had stopped and not a soul was dancing. They had all heard what had just happened. Dean had to be humiliated, on top of being ripped to shreds by the woman who seemed determined to crush him.

Tina needed to see if he was okay. She pushed through the crowd to walk in the direction she had seen him going. Total darkness surrounded her, and the temperature dropped twenty degrees. She snuggled Lucky's coat closer to her body, and squinted trying to figure out where Dean had gone. She knew how fast he walked when he was upset so she picked up her pace, almost jogging toward the woods.

If she remembered right, they weren't too far from the lake and the bluebonnet field. That place seemed to hold some significance for him. Not too far wasn't close though. It had to be at least a quarter mile or so from there. Through the woods. In the dark. Fear of what was in those woods at night made her heart kick up a notch, but she kept going.

She was really afraid what Dean might do.

CHAPTER TEN

Tina stopped at the narrow, rutted dirt path into the woods, and took a deep breath of the earthy, piney air then let it out slowly, before she started walking. She'd only thought it was dark in the field. The blackness once she stepped into the trees was absolute. No moon could penetrate the thick canopy. Dean came here because that's probably how he felt inside after that nasty woman ripped his soul right out of his body in front of everyone at the party.

Even though he was stern with his son, not warm and fuzzy with him, it was obvious to Tina he loved his son completely. If he lost him, it would probably kill him. She wouldn't doubt he'd have ideas of killing himself, or someone else. A man could only take so much before he snapped. The man at the fire had been on the verge of snapping, if he hadn't done that.

Today he'd made it plain he didn't want a relationship with her, but Tina knew he needed a friend. He needed one badly. She could be that friend, if he let her. He wouldn't talk to his family, but maybe he would talk to her if she could find him.

"Dean!" she yelled when she got a little deeper in the woods. Tina hoped he answered, because she wasn't watching the woods, she was watching the path under her feet, what she could see of it, to make sure she didn't trip or step on something. Like a snake.

She'd call out again every ten yards or so, but there was no answer. At least the animals and bugs in the woods had stopped their night calls when she yelled. For a few minutes at least, she could forget they were out there. In the dark. Staring at her. Watching her as she did something stupid like walk in the woods to find a man who didn't want to be found.

Tina walked a few more minutes then a loud roar that sounded like a lion, cougar or bear, split the night. She must've jumped fifteen feet off the ground. Her heart shot up to her throat then dropped to quiver in her chest, and it didn't beat again. Her breathing was short and erratic, as she stopped in her tracks to decide which way she should run. That roar came again, but this time it sounded human, and she thought it sounded a lot like a man yelling, "*NO!*"

Dean. Tina tried to watch the path, but her feet took off running down the path. She ran until she had no breath left. Suddenly the full moon penetrated the blackness and the woods opened up to the clearing she remembered from their ride. She stopped there and looked around at the breathtaking beauty of the bluebonnet field and lake in the full moonlight. She scanned the area and finally found Dean sitting by a tree, hugging his knees and rocking like that was going to soothe him. Tina walked that way, and stopped beside him. He didn't look up, he just kept rocking. She dropped to her knees beside him and put her arms around his shoulders to hug him. "I'm sorry, I get it now. I think everyone gets it."

His voice was a raw whisper when he finally said, "Just leave me alone."

"No, I'm not going to leave you alone. You need a friend, and you just found one. All of us want to help you." There was no way in hell Tina was leaving him out here like this.

"Nobody can help me," he said, sounding so desolate Tina wanted to crawl inside his chest and hug his heart which must be bleeding.

"We can if you let us," she said softly, as she sat beside him.

There was silence for a long, long time, then finally he said, "I'm going to lose my son."

"Not if you let us help you," she said again.

He turned his head toward her and when his eyes met hers in the darkness, she had never seen a man look so hurt, so hopeless. "I can't afford to get an attorney to stop her."

"Use the money you got from selling the horses," Tina suggested.

"We'll lose the ranch," he replied quickly. "I'm not letting my family lose what they've worked for all their lives. My granddaddy left this ranch to my daddy. I'm not risking losing it to fight someone I should never have married in the first place for a child who isn't mine."

Finding out that Jeremy wasn't Dean's biological son back there at the fire had been a shocker, but it explained a lot. But he didn't know that for sure and it didn't really matter. "He's your son," Tina said then his words came back to her. "You provide for him, put food on his plate, clothes on his back. And even though you don't say it, it's obvious that you love him." Tina put her hand on his shoulder. "He is as much your son as a kid can be." A thought hit Tina, and the question slipped past her lips. "Why *did* you marry her?"

She couldn't help but ask, because the woman she'd seen at that fire was not nice. There was nothing soft about her, and she just couldn't imagine why Dean would even like her, much less love her enough to marry the woman.

"She was pregnant," he said and his words echoed through the woods, just like they echoed in her skull. "I met her at the Cowboy. We had sex and she got pregnant." His shoulders stiffened then he added, "I did the right thing."

Tina's heart flipped in her chest. Dean Dixon was a man who lived up to his responsibilities. His ex-wife had taken advantage of that fact, and had trapped him into marrying her when she got into trouble. He was a good man. A man who loved his son, even though he was stingy with the words. That's why the thought of losing Jeremy had him upset enough to be out here in the woods screaming out his anger and frustration. He couldn't just give up without a fight. It just wasn't right.

"Dean, you are a good man who's gotten a raw deal. It's obvious that you love your son, regardless of whether you were the one to get that conniving bitch pregnant. I'm not Laney's mother, but I love her like one. I couldn't imagine just sitting back and watching my sister hurt her without at least trying to fight her." But it hit Tina right then that is exactly what she'd been doing for years. The determination to set her sister straight when she got home cemented itself inside of her. She was either going to love her daughter and be a mother to her, or she was going to get out of her life, and give Tina custody.

"I'm worn out," Dean finally admitted, and that's exactly how he sounded. Tired. Defeated. Done. "I'm dried up in here," he said and hit his chest with his fist. "I'm an asshole to everyone in my life because of it. Maybe everyone involved would better off if I just got in my truck and hit the road. If Cindy gets Jeremy that's probably what I'll do. Cord's here with Daddy now, so they'll be okay."

"Your family loves you, and they would be devastated if you left. Your son would be devastated. He doesn't understand what's going on, and if you just let her have him, Lord knows how he'll grow up. He'll think you didn't love him, and gave him away."

He turned his face away to stare at the lake, and his voice broke as he said, "Probably better than being raised by a man who isn't his father, and doesn't have it in him to show him the love he deserves. I suck at being a father. My life sucks."

Dean sounded so defeated, Tina couldn't stand it. Her heart bled for him. This wasn't just a pity party, he had lost hope that things would ever get better for him. She put her hand on his face and made him look at her. "You can change that, Dean. That kid idolizes you. He wants to be just like you." She smiled and ran her thumb over the rough beard growth on his cheek. "Know why he wanted Paulo to cut his hair today?" Dean didn't reply, but he shook his head. "Because he said he wanted to look as handsome as his daddy did."

Tina felt his jaw tighten under her palm, then his lips opened and she heard the whisper of a breath that escaped from his mouth. She wouldn't have believed it if she hadn't felt the hot drop that hit the back of her hand. A tremor moved through him.

He sucked in a shuddering breath, then before she knew it Tina was sitting on his lap and his mouth was devouring hers. There was desperation in his kiss, and Tina tasted it. It felt almost like he was trying to suck out her soul to console his own. She would gladly give it if he kept kissing her the way he was kissing her. Her own body was desperate to take him inside. To console him, to heal him, and to heal herself in the process. They could help each other forget what waited for them tomorrow. Tonight was the only thing that mattered.

Tina moaned, put her arm around his neck and leaned into the kiss. Dean's hand slid up her thigh, leaving a hot trail until it slid under her skirt and his hot fingers branded her as they dug into her ass to pull her closer. Dean held her to him and eased her to the ground.

His hat tumbled off of his head, then he was kissing her senseless. She grasped at the buttons on his shirt with shaking fingers, and somehow she managed to undo them to the waistband of his jeans. She yanked the shirttail, then smoothed her itching palms up his heated skin to his neck. She felt his heart pounding there, almost faster than her own.

With a groan that sounded more like a growl, Dean pushed his own hand under her shirt and cupped her breast, his thumb roughly stroked her nipple through the thin material of her bra. Tina's breath hitched and she arched into him, but his hard body pinned her to the ground. Suddenly he tore himself away, shrugged out of his shirt then she heard his belt buckle rattle, and the whoosh as he pulled it from the loops to toss it aside.

"Get undressed," he ground out, as he sat back to toe off his boots. He didn't look at her, but he grated, "And throw that fucking jacket as far as you can. Don't ever put it on again. It smells like him."

Lucky's jacket. Tina forgot she'd been wearing it. Evidently Dean knew whose jacket it was, and he didn't like it. "Dean, about Luck—"

"Don't fucking say another man's name when I'm about to fuck you," he said angrily. "Just get rid of the jacket." She heard rustling, as he removed his jeans, then a rip. She glanced over there and saw he was rolling on a condom. Tina scrambled to her knees and pulled her shirt over her head. She unfastened her bra and tossed it aside. She shivered as the cool night air and his words hardened her nipples.

He was going to fuck her. They weren't making love. His words were so harsh, bitter, Tina had to wonder if his cheating ex-wife had done that to him before. Said another man's name when they were making love, or about to. There was too much anger behind his words. But then there was so much anger and frustration inside of this man it kind of scared her a little.

The black mood he was in tonight was extra edgy and dangerous.

Tina didn't have long to think about that though, or even time to take off her skirt, boots and underwear, because he shoved her back to the ground and covered her body with his. The scorching skin of his chest touched her breasts, and Tina rubbed herself against him, as his tongue invaded her mouth. Took control of her senses. Danced an erotic waltz with hers. And man, did this man know how to dance. His hand crawled down her thigh to lift her leg to his hip, and he nudged her legs wider with his body. She felt his hardness meet the barrier of her underwear and absorbed his frustrated growl into her mouth.

She loved that sound. It was a wild, feral sound

that told her he wanted to be inside of her as much as she wanted him there. Dean pulled back to kneel between her legs, staring down at her. Her eyes dropped to his massive erection then she dragged them back to his. His heaving chest and clenched fists told her he wasn't happy. Leaning down, Dean shoved her skirt up to her waist then grabbed her panties in his fist. With one yank, he ripped them right off of her. She gasped and a chill raced up her body. Tina never had a man want to be inside her desperately enough to rip off her panties. This man was that desperate. And he wanted her. Now.

Every ounce of moisture in her body pooled between her legs, and her inner muscles clenched as he laid back on top of her and lifted her thigh again. This time when the head of his hard cock met her wetness, his nostrils flared, his jaw tightened, then his eyes drifted closed as he sucked in a sharp breath. "God, let me go slow," he mumbled under his breath, and she could barely make out the words of his prayer.

The tension in his body relaxed a little, very little as his mouth found hers again. His kiss was slow and deliberate this time. Tina's need inched up inside her. He lowered her thigh then pushed his hand between them. His fingers brushed through her folds to gather moisture. His breathing increased as he slathered her clit then made purposeful circles there. The fire of his touch set the kerosene of his kisses ablaze inside of her, and Tina whimpered as her hips found a rhythm with his hand and mouth.

The first wave of her orgasm was fast and unexpected. It hit her hard and her heart took a giant leap in her chest. Their mouths parted, she turned her head to the side to clamp her teeth down on the scream that wanted to escape. Her body vibrated, and Dean leaned close to her ear. His hot breath teased her hair as he whispered, "We're alone, buttercup. Let it go. Tell me if I'm doing this right. I'm a little rusty."

He increased the pressure of his touch, and dipped a finger inside of her. Her inner muscles clamped down, and her body went into erotic overload. Tina sucked in a gulping breath, her body tensed and the most incredible feeling overtook her. Overwhelmed by it, Tina couldn't help but open her mouth to let it out in a scream that echoed through the woods. Her body shook uncontrollably, she floated toward the moon, her soul danced naked in the moonlight then drifted slowly back to earth.

When she sighed and opened her eyes, Dean was staring at her. "So fucking beautiful," he said and a tremor shook him, as he took her swollen, tender mouth in a punishing kiss. Her body was limp, but Dean sure wasn't when he positioned his cock at her highly sensitive opening. He lifted her hips then his eyes met hers as he made one forceful push with his hips.

Tina screamed against the stinging pain of his entry that mixed with the incredible pleasure of the stretch. Like she was grabbing for her next breath, her fists closed at her sides and she grabbed up fistfuls of pine needles and grass.

His fingers dug into her ass as he stilled. "You okay, sweetheart?" he asked in that dark sexy growl that set every nerve ending in her body on fire. Tina wrapped her legs around his back, and pushed her hips toward him. She needed more now that her body was accustomed to him. She needed all of him. Wanted all of him.

"More," she begged breathlessly.

Dean's roar vibrated in her skull, his grip became almost painful on her hips, as he thrust again to embed himself inside her body. She wasn't sure he was in all the way, but what she had of him was a lot. Maybe he was too large for her. She could barely breathe, she was stretched so much as it was. But it hurt so damned good. Better than ever before. "Oh, God," she groaned, closing her eyes as her body twitched around him.

She heard his labored breathing, felt the incredible control he was showing from the tension in his body. "Tell me if I'm hurting you. I'm trying to go slow, but you're so tight. So fucking tight," he said in a strangled voice, then a low-pitched groan reached her ears.

"I'm fine," she said, even though she wasn't really. He needed this. She needed it too. Wanted it. "Fuck me, Dean," Tina said, relaxing her body.

Dean raised up a little, tilted her pelvis upward more, and the pressure eased. "That better?" he asked and she nodded. His breath rushed out, but he didn't move again. He cupped her mound with his palm, and his thumb circled her clit. Moisture flowed through her body again, and she relaxed more and he pulled back a little and moved forward again making short strokes. His incredible cock brushed a spot inside of her. The same spot over and over. A long low groan built in her chest and worked its way past her vocal chords.

"Oh, yes…wow," she panted, as he increased his pace little by little, went a little deeper. All Tina could do was rotate her hips with him and hang on for the incredible ride Dean Dixon was taking her on. The ride of a lifetime. The best ride ever, better than any rollercoaster. She reached high to grab for the incredible orgasm building inside of her with each thrust he made. When it slammed into her, Tina crumbled into a million tiny pieces that splintered off in every direction. Like it came from the end of a tunnel, she heard Dean roar his own release as his fingers dug deep into her hips with his final thrust.

When she found her breath, and the pieces of her mind, Tina opened her eyes. Dean was still inside of her, still hard. He was staring up at the moon, and she could almost see his heart beating in the center of his muscular chest.

"You okay?" she asked in a raw whisper,

putting her hand on his forearm.

He nodded, but he still didn't look at her. His grip on her thighs was so tight, her feet were going numb now. She unclasped her feet from his waist and laughed. "There's not a damned thing rusty about you, mister. Did you um…"

Dean looked at her then. "What do you think?" he asked and huffed out a breath, as he slowly withdrew and lowered her down to the ground. He pushed back from her and stood, then walked off into the woods.

So much for cuddling, she thought, as she reached for her shirt and pulled it over her head. Typical man. In that department, he wasn't in any different league than any other man she'd been with. In other ways, he was in a whole different ballpark. Tina got to her knees and flinched, then crawled over to grab her skirt. Considering the kind of man he was, she shouldn't expect warm and fuzzy from him. Dean Dixon just wasn't that kind of man. He was about as cuddly as a porcupine.

"Why the hell are you getting dressed?" he asked gruffly, stopping to stand by her, looking like a sculpted Greek god dressed only in the moonlight.

"Well, we're, ah, done, right?" Tina asked with a short laugh.

A slow, sexy smile broke over the lower half of his face. Her inner muscles tensed. "Not nearly, buttercup. I have a lot of ground to make up. But we're moving this party to somewhere a little more comfortable. I have a deer stand over there, and I always keep blankets up there."

"A deer stand?" she yelped. The only ones she had ever seen in magazines were up in trees. Tina did not climb trees. She didn't like heights at all. But another round of what she'd just gotten from this man would definitely be incentive.

"Mama's got the kids all night, and I plan on getting my fill of you by the time the sun comes up. I don't know when this will happen again." He extended his hand to her, and she stared at it for a second, holding her skirt to her chest. His face fell, and dropped his hand to his side. Tina dropped the skirt to grab his hand with both of hers.

Dean was right, in a few days she'd be back in Dallas, and he would be here. She was going to take advantage of the opportunity too.

"Where's the deer stand?" she asked and he finally smiled again as he helped her up. Dean dropped his arm over her shoulders and hugged her to his side, as he led her deeper into the woods.

CHAPTER ELEVEN

Tina's shoulder was suddenly cold, but her lower body felt like it was pressed against a furnace. She rolled toward the heat, and her face rubbed against what felt like sandpaper. Soft snores and hot breath tickled her ear. She opened one eye and panic shot through her, until the events of last night clicked through her mind. She smiled and her other eye opened. Looking around the rough wooden deer stand in the morning light, she thought it was more like a kid's tree house. The flap on the wall was shut right now, so she couldn't see outside, but daylight peeped through the spaces between the boards. That told her it was early morning.

After the night they spent up here, Tina was surprised the damned thing was still up in the tree, and that both she and Dean Dixon were still alive. The man sure hadn't lied when he said he wasn't done with her yet. He more than proved his words once she got past her fear and climbed the rough steps up to the stand. Dean had loved her fifty ways to Sunday. And then twice more on Sunday.

Tina stretched her legs and bit back a groan as her sore muscles protested. Dean's arms tightened around her, and his hand moved to cover her breast. He snuggled his chin into her hair and pulled her closer. Tina decided to catch a few more winks to supplement the ten she might have gotten since yesterday. Besides, she wasn't quite ready to let him go yet.

She turned her face into his neck and inhaled deeply of the few remnants of his delicious cologne that were mixed with sexy male musk. That's what she wanted to remember. How this man smelled, how she felt when he was inside of her. Those sexy growls he made when he got excited. The way he said her name like a prayer when he came. The cute nickname he'd pinned on her. Buttercup. Tina's heart did a little wiggle in her chest, and she mentally cursed herself for letting that make her think he might care about her a little.

Whether he did or didn't wasn't important. Her life was in Dallas. His was here. Last night hadn't been about promises, or the future. They had both needed what happened. Tina knew it had gone a long way to improve her outlook on things. Dean had some serious problems to contend with now, and she hoped it would help him be more optimistic about overcoming those obstacles too.

A soft kiss landed on her forehead, and Dean gave her a squeeze. Pleasure floated through her and she cuddled her face into his neck deeper. "You were playing possum…"

If he could be this affectionate, maybe Dean Dixon wasn't as prickly as he wanted the world to think he was. Or maybe she had slid under those sharp quills of his for a few hours last night. Whichever it was,

Just Shoot Me

Tina liked this softer side of his personality she would never imagine he possessed.

"Morning, buttercup," he said in a sleepy gravelly voice that grabbed her right in the center of her chest. She felt him smile into her hair, and smiled herself. His morning erection pressed into her hip, and Tina couldn't resist turning on her side and sliding her calf over his hip so he was positioned right where she wanted him. Again. Even after last night. Even though she was sore already. She felt sure when she stood, she would have trouble walking. But it was so worth it to have him inside of her just one more time, before the fantasy ended.

Tina wiggled her hips and he sucked in a sharp breath. Before she knew what was happening, he lay on his back and she straddled him. Stretching his arms above his head, Dean slid them under his head and grinned up at her.

"Ride me, baby," he invited in that deep sexy drawl of his.

Tina smiled, shifted her weight, and grabbed him. Slowly she eased her body down over his stiffness, taking him inch by agonizing inch, knowing from experience it would drive him crazy. Dean sucked in a sharp breath, then it hissed out between his teeth as she finally settled herself on top of him. He was so deep, she was so full, Tina felt impaled, totally connected to him.

His mouth relaxed then eased up at corners.

Tina relaxed too and sat up on him a bit more, just enjoying the fullness. "You feel so damned good," she purred and her eyes fell to his mouth. That mouth that had been all over her body last night. But where she liked it most was on her own. The man knew how to kiss. When he kissed her, Tina felt connected to him on a different plane. It wasn't just physical then. This fantasy was going to come to an end soon, and she wanted to hoard every memory of that mouth on hers that she could. It was unlikely another man would kiss her like that. None had to date.

She was greedy though. She didn't want to lose his fullness to get those kisses. But she was too short to pull that off. "I want to kiss you."

Dean's eyes heated, and he surprised her when he sat up, grabbed her hips and put his back against the wall of the stand. "Wrap your legs around me."

Tina did as he asked and draped her arms around his neck. Dean lowered his mouth to hers, and Tina leaned in. Their mouths met in a hot, sweet kiss that short-circuited her brain, so much she thought he said her name, and it sounded like it was coming from outside the stand.

"Hmm?" she murmured, nibbling at his lower lip, while he sucked her upper lip into his mouth. She heard a female voice call Dean's name and knew it wasn't her doing the calling. Panic shot through her and she jerked back. His body tensed and he listened too. A male voice joined in the name calling, then another.

"Holy shit," Dean hissed and leaned his head back against the wall. Tina looked back at him, and started to scramble off his lap, but he held her in place with his hands at her hips. His blue eyes met hers and they glittered with intent. "Just sit still," he said holding her in place. "Be quiet and kiss me," he whispered. "They won't find us."

After a minute, his grip on her hips loosened and he smoothed his hands over her waist up to her breasts. He thumbed her nipples, while he kissed her senseless. Tina was breathing hard when he pulled back. An evil grin spread over his face, and his eyes sparkled as he stretched her back over his arm. Tina held her breath as he lowered his hot mouth to suck her nipple into his mouth. Her inner muscles clenched around him, and she shoved her hands into his hair trying to push his head back.

He sucked harder and Tina bit her lower lip to stifle the scream dangling on the tip of her tongue. All night long, while they made love, Dean had encouraged her to be vocal. Now she had to be quiet while he turned her inside out. It was sensual torture, and Tina didn't know how long she could hold out. She had incentive though. If they heard them up in the deer stand, this fantasy would be over. Reality would come crashing down on them in the most abrupt way.

Dean pulled his mouth back slowly to release her nipple with a wet pop. Tina whimpered, and closed her fists in his hair. He blew on the wetness he left behind and her nipple became painfully hard. She tugged his hair to urge his mouth toward her again. Dean took it between his wet lips again, but instead of sucking he nipped her. Tina wailed, but it was quickly muffled when he covered her mouth with his hand.

"Shh…" he reprimanded. He eased his hand from her mouth to move it to her breast then kneaded her for a second, studied her as if he had all day, or was trying to commit her breast to memory. His dark head lowered and he sucked her into his mouth again. His tongue began tracing maddening circles around the engorged tip. Around and around, over the same path again and again. Tension built inside of her, her breathing became shallow, and her body clamped down on his rigid cock.

The fullness between her legs, his irritating raspy tongue on her breast became pleasure mixed with sensual pain. Agonizing and exciting at the same time. The longer he continued, the less she heard anything around her. The calls of the people outside were covered by the pounding of her heart in her ears. Dean's hot mouth on her body became her sole focus. He was in control of giving her that pleasure pain. She stayed very still so he wouldn't stop. She was scared to even breathe. God he couldn't stop. The sensation finally became unbearable, and a scream built inside her chest along with the orgasm that was barreling down on her.

Having to be quiet while he did this to her increased her discomfort. The knowledge that they could be discovered if she made a sound ramped up her pleasure. His hand moved up between her shoulder blades and he cupped her neck. Tina wondered what he was doing, but wasn't about to ask. His other hand suddenly clamped down over her mouth at the same time he bit her nipple hard. Tina's body went into shock, vibrating uncontrollably. Her arms, her hands, her legs, her insides shook as she screamed into his palm.

An orgasm the likes of which she'd never had before paralyzed her brain, as wave after wave of pain and pleasure warred for control inside of her. Dean hugged her to him and held her tightly until the tremors lessened, then stopped. Tina dragged in a breath and dropped her forehead to his shoulder as she tried to gather her senses.

She felt out of control, and her emotions took over. Pressure built in her chest then moved up her throat to burn her eyes. Before she could stop it a small sob escaped. One hot tear dripped out of her right eye, then a twin followed the same hot path down her face. Tina was afraid being with Dean Dixon had ruined her for life. She would never find another man as exciting, as good at loving her. He just seemed to know exactly what would take her higher than she'd ever been before.

Dean pushed her back from him and cupped

her face in his palms. His eyes were dark and tortured. "Did I hurt you?" he demanded. She shook her head from side to side, but he pulled her tightly to his chest. His breaths were short and agitated, his heartbeat erratic in his chest. "Fuck, I'm so sorry, baby…please don't cry."

Why the hell *was* she crying? Tina asked herself. That was the best, most intense orgasm she'd ever had. She should just appreciate last night for what it was. When she made the decision to make love to him last night, Tina knew what would happen this morning. So why did the thought of leaving this man, this place make her heart hurt so badly?

"Hey, ya'll. I found her skirt! Where the hell are they?!?" Tina's eyes teared up again at hearing Cord's voice outside. She refused to let the tears fall and upset Dean. This was all her problem, and she would deal with it. She knew the score when she allowed this to happen. She sucked in a shuddering breath then pushed away from him. He was still hard inside of her, but Tina made herself get up. As his body slid from hers, it felt like she was ripping her heart out too.

"We have to go," she said softly, and he grabbed her hand.

"Look at me, Tina," he said darkly, and her eyes met his.

"Yeah?" The indecision in his eyes, his sudden tenseness told her he was struggling to find words. She had a feeling she knew what he wanted to say.

When he looked away, she knew she was right. "Um, last night was…"

Dean Dixon had a lot of problems, and Tina wasn't about to add to them, or make him feel guilty about last night. "Amazing," she said lightly with a smile she definitely didn't feel. "But a one-time deal." Tina laughed, instead of sobbing. "We have a problem though."

His eyes flew back to hers. "What?"

"I don't have underwear or a skirt to climb back down that ladder. If I do it now, everyone will see my bare ass. My bra is down there too."

Dean pushed up to his feet, then grabbed his jeans off the floor. He'd managed to remember to bring them, because his supply of condoms was in there. He had used every single one of them. Thank god he hadn't come inside of her that last time. Dean hadn't even thought about a condom that last time.

"I'll go get them." He shoved his legs into the jeans, then managed to zip them over his engorged cock without injuring himself. His underwear was down there too, and his boots and belt. His family was probably having the lake dragged for their bodies. He'd heard Cord's friends' voices as they yelled for them out there too. Dean had no idea how he was going to explain this one to them. He wasn't going to explain. He was a grown man, and didn't care what they thought. Last night was the best night he'd had in three years.

No, it was the best night he'd ever had in his life.

Dean glanced back at Tina, and he didn't want to open that damned door to go down there. What he wanted to do was to keep her up here forever. He could stay here with her, and they'd make love. Pretend the outside world wasn't slowly killing the man he knew he needed to be. The man he was before his ex-wife had destroyed him.

If he stayed up here though, Cindy would finish that job. Dean had to figure out how to hang onto his son. Tina was right. Jeremy was his son, even though they didn't share genes. He was going to fight Cindy with everything he had to keep him from getting hurt again. And his family was depending on him to figure out how to hang onto the ranch.

Tina Montgomery had a life and a big important job in Dallas. She wasn't going to give that up for a broken down cowboy with a needy son. He wasn't going to ask her to. That's not what last night was about anyway. Dean didn't know exactly what it was about, but it wasn't about forever. "I'll be back in a minute," he said gruffly, as he swung the door open.

He turned and laid down on the floor then reached back with his foot to find the first rung. He scrambled down the tree to the ground, and took a moment to adjust his jeans, before he started across the pine needle covered ground. Last night in the heat of the moment, he hadn't felt the prickly pine needles sticking into the soles of his feet. He hadn't felt much of anything, except the overwhelming urge to get Tina Montgomery up in that deer stand and fuck her brains out. This morning, he felt every step he took, just like he felt the bitterness of the regret inside his chest.

If they'd met when he was younger, before he became so jaded. Before Cindy. Maybe Dean's life would be different. Tina Montgomery coming along now wasn't the same. He wasn't the same. Last night up in that deer stand he'd forgotten his problems for a few hours. She'd helped him forget. But when his feet hit the ground again this morning, they were all still there. Last night hadn't solved a damn thing. Dean knew it had just been a temporary reprieve in his shitty life. A welcome one, but just a reprieve. Dean still didn't have a damned clue how he was going to fix things. Or if he could.

Taking a deep breath, he huffed it out then picked his way through the trees toward the place they'd made love the first time last night. Dean looked around under the tree and found his hat behind some scrub, but didn't see her skirt, his boots, or anything else. He mumbled under his breath and turned. A pair of ripped red panties occluded his view. They smelled just like Tina Montgomery, and he couldn't help but take a deep breath.

"Looking for these?" Cord said smugly.

Dean ripped them from his fingers, and shoved

them into the pocket of his jeans. "Where's her damned skirt?" he grumbled.

Cord laughed and pulled it from behind his back to hand it to him.

"My boots?" Dean growled.

"Hope has those in the truck." Cord didn't move to go get them though. His brother stood there with a wide grin on his face. "Figured you took her to the deer stand. I made enough damned noise to wake the dead. You should be saying thank you instead of being an ass. Seems like you should be in a better mood too, considering."

"Would you just go get my damned boots?"

"Hope has Tina's boots too," Cord said in a sing song voice, then his eyes laughed as he added, "I'll go get them on one condition."

"What's that?" Dean asked clenching his fists, wanting nothing more at that moment than to plant one in his brother's face.

"You let her climb down that ladder to get her panties and skirt."

"Fuck you," Dean growled and shoved him hard. Cord laughed as he stumbled back and put his hand on his chest.

"You know I'm just kidding." Cord's face turned serious. "I'm happy for you brother."

"Nothing to be happy about. It's done," Dean said through his gritted teeth. "Now, go get my damned boots before I tell your wife you're ogling

Just Shoot Me

Tina, and she kicks your ass!"

His brother's laughter echoed through the woods, as he walked toward the clearing. A few minutes later, he returned with Dean's shirt, and their boots. Cord dug into the pocket of his jeans and handed Dean a set of keys. "Ya'll take your time," he said with a wink. "Lucky says to take his truck when you're ready to come back. He's riding with us."

A lightning bolt of desire shot through him, but Dean caught it and crushed it. He had things to do. "We'll be there in a few minutes," he said as he turned to walk back to the tree stand.

Two days later, Dean watched out the window of the ranch house as Tina, Paulo and Belinda loaded up their equipment into their cars in the rain. The pouring rain. The bottom had fallen out on their way back from the woods the other morning, and it hadn't let up since. There was no way they could take photos now. He was sure the bluebonnet field on the other side of the lake was knee deep mud. The lake had probably overflowed too, so they couldn't get back there even if a miracle happened and the sun came out.

Dean knew he should go over there and say goodbye, but he just couldn't make himself do it. She was most likely mad at him anyway. After he dropped Tina off at the bunkhouse, Dean had been hiding out to avoid her. Being stuck in the house made that kind of difficult, but she hadn't come out in the rain to walk across the yard to the house.

Who the hell knew, maybe she was hiding out from him too.

The only reason he knew she was leaving this morning, was because Cord came to eat breakfast with the family, and he'd mentioned she got called into a meeting with her bosses in Dallas. He also gave their daddy the check from Texas Tomboy that Tina had brought with her. Their payment for using the ranch for the shoot. That money was going to be combined with the auction money they had to buy spring stock for the ranch. Half a herd was better than no herd.

Dean didn't get a check himself, because he hadn't done the photo shoot. When he did get one, he wasn't going to put it into the herd. He was hiring a fucking attorney to take care of Cindy. According to his brother, Tina was going to call to reschedule when the weather got better, but there was a chance she wouldn't be coming back out to the ranch for the shoot. Hope would handle taking the photos with Paulo and Belinda if she was needed at her office.

Dean could only hope she would be tied up. And hopefully the weather would get better soon, because if it didn't happen soon the money wouldn't mean shit to him. Jeremy would be gone. That money was going to be the difference between keeping Jeremy and losing him to Cindy. Dean felt it in his gut. That fight was coming, even though he hadn't been served notice yet. He was going to be as prepared as he could be, which meant he needed the money from the photo shoot. Regardless of whether he had to see Tina again, work with her.

"Daddy I want to go say goodbye to Laney and Miss Tina," Jeremy said with a tug on Dean's belt. Dean looked down at him. The kid looked afraid that Dean would say no, like he expected him to say no. A few days ago, Dean probably would have said no, or just brushed him off. He didn't want to go over there, but he was going to do it. For his son. If he was going to lose him, Dean was going to make damned sure the kid remembered him fondly at least.

He ruffled Jeremy's hair, and his son smiled up at him. Emotion shot to his throat to form a tight knot. He cleared it, then said, "Okay, go get your raincoat on."

Jeremy squealed and turned to run across the living room, and Dean went to get his slicker out of the closet. They met in the foyer, then walked out into the rain. When they got to the bunkhouse, Tina was inside, but Laney was out on the porch. Dean stopped and pushed Jeremy toward the porch, hoping he would just say goodbye to the little girl, so they could get back to the house. If he was lucky, he wouldn't have to see Tina.

No, if he was lucky she wouldn't be leaving. He shoved that thought out of his head and said, "Okay hurry up. We need to get back to the house and they need to go."

"Yes, sir." Jeremy ran splashing across the yard to the steps. Dean just stood in the rain, hoping he would hurry. Before he had to see Tina. Before he had to say goodbye. Before he had to watch her drive off down that driveway, and watch her leave him like Cindy had done.

Different situation, different woman, he reminded himself. But it sure felt the same.

"Fuck," he said under his breath, as he turned and took a couple of steps back toward the house. Jeremy could just say goodbye then come home.

"Dean!" Tina called from the porch, and he stopped. A gust of wind blew rain into his face and he was glad for it. He tilted his hat lower over his eyes and kicked up the collar of his slicker before he turned around. His heart did a loop in his chest when he saw she had changed into those damned heels of hers again. The ones that made her legs look like three-quarters of her body length. And a navy blue business suit. He'd never seen her in business mode before. She didn't even look like the same woman. This Tina Montgomery he realized was a million miles removed from the one he made love to in that deer stand.

Her smile wobbled and she waved at him. His heart stuttered in his chest again. There was no way in hell he could talk to her. He waved back, then spun on his heel and stormed across the yard. No, he needed just to cut ties and be done with it. Focus on what he needed to be focusing on. Keeping his son. She would go back to Dallas and she would carry on. Probably meet some guy in a matching business suit, and have little boys that wore polo shirts instead of cowboy boots. That was the life she was suited for, not trudging through horseshit and mud in her high heels.

Dean walked through the front door of the house, right past his daddy, who tried to grab his shoulder in the foyer to go straight to the liquor cabinet. It was just ten o'clock in the morning, but he needed a drink. He grabbed the whole fucking bottle, and a glass then headed to his room.

"Watch, Jeremy. I don't feel good," he yelled down the hall before he went inside his room and shut the door.

CHAPTER TWELVE

Tina sat at the long conference table in her nine o'clock meeting with her bosses, staring out the window over the President of Texas Tomboy's shoulder as he talked. She wanted to focus on what he was saying, it was important she was sure, but she just couldn't.

How could she think about anything except the note she found when she got home yesterday afternoon? Her sister was gone on the road with a cowboy. She asked her to take care of Laney, but said she didn't think she'd be a burden. What the fuck did her sister think raising a child was, if not a burden? But then she wouldn't know that. She had never raised Laney.

Laney had cried herself to sleep last night, even though Tina tried to convince her niece that her mother was just taking a vacation. And since she was still on Spring Break from school, Tina had to leave her with the elderly neighbor this morning to come to work. Still crying. Totally unacceptable. She had almost called in sick, but since she got the call from her boss yesterday, specifically requesting her presence in this meeting, she had to be here.

Or lose her job.

Then she wouldn't be able to support her niece, who might as well be her own daughter.

Tina wanted to strangle her sister.

"So, of course we'll need you to travel if you're offered the position," Mr. Jamison said.

The word travel penetrated the fog around her brain, and Tina dragged her eyes back to Mr. Jamison. "Travel?" she repeated dumbly.

"Weren't you listening, Miss Montgomery?" he asked impatiently. She glanced at her manager June, and received a hot look.

Tina looked back at Mr. Jamison, but panic grabbed her by the throat and she couldn't find her voice or words for a second. It finally broke free. "Um, yes of course, I heard, Mr. Jamison. Travel?"

"As our European Marketing Manager, you'd be required to travel overseas frequently. Do you think that would be something you could do?"

"European Marketing Manager? We're not in Europe, sir," Tina repeated, terrified now that she'd missed something vitally important while she was daydreaming. Texas Tomboy was a western wear company. That was as American as you could get. What the hell was he talking about Europe for? Tina pasted on a smile, and her voice was a little patronizing, because she thought surely he had made a mistake. "Um, I was developing the Texas Tomcat menswear line, remember Mr. Jamison?" Texas Tomboy employed a lot of people, she thought surely he had gotten her confused with someone else. "I don't have the photos and presentation together yet. The weather delayed the shoot, but I'm working on it." Tina sat up in her chair and stiffened her shoulders, then said confidently, "I'll definitely be ready for our meeting next Tuesday."

Tina planned on going back to the ranch this weekend to do the shoot. Come hell or high water she was going to get the photos she needed to sell this line. If she was going to have to take care of Laney, that promotion was more important to her now than ever. And the check for that photo shoot would also give Dean Dixon the money to fight his ex-wife to keep his son. Before she'd left the ranch, Tina had only been able to give them the check for the location, since the shoot didn't happen.

Her manager covered her hand on the table, and gave it a squeeze. "Mr. Jamison, this is a huge opportunity for Miss Montgomery. I think she's a little stunned by the offer. Let us talk, and she'll get back to you tomorrow. Would that be okay?"

Mr. Jamison grunted, then shoved his chair back. Her manager grabbed her arm and all but pulled her up to her feet. "We'll just leave you to your work now, sir. Thank you for your offer. I should have an answer for you later this afternoon."

Tina was pushed from behind to the door of the office. June opened it then shoved her into the hallway. Leaning back she shut it behind her. "What the hell is wrong with you Tina?" she hissed.

"I must be living in an alternate universe, June. What just happened in there?"

"You got offered the biggest job you're ever likely to be offered, and you were off in lala land somewhere. What were you daydreaming about?"

"What job offer? I have to do the photo—"

"That promotion is off the table now. Jamison shelved even thinking about the men's line until next year, so the company can do an expansion into Europe. I recommended you for this job, because I can't travel like that with my kids. Now, I'm not so sure I made a good call. You just made me and yourself look like an idiot!"

Good God almighty. Now that Lori had taken off, Tina couldn't take the job either. She had a kid now too. There was no way she could leave Laney here to go gallivanting all over the world. "What happens if I turn it down?"

Nobody here knew her personal problems. These were her co-workers, not her friends or her family. Tina kept her personal like to herself.

"If you'd been listening in that meeting, you would know they're downsizing the staff to help fund the expansion. I'm afraid your job will be one of the ones to be cut. That's why I recommended you."

"But the calendar sales—"

"Made us a record year last year. It was a great idea, and you got full credit for it. But that was last year. And this year, the board has decided to ride the momentum from the increased sales to expand their market, instead of the developing a product line. I'm sorry."

It looked like even though she'd been at Texas Tomboy six years now, she had just worked herself out of a job by recommending that calendar to them. "I see," Tina said fighting valiantly to control the tremble in her voice. "I'll have to think about it."

"Think fast, Tina. I told Mr. Jamison he'd have an answer tomorrow. He wants this settled so they can start talking to distributors."

"Yes, ma'am. I'll let you know by five tomorrow."

June was right, Tina thought as she turned and headed for the ladies room to have the meltdown that was very near to the surface. Tina was about as stunned as a woman could get. She had a little over twenty-four hours to make the decision of her life. And she had not a soul to help her make it. Not a soul to talk to about it.

***

Loud pounding at his bedroom door sounded like it was coming from the inside of his skull. Dean groaned and squeezed the sides of his head. He rolled over and bright sunlight pierced his brain, so he slammed his eyes shut and rolled back over. A noisy thud on the floor beside the bed made it worse. He peered over the edge at the empty whiskey bottle and groaned. A wave of nausea rushed through him, and

Dean held his breath, slapped a hand over his mouth, and hugged his stomach. Collapsing back onto the bed he groaned again. Dumb, dumb dumb, he castigated himself. The knocking started again and he flinched, barely suppressing a whimper.

"Daddy, Miss Tina is on the phone for you," Jeremy shouted from the hall. "And Maw Maw says to tell you to come to lunch!"

Lunch? He glanced over the side of bed at the bottle again and wondered what time it was. Hell what day it was. Friday maybe? He thought it was around midnight when he finally polished it off last night, but couldn't remember. Tina had left yesterday hadn't she? Dean's stomach lurched, and he groaned. He knew one thing, the last thing he wanted right now was food. Or to talk to Tina Montgomery. The pounding started again, and the knob rattled.

Dean sat straight up in the bed. "Alright, Jeremy!" he shouted and swallowed hard, waiting for the room to quit moving. "Tell your grandma I'm not hungry. And tell Tina I will call her back!" *Sometime in the next lifetime*, he added mentally as he laid back. That might be sooner than later, he thought, because he sure as hell felt like he was about to meet his maker.

"Yes, sir…" he barely heard the words, but what he didn't miss was the dejection and concern in Jeremy's tone. Dean sucked in a breath and let it out slowly. He needed to get out of this fucking bed. The sun was shining, and that meant it was a workday. He had work to do, and he also had things to work out. But he just couldn't find the energy to move, or the motivation. Maybe if he just curled up and slept a little more he'd feel better when he woke up. Odds weren't good for that, but it was something to hope for he thought as he drifted off again.

A little while later, or he thought it was a while. It could have been days for all he knew. Dean was just that fuzzy. Scraping at the doorknob woke him up. He sat up in the bed and threw his legs over the side, then hurriedly shoved his legs into his jeans and zipped them up. The door flew inward and Cord stood there looking mad as hell with a butter knife in his hand.

"Get your lazy ass up, Hope needs to talk to you," he grated, taking a step inside.

"I don't feel good. Am I not allowed to be sick once in a while?" Dean shot back, and flinched when his voice echoed in his head.

"You've got a fucking hangover, Dean. Because you're too damned pathetic to face your problems, you tried to drown the fact that you don't have the balls to do something about your situation. To forgive and forget. Move on."

Every word out of his brother's mouth was like a nail driven into his skull. Dean fought the nausea that rolled in his stomach and clenched his fists. He took a step toward Cord, then clamped a hand over his mouth and shoved his brother into the door jamb to get out of the bedroom. He staggered down the hallway to the bathroom, and went inside and locked it. After he worshiped the porcelain goddess for a few minutes, he felt a lot better, but weak as a newborn colt. He staggered to the sink and splashed his face with water then brushed his teeth. When he raised up to look in the mirror he wanted to scream, because he didn't recognize the old man who stared back at him. Old and used up. He had lines at the corners of his eyes, and deeper ones around his mouth. His skin looked pale and his cheeks sunken. Dean felt just as old and used up as he looked. Cord was right, he was absolutely pathetic.

What the hell had happened to him? Cindy had happened. Life had happened. And whiskey had happened last night, which he was sure made things worse. Tina Montgomery must be blind to think he was a fucking model. Maybe she'd taken pity on him because of his financial situation. That's all it could be. Well, he wasn't going to see her again, and he wasn't doing that damned photo shoot. He would just have to figure something else out.

Dean sucked in a shuddering breath, then opened the bathroom door and walked down the hall. He stopped in his bedroom to put on a shirt, because he knew his mama wouldn't be happy if he showed up in the kitchen without one. When he walked into the kitchen his family was all gathered at the table. A sandwich sat in front of his chair.

"Why does everyone look so morose?" Dean

asked as he sat down at the table. "Somebody die?" He picked up his sandwich, and a glob of mayonnaise leaked out the side. His stomach rolled, so he put it back on the plate.

"A courier came by here earlier, son," Silas Dixon said, and his eyes were suspiciously bright. His hand shook as he pulled a sheaf of papers from his lap. He sat them on the table and slid them across the table to Dean.

Dean's stomach rolled again and he sucked in a breath, trying to calm the storm inside of him. He didn't want to look at the papers, didn't have to really. Just a glance at the top of the page told him all he needed to know. "Petition for Emergency Custody of a Minor?"

"She's going for sole custody son. And there's a restraining order in there too. She said you threatened her life, and she's afraid for her son's safety."

"*Bullshit!*" Dean screamed, as his chair scraped back. He stood and slammed his hands down on the table. "She was trespassing on my property! I didn't touch her! And if Cindy was so goddamned concerned about her son, Bobby Jones' son, why the hell did she leave him here for me to have to raise for three years?!?"

Dean heard a whimper and looked at the doorway to the kitchen. Jeremy stood there and his face was white. He looked crestfallen. Devastated.

His mother pushed her chair back and she smothered a wail with her hand, as she ran from the room. Dean's father went after her.

"Oh, God…" he groaned and walked toward Jeremy. Jeremy backed out of the doorway and spun. He ran for the front door, and Dean chased him. "Jeremy, wait!" Jeremy didn't stop though, his feet hit the ground and he ran toward the barn.

Cord ran out onto the porch behind Dean and grabbed his shoulder to jerk him back. "Let me go talk to him, you go talk to Hope," he said sternly. Dean nodded and sucked in a shuddering breath. "I'll bring him back to the house when he calms down."

Dean nodded again then staggered back to the kitchen. The emotion inside his chest built like a pressure cooker. It was so tight he could barely breathe. Spots danced in front of his eyes, his ears rang and Dean thought he might pass out. He sank to his knees, and dropped his chin to his chest. His heart hurt so damned bad he thought he might be having a heart attack. He heard a chair scrape back, then a hand rubbed circles in the center of his back.

"Dean are you okay, honey? Let me help you up," Hope said. She slid her arm through his, and pulled upward with a grunt. Something inside Dean snapped and the lid came off of the pressure cooker. His chest loosened, he sucked in a deep breath, so deep he thought his lungs might explode. The emotions bubbling inside pushed up into his throat, then exploded out of him in a roar. When he was done, Dean felt like a dishrag. He sat back on his butt and hugged his knees to him and rocked. Hope kept rubbing his back, but leaned closer.

"I talked to my father and he recommended an attorney in Dallas. He can help you. I paid him a retainer, and you have an appointment on Monday. You just have to go talk to him. Don't worry about the money, we'll deal with it."

"I can't take your money," he pushed past his raw vocal chords. He put his hand to his forehead. "I'll use the money from the modeling shoot. Has Tina called you yet?"

Hope's hand stopped moving and her body tensed. "Just go talk to the attorney, Dean. He's good. He won't let her win."

Something was wrong. Hope wasn't telling him something. Fear shot through him that something had happened to Tina, or her niece. He met her eyes, because Dean knew his sister-in-law couldn't look him in the eye and lie to him. "Did you talk to Tina?"

She sighed. "Yes, I talked to her earlier when she called for you."

"What did she want?"

"She was pretty upset. Her company has canceled the men's line."

Wasn't that just wonderful. Could it get any worse for him? His mind darted off toward how that was going to affect his situation, but he jerked it back when a thought hit him. "That means she doesn't get her promotion, right?"

"Um, right," Hope said.

No wonder she was upset. The tension in his shoulders eased a little, knowing she wasn't hurt. But he felt damned bad for her. That little girl depended on her, and she wanted to buy a house. That wasn't something Dean could waste what few brain cells he had left on trying to solve though. He had bigger fish to fry right now. And his own problems to deal with.

She still hadn't relaxed beside him. There had to be more. "What else did she say?"

There was another long pause, then breath she'd evidently been holding escaped. "It's a big mess. You need to worry about you and Jeremy right now. I'm going to try to help her."

Hope was always trying to help. Always in the middle of situations that didn't concern her. His situation and Tina Montgomery's situation were prime examples. But then if she wasn't that way, she probably wouldn't be married to his brother.

"I think you need to take your own advice and deal with your problems first."

Sometimes he wondered if she forgot about the Weston lawsuit she needed to take care of. Dean hadn't forgotten. He also hadn't forgotten about owing her money. If it took him until he was ninety, he would pay her back for helping them take care of his father when he was sick.

"I'm handling that too. My father had some advice, and I'm thinking about it."

"You're talking to your dad again?" After the fiasco at Brittany Weston's wedding, because of her camera malfunction, her family had basically disowned her. She had embarrassed them. Those snobs needed embarrassment. If that was the worst of their problems, then they were doing good. But everyone needed family. At least hers was talking to her again. He knew it had to be a relief.

"Um yeah, a little." That was another thing about Hope. She kept everything entirely too close to her chest. If she'd let people in on her problems, maybe they could help her too.

That thought sent off bells inside of him. "What the fuck happened to Tina?"

"She quit her job."

Shock rocked Dean, and he sat back. Cord walked into the kitchen. "Dean, go talk to Jeremy, he's in his room."

He looked up at his brother for a second without even seeing him. Dean was that stunned from the news that Tina hadn't lost her job, she quit. "Did she say why?"

"They wanted her to travel to Europe, and she couldn't do that." Hope said.

"Dean, you really need to go talk to your son," Cord said shortly.

Yes, he needed to go talk to his son. Explain

why he said what he'd said. He would think about Tina Montgomery later. When he could actually think again. Right now he had to deal with explaining to Jeremy that his mother was a faithless whore without saying that. A six-year-old was not going to understand that. And he was afraid Jeremy wasn't ever going to forgive him for saying what he had. Jeremy would become just one more member of his family that hated him.

Because of Cindy.

No, he wasn't letting that happen. "What did you say to him?" Dean asked trying to figure out what he was going to say.

"I told him that you loved him, and that you didn't mean what you said. If I were you, I'd start there," Cord recommended.

Dean nodded and got up then walked on leaden feet toward his son's room. He knocked on the door, but there was no answer so he just opened the door. Jeremy was laying on his bed facing the wall. Dean walked over to sit on the side of the bed and put his hand on Jeremy's hip.

Emotion choked, but Dean swallowed it down. *Words are cheap.* He gathered his courage and forced the words past the lump in his throat, "I love you, son." Jeremy's shoulders tensed, but he didn't roll over, so Dean continued, "I'm sorry I said what I did. It's not true. You *are* my son, and I love you very much."

"I'm not your son," Jeremy said sadly.

Dean's eyes burned, he rolled them and sucked

in a deep breath. "Jeremy, do you remember when your Mama left?"

"Not really," Jeremy replied in an even sadder voice.

His shoulders shook and Dean leaned over the bed and slid his arms under him to pick him up. He pulled him onto his lap and hugged him tight to his chest.

"Well I remember. She did both of us wrong when she left. But you know what, Jeremy?"

"What?" Jeremy said with a sniffle.

"She did me the biggest favor she could have too."

"By leaving?" he asked with confusion.

"No by leaving you here with me," he said brushing the hair off of his forehead. "I didn't mind that she left so much, but if she had taken you with her, I would have been crushed. I was there when you were born, and I was the first person to hold you. To love you. You *are* my son, and I'm glad you are." Dean hugged him so hard, his muscles quaked.

"But you said Bobby Jones was my daddy," Jeremy mumbled against his chest.

"Bobby Jones is *not* your daddy," Dean said gruffly. "Daddies are the men that take care of their kids. They make sure they are fed, clothed…and loved." Dean hugged him tighter. "I love you, Jeremy and I will fight for you. That's what daddies do."

"Maw Maw says you're not posed to fight," he

said and Dean laughed.

"Maw Maw is right," he said and ruffled his hair. "I just mean I will *never* let anyone hurt you or take you away from me," Dean said then determination hit him in the gut. "You're mine, and I would fight for you with my last breath."

"Can I have a brownie?" Jeremy asked hesitantly.

"You can have the whole pan. Except for one, I want at least one," Dean said as relief flooded him that evidently he'd said something right. Something that made Jeremy feel better.

"Deal…and Daddy?" Jeremy said looking up at him.

"Yeah?" Dean replied meeting his green eyes.

"I'm glad you're my Daddy too."

CHAPTER THIRTEEN

Dean tugged at the collar of the dress shirt, which felt a size too small. Smaller even with the tie his mother tied for him before he left the ranch that morning. Making matters worse was the huge knot of fear in his throat that felt like he'd swallowed a brick. That feeling had been with him since he got those papers from Cindy's attorney on Friday.

Jeremy was counting on him to work this out.

His family was counting on him. He was counting on himself. And he was putting his eggs all in the same basket. The attorney that Hope's estranged father had recommended. The man was a socialite. His daughter had been too before she married his brother. They knew people, he reminded himself. To get a recommendation from someone like Liam Carlisle meant you had clients in that circle. Those people didn't mess around. They only hired the best attorneys, because they had the money to do so.

Dean needed the best, but he couldn't afford that kind of attorney. He was only here for a consultation, he reminded himself, as he forced himself to push the button on the wall to call the elevator. According to Hope, the man would give him advice on what he needed to do to stop Cindy. To keep his son. The door swooshed open, and Dean stepped aside for two fancy looking women to exit. They were talking, but one woman glanced at him, did a double-take then smiled widely and stopped. The other kept walking. "Cord Dixon?"

Dean pushed his hat back on his head, so she could see his face. He knew that would answer her question whether he was his brother or not. He waited. She smiled and waited. He huffed out a breath. "No, I'm Dean Dixon, Cord's brother."

"Twin brother?" she asked with a laugh then shook her head. "Damn, two of you?"

"*Older* brother." Ancient brother. From the looks of it at least five years older than this woman who obviously knew his brother. Dean gave her a tight smile and tried to step around her to get into the elevator. He had things to do other than flirting with his brother's old girlfriends.

But she put a hand on his arm. "Wait. I heard what happened to your brother at Laramie Jeans. That Tonya Laramie is a piece of work."

Dean stopped because he was too damned curious not to. His brother had never told him the whole story about what happened to end his reign as Mr. Laramie Jeans. Dean stepped back out of the elevator. He had a few minutes. "What happened?"

Her face flushed, but she smiled again. "Well, Tonya Laramie propositioned your brother, then when he turned her down she fired him and had him blackballed in the Dallas modeling world. She did that to a couple of other guys there too. The man she replaced him with even. I'd like to talk to Cord, but didn't know where to find him."

"Why do you need to talk to him?"

"Because I'm representing those other men in a harassment suit against Laramie, and I think he needs to include himself. It's public knowledge now, in all the papers. We're getting ready to go to court, and I'm going for broke," she said with a cocky smile. "I believe we have a damned good shot at winning the case. His testimony would be the icing."

Dean knew about broke. And right now his brother did too. He wondered what that term meant in this woman's world. "Broke?"

"Ten million. If Cord includes himself, I'll up that another five."

Dean's breath caught in his chest and he whistled it out. "Damn."

The woman reached into the pocket of her skirt and pulled out a card. She handed it to Dean and smiled. "Tell your brother to call me."

With a saucy wink she left, and he watched her walk across the rotunda toward the door.

Dean was sure his brother would be glad to call her. Five million dollars? Damn, Dean would like to have even a tenth of that. He wouldn't take Hope's money, but he damn sure wouldn't hesitate to take it from his brother. Maybe things would work out after all. He felt better about getting into the elevator and pushing the button for the eleventh floor.

An hour later, he finished the story about his

and Cindy's situation then took a deep breath. He felt like he had purged himself of it. Having it out in the open now felt damn good. Dean had never talked to anyone about it. He would have paid this man the two-hundred-fifty dollars an hour he charged, just to be able to do that again.

"Now, she's married to the man she left me for, the man she claims is Jeremy's Fa—" He just couldn't push the word out of his throat. The word tasted like bitter acid on his tongue when he finally heaved a breath to finish, "Father."

The man who had thus far just sat there either staring at him, or scribbling notes on the pad in front of him, sighed too. He sat back in his chair and put his hands behind his head. "Have you had a DNA test done?" he asked bluntly.

"No…I thought it was better for my son if I didn't know." Dean dragged his eyes away. "Still think it's better. He's my son. That's all that matters."

"Not now. You need to have it done. If he's your biological son that will make things a lot clearer in the judge's eyes."

"Okay." He didn't want to know, but if this man said he needed to do it, he would.

"You said you're single on the information form. Are you dating anyone?" the attorney asked easing back to lay his elbows on his desk.

"What the hell does that have to do with anything?" Dean asked gruffly.

"If you're married, that will also look better to the court. She's married, and could provide a stable home for him."

"Single isn't stable? He has a home, a roof over his head, food on his plate." Even Dean heard the defensiveness in his tone and flinched.

"If he's not your son biologically, and his mother is married to his biological father now that could look a lot more stable to the court than a single father who might have raised him for the last six years, but isn't his *real* father."

"I'm about as fucking real as you can get. I'm the one who stayed up with him when he had a bug and threw up all night. I'm the one who busted his ass to make sure he had clothes on his back, and food on his plate. I'd say that's pretty damned real."

"Yes, that's true, but the court is going to look at the big picture. The whole picture. They will think about the future, and what's best for Jeremy. If your ex-wife can prove she can give him a stable home with both of his biological parents, it may not go well for you despite all that."

"Fuck," Dean said as he shot to his feet. "Thank you for your time."

"I want to work with you, Dean, and I don't take on cases I can't win." The man held up his hand, and Dean eased back down into the chair, but sat on the edge. "But I'm not going to candy coat anything for you. I'm going to tell you what I think. You may not like it, but that's what is best for you to hear. Have the DNA test done, and have the lab send me the results. Here's a lab that's nearby." The man scribbled something on a notepad then tore off the sheet and handed it to him. "I'll call you when I get the results. In the meantime, I'm going to file a request for a stay on that Emergency Custody Order and file one of my own. I think the court will allow him to stay with you at least until the test results come back."

Let him stay with him. That sounded so strange to Dean. For years now, since Cindy left him, Dean had blamed her for strapping him with a kid who wasn't his. Now, all he could think about was fighting her to keep his son. He was so damned scared of losing him, he felt like he would lose himself if Jeremy wasn't with him anymore.

"I'll get the test done right away," Dean said as he stood. He extended his arm over the desk, and the attorney shook his hand.

"Try not to worry. We're going to give Cindy and that jackleg attorney of hers a run for their money. If we can drag it out long enough, maybe your son will be old enough for the court to let him decide himself who he wants to live with." A smug smile eased up the corner of the man's mouth and he winked at Dean.

The confidence this man had was contagious. Dean needed that confidence in his court for this fight. "Thank you so much. Let me know if there's anything else you need."

Dean left the man's office and didn't know how he felt. He didn't really give Dean good news about the situation, but he didn't think it was a hopeless situation either. That in itself was good news to Dean, because before he talked to him that's exactly how he'd felt.

According to the paperwork Dean had finally made himself read last night, he was supposed to turn Jeremy over to Cindy tonight. Now he didn't have to do that. If nothing else, meeting with the attorney had bought him more time with his son. Maybe years, if the man was right. Dragging things on for years though, playing legal football with Cindy, would cost him a lot of money. His son was worth every penny. He would sell his soul if that's what it took to keep his son. His sanity was worth more though.

If he lost his son, Dean would lose his mind.

He was sure Tina Montgomery was losing hers too at the moment. She had lost her job. Or quit it. Hope still hadn't told him the entire story. But she did ask him to stop by Tina's apartment to check on her on his way back home, which worked out perfectly. That gave him a good excuse to go by there without having to answer a million questions from Hope. Seeing her was the last thing Dean wanted to do, but he was worried about her. Damned worried. Like his son was to him, Dean knew that job meant everything to her.

When he was having a breakdown out by that

lake that night she had been there for him. He owed it to her to be there for her, drag her back from the edge, or just listen.

Right now though, he was going to have that test done then pray like hell while he waited for the results to come back.

***

Tina paused the movie for a moment so she could shuffle to the bathroom to get another box of Kleenex from the cabinet. When she walked back to the sofa, she picked up the wastebasket, shoved the empty Oreo bag inside, then gathered up the full trash bag and tied it off. She didn't take it to the kitchen, she just didn't have the energy. Instead, she set it beside the other full wastepaper bag she'd changed out last night, before she plopped back on the sofa.

She had to finish the movie and her newest crying jag before Laney got home from school in two hours. Her pity party was only allowed when her niece was sleeping, crying herself, or at school. Tina jerked up the remote and pressed the button, then threw it down beside her to pick up the bag of nacho chips she still had to finish. Between the Oreos, chips and flat soda she had in her stomach, Tina felt sick, but she couldn't seem to stop herself. Last night, she'd eaten an entire box of chocolate covered cherries she'd gotten as a Secret Santa gift from someone at her office for Christmas. Yeah, she'd thrown them up, but they had been good going down.

The same would probably happen when she finished the chips.

Since Friday when she'd quit her job before they could fire her, Tina had done nothing but cry or throw up. When Laney wasn't watching that is. Her niece did enough crying of her own from missing her mother, and Tina could at least justify her tears to the kid then as sympathetic tears. Otherwise, she held her own in until she could wallow in her misery alone.

Like now, she thought as her eyes welled up again. She jerked a tissue from the box to blow her nose. The scene in the sappy movie she was watching caught her attention. The guy had just told the woman he was dying. Fixated on the scene, Tina bit her lower lip, then sucked in a sob when the woman started crying. She jerked the blanket beside her up to her chin, and the chip bag fell, scattering chips all over the floor. Tina didn't care. She eased down on the couch, pulled the cover over her head and just cried.

A heavy knock at the front door woke her up. Tina's eyes popped open like rusty shutters, and she was scared for a minute, because it was pitch dark, then realized the blanket was over face. She shoved it off and looked toward the door when another round of knocking started. It wasn't Laney coming home, knocking because she'd forgotten her key. The knock was too heavy.

Tina groaned, and thought about ignoring whoever it was. She sure as hell didn't want to see anyone. She glanced at the clock hanging beside the refrigerator. And she still had thirty minutes left to party. The knock came again and Tina sat up on the couch, knocking over the trash can.

"Tina, I know you're in there, I saw your car in the parking lot!" Dean shouted and knocked harder.

Oh, Lord. The absolute last person in the world she wanted to see. She ran her hands through her hair, knowing it was a bird's nest. She had seen it this morning in the mirror and almost scared herself, but was too exhausted to run a comb through it. Screw it. He needed to see this. Maybe then he'd leave her the hell alone for good.

What the hell could he want anyway?

Dean had pretty much told her she was just a good fuck to him, that he couldn't give a shit less about her. The pathetic way he'd said goodbye to her when she left the ranch said it all. The fact that he hadn't even bothered to come a hundred yards in the rain to see her at the bunkhouse for two days after they had sex should have been her first clue to how he felt. But not Tina. She had been stupid enough to hold out hope, until he gave her that flip of his hand that he tried to pass off as a wave on her way out the door.

She had nothing to say to the man. Anger replaced her sorrow as she stood and crunched her way across the chips on the floor to the front door. She slid the chain free, flipped open the deadbolt, then opened the door and Dean's fist almost knocked on her forehead.

He dropped his hand to his side, and had the gall to smile at her. "You look like shit, buttercup," he said cheerfully.

Tina shoved the door closed in his face, but he put his foot between the door and the jamb. "Open the door, Tina.'

Well, with his big ass boot in the door, she wasn't going to be able to close it, so she huffed out a sigh then walked back to the sofa. The movie had ended, so she flicked the TV off and threw the remote onto the coffee table, then plopped back on the sofa and brushed the chip crumbs off of her feet, before she curled them under her. She jerked a pillow from beside her and hugged it to her chest. Dean pushed the door open and walked inside then shut it behind him. Her eyes took in his cowboy hat and the dress shirt and tie he wore, and her heart tried to do a little wiggle in her chest. She slapped the shit out of it and said, "What do you want?"

His eyes didn't meet hers, they traveled around the room. The smug bastard evidently passed judgment that it looked like a nuclear wasteland, because when he finally looked at her his lip curled a little. "Good God, honey. This place is a mess."

"It looks exactly how I feel. I'm sorry it doesn't meet your expectations. I won't be living here much longer, so I'm not too worried. Now what the hell do you want?" she asked shortly, hugging the pillow tighter.

"Hope asked me to come by and check on you," he said evenly.

It figured, he wasn't here of his own free will. He was doing his sister-in-law a favor. Well he sure wasn't doing her one, and Hope hadn't either. Emotion shot up to her throat, but she swallowed it enough to say, "Well you can tell Hope if she wants to know how I am, she can come here herself. She's welcome here, you're not. Now get out." Tina pointed toward the door, and bit her lower lip to stop the trembling.

Dean didn't move. He stood there staring at her with his stormy blue eyes.

"I said *get out*!" she repeated, dragging her eyes away, as the emotion got closer to the surface. Her eyes watered, and she sucked in a shuddering breath.

She heard a sigh, then footsteps, before a big body plopped beside her on the sofa. Dean dropped his arm over her shoulders. "You talked me down off the cliff the other night. It's my turn. Spill it, what's wrong? What happened with your job?"

Too late to pretend you care cowboy. Tina stiffened her body, lifted her chin and pinched her lips tighter. His arm slid behind her neck, as he pushed his other under her legs. Before she knew it Dean dragged her onto his lap and hugged her. Tight. His scent worked its magic, and Tina couldn't help but inhale it. It made her mad that it comforted her a little.

"Let me go," she growled pushing against his chest. His arms tightened even more, so she quit pushing. He was too strong.

"I'm not leaving until you talk to me," he said calmly.

"I got a promotion," she mumbled into his chest taking one more sniff of him, because she couldn't help herself. It was a little different mixed with the starch in his dress shirt. She wasn't sure she liked it better. Dean wasn't a starched shirt kind of man. The outdoors is what mixed well with his unique scent. "Why are you dressed up?" she muttered, because she couldn't help but ask. Surely it wasn't to impress her. Dean struck her as the kind of man who would rather be hanged than put on a tie. Probably thought it was the same thing.

"I went to see an attorney this morning. Cindy is suing me for custody of Jeremy," he said as if he were relating the weather. "Now why the hell would you quit your job if they offered you a promotion?" he countered angrily. His arms loosened a little so he could look down at her.

He waited. She held her tongue. His eyes narrowed, and she finally said, "It wasn't the promotion I wanted."

"So you quit your damned job?" Dean asked incredulously.

"They would have fired me otherwise, because I can't travel."

Dean shook his head. "Why the hell not? You're single. That sounds pretty exciting, actually."

"If I was five years younger, and not a single mother now, maybe it would be." He gasped and almost dumped her off of his lap. Tina grabbed herself with a hand on the coffee table, then he pulled her back up.

"You have a *kid* and didn't bother to tell me about it?" Dean all but shouted.

"You've met her. My sister left town, and left Laney with me."

"Good Lord," Dean whispered.

The phone on the wall in the kitchen rang, and Tina eased off of Dean's lap, crunched across the chips and walked over to answer it. "Tina Montgomery."

"Miss Montgomery, I need Laney's mother down at the school right now. We have a problem."

Tina's heart jumped to her throat. "Is Laney okay?"

"Yes, ma'am, but she's in a lot of trouble. I need her mother to come down here and pick her up. The principal wants to talk to her."

Tina's heart rate went off the charts. Being called in to talk to the principal was never a good thing. It hadn't been a good thing when she was in school, and she was sure that hadn't changed. Laney was never in trouble at school, so she couldn't imagine what she could have done.

"Um, her mother, is uh…out of town," she

stuttered.

"Well, we need someone to come down here and get her, and until we talk to her mother, she isn't allowed back at school."

"Can't she ride the bus?"

"I'm afraid not, ma'am. This is very serious." Tina eased the phone back onto the hook, then leaned her forehead against the wall.

Dean walked up behind her and put a hand on her shoulder. "What's wrong?"

"Laney's in trouble at school and they want to see Lori before she can go back. I have no idea where my sister is. All I have is a note that said she was leaving with some cowboy. She didn't say where she was going, but she asked me to take care of Laney. If the school finds that out, they'll probably call somebody, and they'll try to take her away from me."

"You're a good person, and take good care of her. Why would you think that?"

Tina laughed bitterly then turned around. Dean's arms trapped her against the wall. "I'm unemployed now. My savings won't last forever, so I'll eventually lose my apartment. We'll be homeless." She rolled her eyes to disperse the tears gathering there then ducked under his arm to walk toward the bedroom. She stopped there, but didn't turn around. She didn't want him to know how upset she was. Dean Dixon had enough problems of his own.

"I'm single, which would be good for traveling,

but not so good when they are gauging your fitness as a kid's guardian."

"Funny, my lawyer said almost the same thing to me today," he replied with a strange tone to his voice. Almost reflective.

Tina wondered at it, but didn't have time to talk. She had to go pick up her niece. And she had to figure out what she was going to do. "You can show yourself out. I've got to get ready to go pick her up," Tina said as she walked inside shutting the door behind her.

CHAPTER FOURTEEN

Tina was sure she was out of tears. That last round in the shower made her feel practically dried up, and stopped up too. She walked to the mirror, cringing when she wiped the steam from the mirror and saw her red-rimmed eyes. She was not a pretty crier like her sister. She looked like a damned Puffer fish when she finished. Her face was swollen and her lips were too. That was not going to look good at the school, so she turned on the cold water in the sink and splashed it on her face until her cheeks cooled. She turned the tap off and breathed deeply of the steam cloud in the bathroom to clear away some of her stuffiness.

Jerking a towel off the rack, she dried off quickly, then wrapped it around her wet hair turban style. She'd towel dry it in the bedroom, and put it in a knot of some kind. Maybe one like the one in her stomach, she thought as she grabbed the knob and opened the door. She took one step out then squealed when she came face to face with Dean Dixon, who was still in her apartment. It looked like he had been about to knock on the bathroom door.

He looked as surprised as she did, but then his eyes tracked slowly down her body to her toes and she thought she heard him groan. Tina put one arm over her breasts and the other across the top of her thighs. "What the hell are you still doing here?"

"I was thinking that I have a helluva lot of

experience talking to principals. Jeremy likes to visit his principal's office frequently. You could probably use my help."

Tina walked past him with her chin held up, pretending she didn't feel him staring at her ass. She had to get dressed and get to school. She didn't have time for this. And she didn't want Dean Dixon's help, or interference in the situation.

"I don't need your help," she said as she walked into her bedroom. The man had a habit of putting his foot into doorways, she found out when she tried to close the bedroom door. She'd like to pinch his damned toes off in there. Her eyes flew up to his. "Don't you have anything better to do than bug the crap out of me?"

"Not really," he said, leaning against the jamb.

Dean didn't move his foot, and she couldn't wait or fight with him. Tina left the door open and walked to the closet to yank down a skirt, and shirt. She figured if she had on professional armor she might be taken more seriously than if she wore the pair of blue jeans she really wanted to put on. The only pair she owned. The pair she'd bought to wear to the ranch for the photo shoot with Dean. A sob escaped her throat, and she found out she wasn't out of tears just yet. One leaked out of her left eye, then another out of her right. She swiped them away with her wrist and turned to lay her clothes on the bed, but ran into Dean's broad chest. He grabbed her shoulders, and her eyes flew up to his. The skirt and shirt dropped to the floor, and he slowly pulled the towel off of her hair.

"Let me help you, buttercup," he said in that low growly voice that sent her hormones into overload. He tipped her chin up with his finger. "Please," he added.

Tina's heart stuttered in her chest, then sped up to road racer speed. Dean dropped the towel to the floor to put his hands on her hips, then bent and his lips met hers, in a slow comforting whisper of a kiss. Tina was confused by his gentleness, his concern, and Lord knew she didn't need to be any more confused. But Dean's presence there did make her feel less alone. If he went with her to the school, she'd probably feel the same there too.

"Okay, you can go, but don't say anything."

His eyebrows shot up. "Really?" he asked.

"Really. You can go, but I can't let them know Lori is gone. I have no idea what Laney did, but her teacher said it was bad. I know they can be dramatic sometimes, but the way she sounded makes me believe I'm going to have to do some quick thinking to get Laney out of this mess. To keep myself from getting into more of one."

"I'll let you do the talking," he promised. "I'll just be there for moral support."

Tina huffed out a breath and took a step back. "I damn sure could use some right now."

"Well, I'm here for you," he said, surprising

her, as she bent to pick up her clothes.

When she stood back up he had *that* look in his eyes. The one he got a lot while they were up in the deer stand. A tingle floated through her body, but she snuffed it out. "Don't go there, big boy," Tina said putting her hand in the center of his chest to give him a push so she could get by. "I don't have time for it."

They had a lot to talk about before she let that look get to her again. And she had things to do that were more important right now. She pushed him again and he stepped back into the doorway. When he just stood there looking at her, she flipped her hand at him then grabbed the door knob. "Keep on going. I need to get dressed."

"What if I want to watch?" he asked in that gravelly voice again. His eyes tracked down her still wet body, and he whistled. "It's not like I haven't seen it all before."

Tina lifted a brow. Enough was enough. "At the rate you're going, cowboy, you won't ever be seeing anything again if you don't *MOVE!*" she shouted.

Dean laughed as he stepped back out of the doorway. She closed the door, holding back a laugh herself. Why the hell did she always feel better when she was with him? It just didn't make sense to her. He was just about the grumpiest, crankiest, most unpredictable man she'd ever been with. But he was also the sexiest and most exciting man she'd ever met because of that. She kind of liked never knowing what to expect from Dean. Tina shook her head and hurried to dress.

Two hours later, Tina wondered what she'd been thinking bringing Dean Dixon with her to the school. "Principal Landers, I think what my *fiancé* is trying to say here," she said the word through her teeth, then shot Dean a hot glare, hoping he would take the hint to shut the hell up. "What he's trying to say is that Laney was provoked into pushing that girl."

Snipping off the end of the little shit's braid in art class before that, though, was just a little added bonus for her niece, Tina was sure. That hadn't been discovered until some other child tattled after the altercation on the playground.

"Well it resulted in bodily injury, so I'm afraid your niece will have to be suspended for ten days. It's school policy. And as I said, before she is allowed back in school, her *mother* will need to speak to me," he said with his nose up in the air. Tina wished it would rain, so the red-faced bastard would drown.

"Let me ask you this," Dean said sliding to the edge of his chair. His jaw tightened and his eyes grilled the principal. "If someone called your mother a skanky whore, what would you do, Principal Landers? Would you just turn the other cheek? Or would you defend your mother? And where does a six-year-old learn to talk like that? Is the other child being disciplined at all here?" That seemed to be the theme of every comment Dean had made so far during this meeting.

Just Shoot Me

Instead of being appalled that Laney had not only cut the end of the other girl's braid off, she had pushed her at recess. The bodily injury was from the girl falling on a tree root and breaking her arm. That hadn't been intentional, but the pushing had been.

Unacceptable. And even though it secretly pleased her, amazed her, so was Dean's defense of Laney's actions. Among other things. Like introducing himself to Principal Landers as her fiancé. Tina had been so speechless there for a second, she wasn't sure she'd be able to introduce herself.

Tina stood and stepped in front of Dean to stick her hand out to the principal. "Thank you for your time, sir. I will make sure that Lori comes back to school with her in ten days." Tina would make sure of that if she had to buy hunting dogs and a shotgun to find her damned sister.

This was all Lori's fault. If Laney wasn't upset because her mother was gone, Tina knew there was no way her niece would be in trouble right now.

"You're welcome, Miss Montgomery. You may pick your niece up in the nurse's office. I believe the nurse is attending to her scrape."

That was another thing. When that little hussy got up from the ground, according to Mr. Landers, she had hit Laney in the face with her good hand. Hell, Dean was right. Why wasn't Camille Petersen being raked over the coals like Laney was?

Tina bit her tongue though and said, "Thank

you."

Dean stood behind her, and Tina wasn't sure, but she thought he growled as he put his hand at her lower back, and leaned around her to open the door for her. She could practically feel the anger radiating off of him.

"You have experience in the principal's office, huh?" Tina hissed under her breath as they walked down the hall toward the nurse's office. "Probably because you were in his office more than the classroom when you were a kid."

"You didn't ask what kind of experience I had," Dean said with a dry laugh. "And that man deserved to be grilled. How he's treating her just isn't fair."

"Fair is subjective, and he is the one who determines the rules, Dean."

"Our taxes pay for this damned school. That makes him a public servant. Last time I checked, the school board makes the rules. He just enforces them. Interpretation of those rules is what is subjective. And his was damned wrong."

"You should have been an attorney instead of a cowboy," Tina said with exasperation. They stopped at the door of the medical office, and Dean opened it to let her go in first. The nurse, who was leaning over Laney, stood and stepped to the side to toss a gauze into the trash, giving Tina her first look at Laney's injuries. Fear shot through her when she saw the huge gash on Laney's forehead, and her quickly blackening eye.

"Oh, God, baby…" she groaned as she stumbled over to her niece. Kneeling in front of her she swiped her bangs to the side to get a better look at the gash.

Laney's blue eyes filled and her lower lip trembled. "She called mama a skank and a whore." Tina knew her niece had no idea exactly what that meant, but she'd bet the other girl did. Laney had just known that girl was insulting her mother. And she was upset enough that she was gone. Tina could understand why the fight happened. Laney was hurting in more ways than one.

"Oh, I know, honey," Tina said and hugged her tight.

The nurse cleared her throat and Tina released Laney to step back. "I just need to put a Band-aid on her cut."

"That is *not* a fucking *scrape* or a *cut*," Dean grated angrily.

Tina gasped as the nurse rounded on him. Her eyes narrowed, and her face looked like she thought he was the scum of the Earth. "Watch your language, sir!"

Dean wasn't afraid of Betty Ballbreaker though. He took a step forward, almost going nose-to-nose with the woman. "Language hell, we're going to the *emergency* room. Maybe someone *there* can determine the difference between a *fucking* scrape and a gaping laceration that might require stitches," he grated, taking another step forward. Miss Ballbreaker took a step back and put her hand on her chest. "And then we're going to the school board! After that maybe the medical board might also be interested to know on top of being incompetent, you must be fucking blind, if you call *that*," he pointed to Laney's forehead. "A scratch, Lady!"

Tina flinched at the volume and content of Dean's tirade, but her soul smiled.

"I'm afraid I'm going to have to ask you to leave, Mr. Dixon," the principal said from the doorway. "And when your sister comes back to meet with me, I would ask that she not bring *him* with her, Miss Montgomery."

Tina groaned and helped Laney to her feet. The nurse took a step forward with her bandage, but Tina held up a hand. "I'll take care of it," she mumbled as she grabbed a stack of gauze out of the box on the treatment table. Putting her arm around Laney, she led her past Dean, whispering as she passed him, "Come on, before I kill you right here."

They got into the hall and Laney sobbed, then started crying. Dean rushed up beside them and grabbed her arm. "I'll carry her," he said swooping her up into his arms. "We are going to the damned emergency room to make sure she's not hurt. That could leave a scar if it's not taken care of. Or she could have a concussion."

Just Shoot Me

Laney wrapped her legs around him and hugged his neck as he carried her toward the front entrance. Tina's heart wiggled at the sight, but then she got a grip on her emotions and ran after him. She couldn't afford a hospital visit.

"Dean it's a cut. I can bandage it when we get back to the apartment."

He didn't stop, he went out the front door of the school and straight to his truck, which he insisted they take since he wouldn't fit in her car. Two hours later, they were finally escorted from the waiting room to a treatment room at the emergency department. No matter how much she protested, Dean insisted they stay until Laney was seen. She decided to try one more time.

"Dean I don't have insurance to cover this," Tina grated after he laid a sleeping Laney down on the bed. "Let's just go back to my apartment."

His response was a pointed look, as he sat in one of the chairs in the room and folded his arms over his chest. Tina huffed out a breath and sat in the chair beside him. By the time they dragged themselves back to the truck with butterfly stitches on Laney's forehead and an icepack on her eye, Tina was worn out and strung out. But she wasn't broke. Dean had insisted they bill him for the visit. Where he was going to get the money to pay the bill, she didn't know.

But he wouldn't let her pay.

After he put Laney in the backseat and made

sure she was buckled in, he opened the passenger door for Tina. His truck was so tall, she had a hard time getting up inside, so he picked her up and set her in the seat, then like he had with Laney he reached across her to fasten her seat belt. Who was this man, Tina wondered, as she watched him walk around the front of the truck and get behind the wheel. He sure wasn't Mr. Cranky Pants anymore. He reached for the keys to start the truck and she said, "You feeling okay?"

He looked over at her with a confused look on his face. "Yeah, fine, why?"

"I don't know, you just seem…different today." He smiled widely and her heart did a little flip in her chest.

"I am different." Without explaining his cryptic statement, Dean cranked the truck and headed toward her apartment. Whatever had caused the change in Dean, she liked this new version. But she was scared too, because those soft feelings she had developed for the man were quickly getting softer. In fact, her feelings for the handsome cowboy had definitely taken on a new dimension. One that went way past infatuation. If she let herself bask in those feelings though, she knew Mr. Cranky Pants was still in there somewhere, and she'd probably wind up with a broken heart.

Tina couldn't deal with that on top of trying to figure out her current situation.

When they got closer to home, Dean spotted a

fast food joint, and insisted they stop and pick up burgers, so neither of them had to cook. Tina didn't feel like eating. After her Oreo and chip binge, she probably shouldn't eat for a month. Especially fast food, but she ordered a burger anyway, and a shake, and it came in a combo so she ordered fries too. She was definitely going to have to find time for the gym soon. As soon as her life wasn't falling apart.

Laney was sleeping so Dean just ordered her a kid's meal for later. Dean parked in the space next to hers at the apartment complex, then hopped out of the truck. Before she could open her door, he was right there lifting her down. Once her feet hit the ground, he bent and kissed her, before he reached inside for the bags and handed them to her. "I'll carry Laney inside, so we don't have to wake her."

Tina's mouth opened and she started to tell him Laney could walk, but decided it wasn't worth the argument she knew she'd have with him. Like at the school. And at the hospital. Laney slept on Dean's shoulder as Tina shuffled the bags to stick the key into the lock of her door. Tina flicked on the light and groaned at the mess.

Dean walked inside and turned back to her to ask quietly, "Where's her bedroom?"

Tina laughed. "Our bedroom?" She pointed to the bedroom.

"This is a one freaking bedroom apartment?" he asked with surprise.

"Yeah, I was saving up for a house, but that's not happening now."

Dean walked to the bedroom, and Tina kicked off her shoes, sat the dinner bags down on the table, and started cleaning up. She was on her hands and knees with a whisk broom and dust pan sweeping up the chip crumbs from the carpet when his large boots suddenly appeared near her knee.

"We need to talk." He reached down and took the dust pan and broom from her. "But let's eat first," he said, as he walked into the kitchen and dumped the crumbs into the trash. Dean sure was making himself at home here. And inserting himself into her life. She should probably get him out of there, but she just couldn't make herself do it. Having him here made her feel better about her situation, and she just couldn't figure out why. Tina got back to her feet, and folded the blanket, picked up the two trash bags and walked to the front door.

"Where the hell do you think you're going?" Dean demanded.

She glanced back at him, as she opened the door. "I'm going to the dumpster, of course."

"It's nearly midnight. And if you haven't noticed, this isn't the greatest neighborhood."

Tina laughed. "I know what kind of neighborhood this is, country boy. I go out to the dumpster at night all the time. There's a light out there."

"Well, you're not going out there this time,'" he growled and walked over to snatch the bags from her hand. "Where's the damned dumpster?"

"At the end of the building around the corner."

"I'll be back. Get us a drink." Was Mr. Cranky Pants back? If so, his transformation into Prince Charming sure hadn't lasted long.

"I have water or milk," Tina fired back. She didn't know what Dean expected here, but she wasn't a rich woman. If he expected wine or whiskey with his take-out he was out of luck. She didn't even waste money on soda. Except for the flat soda that Lori had left here, she hadn't had that in her apartment in a year. That's why she had ordered a shake. He hadn't ordered a drink.

"Water's fine," he said grumpily and walked outside. He shut the door with a snap, and Tina walked to the kitchen to make his drink, then pulled mismatched plates down from the cabinet. She had pieces and parts of her mother's dish sets, but hadn't bought a new set for herself after her mother died. They had dishes, that's all that mattered. She had been too worried about taking care of her sister and herself, then Laney to worry about much else than survival.

She brought the plates and drink into the living room and set them on the coffee table. Dean came back in and he didn't look happy. "What are you frowning about?" she asked, as she pulled the burgers out of the bag.

"This place isn't fucking safe, Tina. That damned school isn't safe for Laney either."

"What happened?" she asked as she stood back up.

"Some dumbass was messing around your car, but I ran him off." Dean slammed the door and stomped over to the sofa then sat down. He huffed out a breath, and took off his hat to balance it on the arm of the sofa. He ran a hand through his hair. "Marry me," he said shortly.

Tina thought she was hearing things. She actually smacked her ear with her palm thinking her hearing was going out. Surely Dean Dixon hadn't just asked her to marry him?

"Come back?"

His eyes met hers and they were a filled with swirling emotions she couldn't name. He cleared his throat. "I said, marry me."

Tina's knees went weak, and she reached behind her as she fell back on the sofa. Since she was a little girl she had always envisioned the exact moment when the man she loved would ask her to marry him. In her mind, it happened in a variety of different ways. This surely wasn't one of them. As much as his protectiveness of her niece touched her heart, as attentive and helpful as he'd been to her, Tina never imagined he was leading up to this.

There had to be a reason, because he certainly didn't appear to be in love with her.

Funny, my lawyer said almost the same thing today.

"Say something," Dean said, dragging his eyes to his hamburger, which he proceeded to unwrap and put on the plate.

"You're out of your mind."

"Maybe I am, but I'm still asking," Dean said as he took a bite of his hamburger. Tina didn't touch hers. Her Oreos from earlier were now doing a tango with the chips in her stomach.

"Why?" she asked the burning question that might give her a clue to what he was thinking.

"My lawyer said it would look better to the court. You said it would help your situation. We could go to the courthouse in the morning, then go see the lawyer and start things rolling to adopt her." His emotionless tone, the straightforward words, his damned reasons were definitely not what her romantic heart wanted.

And his idea was way out in left field. She was as broke as he was. "Adoption costs a lot of money, Dean. I can't afford an attorney right now, and you can't either, unless you hit the lottery and didn't mention it."

He set his hamburger down, and his eyes met hers. "If we're married, you won't need a house, you'll live at the ranch with me. Use the money you have saved to buy a house."

Tina gnawed her lip. Why the hell was this idea making sense to her?

"What happens when all this is settled? Once I have custody of Laney, and your problems with Cindy are resolved?"

"We cross that bridge when we get there. Decide whether we stay married or not."

God, it sounded so cold. He sounded so cold. This was not at all what she wanted.

"So we'd get a divorce?"

Dean stopped chewing to suck in a sharp breath. He set his hamburger down on the plate slowly, then turned on the sofa to face her. "I hope not. Jeremy needs a mother. I need a wife. I think we're a good fit. I know we are in one area," he said and his eyes heated. "I'm hoping things will work out in other areas too."

"The kids would be devastated if we got them comfortable with us being their parents, then decided to get a divorce. It would be worse for them than it is now." Tina did not ever want to be divorced. She knew firsthand that kids from broken homes had it much worse than kids from single-parent families most of the time.

"It worked out for my brother and Hope. I think it will work out for us too," Dean said.

Her stomach did a rumba now, and she put a hand on it. Seeing the glob of mayo that leaked out the side of Dean's hamburger added sound effects. Tina's stomach lurched and she sprinted for the bathroom. Tina leaned over the toilet and breathed in and out slowly until her stomach decided whether it wanted to evict the Oreos. Dean lifted her hair off of her neck, then caressed her nape with his thumb. It was a weird combination, this nausea and the chills his touch sent racing down her spine.

"You okay, sweetheart?" he asked, his voice full of concern.

"Yeah, I'll be okay. Must have a bug." *Or be totally stressed out, because you just dumped something else on my plate I didn't need.* Plate. Greasy Hamburger. Mayonnaise. Tina's stomach lurched and she pinched her lips and sucked in a breath through her nose. "Maybe you should just go. I don't want you to get sick," she said. *And I don't want to have to tell you no, because I'm only going to marry a man who loves me.*

"I'm pretty resilient," Dean said, as if she hadn't told him to leave. "C'mon you need to lay down." Tina wanted to say no, but she felt too damned bad to say anything. Maybe if she laid down a second she would feel better. Dean didn't wait for her to decide though. Mr. Caveman bent and put his arm under her knees and lifted her. He walked with her into the living room and sat down on the couch with her on his lap.

He turned off the lamp on the side table, then reached behind him and grabbed the blanket she had folded over the back. With a whoosh he shook it out then covered her, tucking the end of the blanket under her chin. He leaned down and kissed her forehead, then whispered fiercely, "Sleep. You'll feel better in the morning. We'll talk about it then." He grabbed the remote off the coffee table and flicked on the television, then put it on mute.

In the morning. That meant he wasn't leaving. Dean Dixon was going to spend the night holding her while she slept. And he'd asked her to marry him. How the hell was she supposed to sleep? Tina shut her eyes, Dean rubbed her hair in slow monotonous strokes, and her body must've figured it out, because it wasn't long before she drifted off dreaming about a white dress and Dean Dixon.

CHAPTER FIFTEEN

Tina could not believe she was actually doing this. Maybe she was still sleeping, and this was all a dream. She glanced at the stone-faced man beside her and flinched, then looked down at herself. No white dress. She wiggled the fingers of her left hand, looking particularly close at her ring finger. Nope, no ring either.

The man in the suit behind the scuffed up wooden podium cleared his throat, and Dean Dixon squeezed her hand. Like he wasn't already holding it tight enough. She couldn't even feel the fingers of her right hand, and her palm felt like it was stuck to a hot plate, Dean's palm was so hot. She shook her head, and just said, "I do," because she figured that was the expected response.

Considering this was a marriage ceremony that had to be it. A bead of sweat trickled from the base of her skull, slid slowly down her neck, then inched down her spine. The man started speaking again, so she must've gotten it right. Why the hell did his voice sound like it was coming from the end of a tunnel? He needed to speak louder. And Tina realized she needed to unlock her knees before she passed out.

She relaxed them as much as she could, and Dean tucked her arm under his and pulled her closer to his body, seeming to know she needed support. Or making sure she didn't turn and bolt from this small, hot room where she was becoming his wife. That is what she was really considering doing, when Dean suddenly released her hand to grab her left hand. He roughly shoved a thin gold band over her knuckle, before putting his hand on her back and facing the judge again. The scrambled eggs in her stomach, the breakfast Dean had cooked and insisted she eat before they dropped Laney off at the neighbors to come here, did a jig in her stomach. Tina covered it with her newly-adorned left hand and held back a groan.

Dean tensed beside her and looked down with concern in his eyes. She forced a smile and looked back at the man in the suit. He smiled, and closed the book on the podium.

"Congratulations," he said cheerfully, and Tina's stomach lurched again.

Dean turned her then lifted her against him to close his lips over hers in a hot kiss that went on a second too long. That was when she knew this had actually happened. She was now Mrs. Tina Dixon, Dean Dixon's wife. A whimper worked its way up from her sternum to her throat, but she stopped it from escaping through her lips by pinching them together.

What the hell had she just done? She had just saved her niece, helped Dean save his son, and maybe saved herself in the process. If she had lost Laney, Tina had no idea what she would do. This morning, she had weighed the odds of finding her sister, and realized they were next to zero. Texas was a big state. She could be anywhere. She could have even left the state. The cowboys she hung out with were on the rodeo circuit. Many different circuits that traveled all over the country, even to Canada.

The only thing she could do was say yes this morning when Dean asked again. This morning his proposal had been a little softer, with more feeling, but he still hadn't mentioned feeling a damned thing for her.

After they met with his attorney, before they came here, Tina had felt a little better about her decision. She could petition the court for temporary guardianship since she was a close relative, then go for adoption in a few years if her sister didn't show up. The attorney also confirmed her thoughts on the situation by telling her it would look better to the court, she'd have a better chance of getting guardianship and adopting Laney if she was married.

That had sealed the deal for her. And sealed her fate too. She was a married woman, and she was moving to Tyler, Texas to live on the ranch with Dean and his family. At least Hope would be there too. When things got hairy, and Tina knew that was likely to happen, she would at least have someone to talk to, someone in her court.

Dean put his hand at her lower back and ushered her out of the Judge's chamber, then guided her down the hall to the elevator and pushed the button. "You okay, buttercup?" he asked, looking down at her.

Under the brim of his black hat that he'd put back on when they left the judge's office, Tina could see relief in his eyes. She wished that's how she felt. As well as Dean was treating her right now, as *nice* as he was being, she couldn't help but believe she had just made the biggest mistake of her life. But it was the only decision she could make. She would just have to make the best of it. For Laney. For herself.

The elevator opened, they walked inside and Dean smiled down at her. His eyes actually smiled too, and Tina felt a little better. "We'll just go back to the apartment and pack some of your things up, then I'll get Cord to get a few buddies to help move the rest of your stuff to the ranch."

She was moving. To the ranch. With Dean. With Laney. "We'll have to get Laney enrolled in the school where Jeremy goes."

"Yeah, there are a lot of details, but we'll take care of it," he said with a squeeze to her shoulders. "Don't worry, buttercup. Things will be fine."

They drove back to her apartment where Tina packed up four heaping suitcases, which constituted most of her and her niece's things, then Tina walked to the neighbor's apartment to pick Laney up. Dean loaded the suitcases into the back of the truck. Laney asked if they were going on vacation to see her mama. Tina's heart broke, and so did the dam holding back her tears. Laney started crying too. Dean looked like he would lose his mind as he shuffled them into the truck and headed to Tyler.

With every mile that passed by outside the window of the truck, Tina's tension grew. She had no idea how his family was going to react, how Jeremy and Laney would react, when they sat them down and told them what they'd done. Now that she thought about it, what they had done was rash, a knee-jerk solution to their situations. They could've just jumped out of the frying pan straight into the fires of hell.

A warm hand covered hers on the seat. "Stop worrying," Dean said, giving her hand a reassuring squeeze. But he wasn't fooling her at all. Tina heard the worry in his voice too. But he laced his fingers with hers, and surprised her when he carried her hand to his mouth to drop a kiss on the back, before he pulled her toward him. "Come over here, wife," he said gruffly.

Tina scooted across the seat to sit beside him and he dropped his arm around her shoulders. "That's better."

It *was* better. His scent wafted down to her and she inhaled it, letting it comfort her. So did the connection she felt with his arm around her. Maybe things would be fine, she thought. Tina relaxed against Dean, and before she knew it she drifted off to sleep.

When Dean shook her shoulder, Tina opened her eyes and looked around, disoriented for a moment. "We're home, baby," he whispered in that sexy growl.

Tina leaned forward and looked over the dashboard and bit back a groan. There on the front porch of the ranch house was his mother and father, Dean and Hope and Jeremy. All of them looked pretty excited to see them.

"Did you tell them already?" Tina asked.

"I called Cord earlier and told him."

"What did he say?" she asked anxiously.

"He said it was about time I got my head out of my ass," Dean replied with a laugh, then smiled. "I hate to admit it, but I think he's right this time." Dean put his forearm behind her neck, and bent to drop a gentle kiss on her lips. "Thanks for marrying me."

Tina's heart melted in her chest. He may not have said he loved her yet, but Dean Dixon just told her without saying it. The look in his eyes said it. Everything he'd done the last few days told her that too, she realized. *I show him every day that I love him.*

His statement to her about not telling Jeremy he loved him came back to her. That was evidently how Dean operated. He showed those he loved that he loved them.

"I'm glad I married you," Tina said and her lips wobbled.

His eyes heated, and he drawled, "I think we need to go hunting tonight."

"What?" Tina asked not following his abrupt change of topic.

The door flew open behind Dean and Hope

said impatiently, "We've been waiting hours! Get out here so we can celebrate!" That answered her question about what his family would think of them getting married. Dean kissed her quickly, then got out of the truck and reached back up to help her down.

He dropped his arm around her. "Meet the newest Mrs. Dixon," he said proudly, and squeezed her shoulders.

"Aunt Tina, what's going on? Where are we?" Laney asked groggily from the backseat.

Tina's happiness faded. Finding out like this would not be good for Laney. She pulled away from Dean and leaned back inside the truck. "Nothing baby. We're just back at the ranch. Wait a second, and Dean will help you out."

The backdoor opened, and she breathed a sigh of relief that he was already there. Now, the fun would begin. She wondered if Jeremy knew, and glanced back at the front porch. He stood behind Mrs. Dixon, looking uncertain about what he should be doing. Tina closed the truck door then walked up onto the porch.

"Can I have a hug, Jeremy?" she asked, opening her arms to him. He took one unsure step, then threw his arms around her waist. She put her head on the top of his and hugged him tightly.

"Does this mean you're my Mama now?" Jeremy asked when she released him.

The hope-tinged uncertainty in his voice tugged at her heart. But how the hell was she supposed answer that question? Tina didn't know what she was to him now. She just knew that she loved the kid. Cared about him. And would fight for him, just like any mother would.

Well, except for his own.

Laney pulled on the hem of her shirt. Tina looked down into the girl's terrified face, and her heart took a plunge. "If you're his Mama, who's gonna take care of me now since my Mama is on vacation?"

Tina looked over her shoulder at Dean, who was standing in the yard talking to his brother. They looked to be having an argument of some kind. Neither was smiling anymore, and Dean's fists were clenched at his sides. "I'm going to take care of both of you," she replied with determination. It looked like Dean was going to be too busy arguing with his damned brother to help her with anything. She pulled both children to her and hugged them. "We have a lot to work out, but that's not for you two to worry about."

"And I'll help," Hope said, stepping up to hug them too.

Mrs. Dixon joined the huddle to add her comforting arms around all of them. "That's right. We're all family now," she said in a trembling voice. The Dixon women had banded together, and there was nothing that could penetrate that to hurt these two kids. Not the loud voices of their men who were out in the yard arguing, not her squirrely sister, and certainly not Dean's horrible ex-wife.

Mr. Dixon's deep, booming voice joined Dean and Cord's very loud *discussion,* and Mrs. Dixon must've decided it was time for them to go inside. She pulled back and wiped her eyes. "I made cherry cobbler earlier. Ya'll want some? I bought ice cream to go with it."

"Daddy'll get mad. It's too close to supper," Jeremy said, glancing at Dean out in the yard.

Tina ruffled his hair, then leaned close to his ear to whisper, "We're celebrating tonight. That cobbler and ice cream will be our dinner, not dessert. We'll just hurry and eat it all before Mr. Cranky Pants comes inside. He can have vegetables for supper."

Laney giggled. "Yeah, Mr. Cranky can have the vegetables."

Jeremy eyes lit up, and he giggled. "You're being bad."

Tina laughed, and so did the other women, as they led the kids into the house. They sat the children at the table, before Tina and Hope got the bowls down from the cabinet. Mrs. Dixon pulled the hot cherry cobbler from the oven and spooned some into the bowls, then sat the dish in the middle of the table on a hot pad.

"Let me get the ice cream," she said with a smile in her voice as she walked to the refrigerator. The rich pastry and baked cherry smell wafted up to Tina's nose and her mouth watered. Mrs. Dixon took the lid off of the ice cream and put huge scoops on top of each serving of cobbler. "Eat up, before they come in," she said with a wink for the kids.

A few hours later, Tina realized they needn't have worried about eating fast. It was a long time before Dean and his father dragged into the house. Way past the kids' bedtime. Two hours past the time Mrs. Dixon went to bed. And an hour later than Hope had finally headed to the bunkhouse.

Tina had no idea where she was supposed to go, so she just sat on the sofa and waited for Dean to come inside. The longer she waited for her new *husband* to come inside, the madder she got. This was their damned wedding night, and he was out at the barn with his brother and father half the night, probably arguing. Tina had a feeling their first fight was coming when she saw his face when he walked into the living room.

He didn't say anything, he just shook his head as he breezed past her, huffing out a breath as he walked toward the hall. Mr. Dixon at least said goodnight, before he followed his son down the hall. Tina sat there stewing. Her suitcases were still in the back of the truck, so she didn't have anything to change into. She slipped off her boots, pulled her ponytail down then jerked the hem of her shirt out of her jeans. Grabbing a pillow from the sofa, she punched it a few times, before she slammed it down and laid down, wondering just what kind of mess she'd gotten herself into by marrying Dean Dixon.

"What the hell are you doing out here?" Dean asked gruffly, and Tina sat straight up out of a dead sleep, her heart racing in her chest.

"Sleeping! What the hell does it look like?!?" she shot back, putting a hand to her chest. Her eyes latched onto his wet muscular chest and slid down to the waistband of his loose pajama pants. Her mouth watered, and she forced them back up to his face.

"I thought you'd be in bed when I got out of the shower," he said.

"I might have been if I knew where your bed was located."

His eyes widened, and he looked a little stunned. "I'm sorry."

"You should be, mister." Tina harrumphed. "I've been sitting here for hours waiting for you to finish your argument and come in, then when you do, you've got your ass over your shoulders and ignore me."

"I was upset when I came in. I'm sorry, I wasn't thinking."

"Seems to be a habit for you," she accused.

"What, arguing?" he asked tilting his head. "Or not thinking?"

She tilted her chin. "Both."

He hesitated a moment, his jaw worked, then he said, "You're right. I'm sorry."

"Three sorries in three minutes. Wish you

meant even one of them," Tina said and punched her pillow. She was about to lay back down, but he grabbed her arm.

"I meant all of them, buttercup. I don't apologize. For anything. I'm trying to change that, but it's going to take time." Tina looked at his hand, then followed the delicious curves of his muscled arm up to his eyes.

"I hope you mean that too." Unless that change was permanent, Tina didn't hold out a lot of hope for their marriage, even though she was trying to stay positive. Dean Dixon didn't make that easy for sure.

"I do mean it," he said firmly.

Tina set the pillow beside her and held her hand out to him. Dean jerked her up to her feet and pulled her into his chest. He bent and picked her up by the back of her thighs. Tina wrapped her legs around his waist and put her arms around his neck, then Dean was kissing her. This making up was pretty damned good, she thought. Maybe she needed to get mad at him often. Dean pulled back and nibbled her lower lip then growled, "That's more like it, Mrs. Dixon."

"Show me where your room is, cowboy," she said nipping his lower lip back.

"Gladly, ma'am," he said with a laugh as he carried her across the living room, down the hall, and into the bedroom. He kicked the door closed behind him, then sat her on the bed. "Welcome to my room, buttercup. Now get your damned clothes off, before I rip them off."

Dean stepped back and stood there staring at her. He saw her shiver, and wondered if Tina was remembering him ripping off her panties the other night when he made love to her by the lake. A look came into her eyes that made him think she might tease him into doing it again, and Dean would do it. Her fingers shook as she unbuttoned her blouse, and slid it off of her shoulders. She stood and removed her jeans, and Dean was a little disappointed she decided not to tease him. But then she stood back up and his eyes tracked over her beautiful body.

Goddamn, how had he gotten so lucky? Something in his life was finally going right. Tina Montgomery had married him. Not only would she be a good mother to Jeremy, and a good wife to him, she was a walking wet dream. A dream that he'd thought about every minute of every day since he met her. Now he could have her any damned time he pleased.

He lifted an eyebrow, because she didn't make a move to remove her bra or her panties. He took a step toward her and Tina squealed as she scrambled up onto the bed, her hands fumbling behind her to remove her black lace bra. She threw it over the side of the bed, then he saw her staring at something with a strange look on her beautiful face, while she removed her panties.

His eyes followed hers and he realized she was staring at his tie, which was laying on top of his wrinkled dress shirt. She dragged her gaze away, but it snagged on the bedpost before she looked at him again. Dean read her like a book. He knew what was going through that gorgeous head of hers. He heard her gasp when he walked toward the dresser and snatched up his tie.

"Lay down at the foot of the bed," Dean said roughly as he turned back toward her.

Tina gnawed her bottom lip for a second, before she scooted to the end of the bed and laid down with her hands resting on her midsection. "Grab the bedpost, Tina."

A shiver passed through her, as she hesitantly reached above her head to loosely grip the wooden post. Yes, this is definitely what his beautiful new wife wanted. Dean had no problem with giving her what she wanted. At all.

Dean's dick got rock solid as he straddled her body, and reached above her to loop the tie around her wrists. He pulled the knot tight, then jerked it even tighter. She whimpered and squirmed beneath him and he felt her knees clamp together. That wasn't going to work.

She wanted this, but she needed to relax to be able to enjoy it. He scooted back off the bed and went to the closet. He flipped on the light inside, then searched around on the top shelf until he found his pigging string from when he did tie-down roping in high school. He'd saved it as a memento, and was thankful he had now. He flipped off the light and walked back to the bed. Tina's wide eyes fell to the rope in his hands.

"What's that for?" she asked in a trembling voice.

"You ask too many questions, buttercup," Dean said, as he walked to the bedpost.

He quickly looped the string around her wrists, then removed his necktie. He checked to make sure she was tied tight, then he took the necktie and lifted her head. He put the thick part over her eyes and tied the ends. Tina bit her lip, and pulled against the rope. It looked like she was having second thoughts. Or she was making him think she did. He'd find out.

"Be still, or I'm going to tie your feet too," he threatened, as he took a moment to let his eyes soaked up the sight of her full cherry tipped breasts begging for his mouth. Tina gasped, but her body stilled, and she seemed to relax.

Dean stood over her and stroked his hand over the smooth skin of her shoulder to her breast. Her skin felt like silk under his hand as he passed his palm over her hard nipple. Tina groaned arching her back into his hand, and Dean got harder, painfully hard.

This woman was as hot and responsive, hotter, than any woman he'd ever been with. She evidently loved his touch. And he loved fucking touching her—

loved—no he didn't. Not yet.

He wasn't falling into that trap so soon. Trusting her yet. He thought he knew her, but Dean was taking his time this time. Using his head, instead of thinking with his dick. But who the hell knew what the future held? All he knew was he wanted this woman every minute of every day. And now he could have her. Would have her over and over again. Any damned time he pleased. That was something to build on right?

Her muscles quivered under his hand as he slid it over her stomach down to her navel. He rested his hand right above her mound. "Spread your legs, Tina," he said and she unclamped her knees a little. "Wider," he growled, grabbing her knees to shove them apart. The muscles in her legs jerked, and he saw her throat bob a few times, but she didn't resist.

"Good girl," he praised, patting her thigh as he went to the side of the bed to crawl between her legs. Dean was about to have his answer to the question about whether his wife tasted like honey between her legs. "Don't you dare scream, or I'll gag you too," he warned as he eased down onto his elbows. Dean took his time, letting her anticipate what he was going to do.

He spread her folds and saw the glistening pearls of her excitement. Her breathing got faster, her stomach muscles rolled, but she didn't scream. He looked up to see her head to the side, her lower lip being mangled by her teeth. Dean hadn't even touched her, and his wife looked to be near an orgasm already. He pushed back from her sat up to watch her.

Dean had all night, and he owed her for being pissed at him when he came in when he was already upset with his family. He was going to teach her a lesson about patience. He folded his arms and waited. Her stomach continued to quiver for a few minutes, then her breathing slowed and her forehead wrinkled. Her jaw finally relaxed and her teeth loosened on her lip.

"What are you doing?" she asked in a hoarse whisper.

A smile curved his mouth, but he didn't answer. He did, however, shove his hand under the waistband of his pajama pants to fist his erection when her hips moved as if she were itching for him to be inside of her. She was probably itching just as badly as he was right about then. Feeling her tight walls squeezing his cock was the ultimate goal, the reward for his own patience. But they had a long way to go, before that happened.

Dean upped the ante. He got up off the bed and knew she realized it. He walked to the bedroom door, and opened it then went outside, closing it behind him loudly enough that he knew she heard. He heard a whimper of protest from behind the door. Dean grinned as he walked to the kitchen to get himself a snack. His mother had made cherry cobbler today, and that was his absolute favorite.

He took his time getting there with anticipation building inside him too. He could only imagine how Tina felt. Tied to the bedpost, wondering where the hell he went. He chuckled as he opened the door of the refrigerator and leaned inside. He shoved things around looking for the baking dish he knew his Mama always used for her cobbler, but he didn't see it. That was damned weird. He shut the refrigerator, then saw an empty carton of vanilla ice cream on top of the trash. They fucking ate it all?

Dean walked to the sink and looked down. Sure enough, the empty casserole dish was sitting there. All that was left of the cobbler was thick gooey cherry filling around the sides and pastry crumbs. Disappointment filled him as he turned away from the sink, then a thought hit him. That was something else his wife was going to pay for. He grabbed the dish from the sink and headed back to the bedroom.

He would have his cherry cobbler in a way much better than a bowl. He opened the door and she gasped. Dean shut the door and locked it then walked over to Tina, who was grumbling as she struggled with the rope ties. She had managed to push the blindfold almost to her hairline.

"I thought I told you to be still," he said sternly.

"You tied me up and left me," She accused, struggling again.

"And I'm going to spank your ass if you don't settle down," Dean growled yanking the blindfold back over her eyes.

She gasped, bit her lip then finally relaxed. Dean smiled and sat the cobbler dish down on the other side of her on the bed. He could definitely get to like this. Tina Dixon was going to *love* it by the time he finished with her. Dean leaned across her to swipe his finger through the cherry filling then brought it to her mouth. He circled her lips with his finger, and her tongue came out to make a pass over her lips.

She sucked in a breath and her body tensed. "I'm sorry," she whispered.

"Sorry isn't going to fix this. You thought you didn't leave me any, but there's plenty left for me to teach you a lesson about being greedy," he said and smeared some of the filling on her neck down to her collarbone. "That wasn't right, because I love cherry cobbler," he said as he lowered his mouth to her neck. Her breath hitched, and she moaned when he licked the trail up to her earlobe. The sweet taste of her skin mixed with the sweet filling excited his taste buds into a frenzy.

"Fucking love it," he said gruffly, as he nipped her earlobe.

Dean leaned up to swipe his finger into the dish again, then slowly circled her nipple with it. Tina groaned loudly, and he leaned down to her ear. "Don't you dare scream, or I'll gag you, I promise," he warned and a low-pitched moan sounded in her throat as she nodded.

He smiled and lowered his mouth to her breast. He ran his tongue around her nipple in slow monotonous circles until she squirmed, then he nipped it. Tina didn't scream, but he glanced at her face and saw she wanted to. Badly. Her lips were pinched, her nostrils flared, and her breathing was swift and shallow. Dean smoothed his hand down her flat stomach to shove his hand between her legs. He dipped a finger inside of her and her thighs clamped around his hand, trapping it there. She whimpered and moved her hips against him.

"Open your legs, Tina." She shook her head, and grumbled.

Dean pulled his hand away and she huffed out a frustrated breath. He didn't touch her, just waited. Her knees finally relaxed and she slid them apart, but he could see her fingernails curled into her palms above her head. She was frustrated. Well Mrs. Dixon had no idea what frustration was yet.

"Good girl," he said with a laugh.

He dipped his finger into the cobbler leftovers then slathered it on her clit. Her hips jerked and she tried to get away. "Nooo…" she protested in a harsh whisper, arching her back.

"Oh, yes, baby," he drawled, as he stood and shoved his pajama pants down his legs. "And shh…" he reminded as he knelt between her knees. Dean leaned over her to scoop up more of the cobbler and painted it down her body. From the dip at the base of her neck, between her breasts to her navel, where he left a huge dollop.

"Your belly button is so damned cute," he said leaning down to swipe his tongue inside. Tina giggled and wiggled, but Dean gripped the back of her thighs to hold her still until it was licked clean. "Best damned cobbler I've ever had." He lowered her hips, then licked every inch of her up to her throat. He ran his tongue over her lips, then closed his mouth over hers in a soft sweet kiss that went on forever as he soaked up her taste. He swallowed her moan, then with a growl, he nipped her lower lip as he pulled way, and she groaned.

Dean swiped more cobbler from the dish, as he kissed his way back down her body. He moved where he really wanted to be and shoved her knees apart. Dean smoothed the gel along her folds with his finger, then took a dip inside her body.

"Dean, that's enough," she growled, writhing her hips.

"Remember, no screaming," he said as he lowered his mouth and made a pass over her sweet clit with his tongue. She didn't scream, but she let out a long low wail that vibrated through his body and settled in his groin.

He lifted his head. "Quiet!" he hissed and smiled when she bit her lip and nodded.

Opening her pink folds, Dean slowly licked her from bottom to top. By the time he reached her clit, her body shook violently. But she didn't wail, and she didn't scream. Her chin dropped to her chest, she clenched her teeth and he saw the most incredible look on her face.

Ecstasy had never looked more beautiful. He sucked her into his mouth, and the sweet flavor of her orgasm mixed with the cobbler there, and he took her higher. She threw her head back on her shoulders and shook harder. But she didn't scream. Dean dropped down and entered her sweetness with his tongue, and she finally broke. Tina sobbed, then wailed her release and the sweet sound danced through his soul. Her body finally went limp, and he released his grip on her thighs to move up her body. Leaning down, he dropped a gentle kiss on her mouth, then another, before he untied her hands and rubbed her raw wrists.

He had to get something better if they were going to play like this again. It made him angry to see the welts he had put there. He lifted her wrist to his mouth and kissed it, then lowered her arms to her heaving chest.

"You okay, buttercup?" he asked, moving to lay beside her and pull her into his arms.

She didn't speak, she just nodded. He kissed her cheek, then the corner of her mouth, before he hugged her to his side. When he released her, Tina didn't just settle at his side like he expected, she shot up and scrambled on top of him to straddle his waist.

"Ut uh, it's my turn," she said hoarsely.

Dean grinned when she leaned over him to swipe her finger through the cobbler, dangling her beautiful breast near his mouth. She ordered him to put his hands behind his head and Dean complied. He had a feeling, before this night was done, he would never think of cobbler the same way again. And every time he ate it from here on out, he would think of his delicious wife, and get hard as he was right that moment.

Tina Dixon was his new favorite dessert.

CHAPTER SIXTEEN

Dean kneed Blaze and he danced to the left to catch a bronco who had broken from the herd. He, his brother and father were moving them to an adjacent pasture. It had only taken two weeks for the herd of twenty horses to chew through every last blade of grass in the pasture. With the rain they'd had recently, the pasture was also now a big mud pit.

Now, they had to reseed the pasture. Seed cost money.

Dean had apologized to Cord for going off on him for buying this damned rough stock instead of the beef cattle he'd told him to buy. But dammit, the way things were going he'd been right. Managing this rodeo stock was a lot of work, and they didn't have any help. They hadn't even started using the dummy to see if they could even buck well. Cord told him that every head he bought was proven, had been successful at various levels of rodeo competitions. But Dean wanted to see it for himself. According to his brother, Zack and Ryan were coming down next weekend to work with the bulls using the remote controlled dummy they had bought.

They couldn't afford to hire any hands, so those two better get out here to help, or their bulls wouldn't be bucking. It was enough for the three of them to make sure the animals had enough grazing. The ten bulls were in the biggest pasture and were doing a good job of clearing it too. If they didn't start supplementing the natural grazing with feed and hay they would have a barren ranch before long.

The hefty lease check from the rodeo company that his brother had thrown in his face the night he got back from Dallas was getting smaller and smaller by the day. Cord's two friends were bringing the retired breeder bull out this weekend with the cows that they'd bought too. More mouths to feed.

Dean was going to go with the flow, his new mantra, but he didn't like it. He just hoped switching the ranch from beef cattle to rodeo stock didn't finish sinking their boat. It had enough holes in it already, and Dean had been bailing as fast as he could for years. But at least now he had help, and maybe Cord was right to look at a change. It burned his ass to say it, but they needed to do something to get out of the financial rut they'd been in for three years. Like Dean was trying to get out of the personal rut he had fallen into.

It was an every-day, all day fight to maintain the motivation to do that. Just this morning, he called the attorney's office to see if they'd gotten the DNA results back yet. The secretary told Cord he was out of the office in court and said he would call him back when he was available. To Dean's way of thinking, considering the price he was paying the man, he should always be available. But then everyone was paying the same hourly rate with the man. He didn't get priority. And neither did Tina either evidently. Her guardianship order hadn't been signed by the judge yet. They were playing the waiting game and Dean was losing patience.

He'd done everything the attorney had asked him to do. The week after he got back he took Jeremy to a local lab to have his blood drawn, and had it overnighted to the other lab. He'd signed the paperwork the attorney faxed to him and overnighted it back. Hurry up and wait was getting real old, real fast. Dean wanted this over with. Wanted Cindy out of his and his son's life for good.

"Dean, look out!" Cord shouted, just as one of the broncs reared, flailing his sharp hooves and baring his teeth. Blaze snorted, then reared too. Dean used his body to try and push him back down to the ground, but he just reared higher until Dean was almost vertical.

Dean shoved off against the saddle, because he knew if Blaze went over backward he would be crushed. He hit the ground hard, jarring his teeth then rolled to the left, about the same time that Blaze landed and rolled the other way, thank God. If he'd have rolled the same way as Dean, he still would have been crushed or trampled. Blaze got up to his feet, danced around wild-eyed for a second, then took off back toward the barn. Damned barn sour fucking horse, Dean thought as he sat up to cradle his shoulder, biting back a moan.

Cord's horse slid to a stop, and he vaulted out

of the saddle, then knelt beside Dean. "Are you okay?" he asked with concern.

"Think I dislocated my shoulder," Dean said with a grunt.

"If you were paying attention, you would have seen that coming!" Cord grated.

Dean's phone went off in his pocket, but he couldn't let go of his shoulder just yet. "Answer that will you?"

"You can call them back later," Cord said as he grabbed Dean's good arm to help him to his feet. "Now how the hell do you think you're going to get back to the ranch?"

"Ride double with you?"

Cord laughed and shook his head. "I don't think so, bitch."

"Well you better call Tina," he said then groaned. "No, don't call her." Dean closed his eyes against the throbbing pain in his shoulder. That pain would move to his ass if his wife came out here. She would probably mother him to death like she was doing Jeremy. Of course Jeremy was loving it since he hadn't had a mother in his life in so long. He thought about it, and there wasn't anyone else he could call. "Fuck, you have to call Tina to come out here in the golf cart, or ride back to the house to get the truck. Either way she's coming out here, I know her. Just call her."

Cord saluted and pulled out his phone. He

dialed, then waited. A smug smile eased up the corners of his mouth. "Hello, Tina. Your dumbass husband has hurt himself and needs you to come out in the golf cart and help him." Holding the phone out from his ear, so Dean could hear her yelling into the phone, Cord laughed and waited until she wound down. "No, we don't need an air ambulance honey, he just has a little boo-boo on his shoulder. I'm sure an icepack and a kiss from your pretty lips would fix it."

She started ranting again and Cord held the phone out again. Dean flinched as he listened to the ten-pounds of dynamite in a five-pound sack that was his wife. God he loved that woman, but she scared the shit out of him sometimes. When he saw her reading to Jeremy night before last before he went to bed, Dean finally admitted to himself that he loved her.

Other than his sister-in-law Hope, he hadn't met a better woman in his life. She was real, and she actually fucking cared about people. But Dean was scared to tell her, because he wasn't sure she felt the same way about him yet.

"Yeah, be sure and tell Mama too," Cord said, before he hung up the phone.

"You are a bastard," Dean growled, hugging his shoulder.

"Takes one to know one, brother."

Dean's phone went off in his pocket again, and he said, "Answer my damned phone. It could be the attorney calling back."

Cord huffed out a breath, then leaned down and shoved his hand into Dean's pocket. He pulled out the phone and pressed the button. "Hello?" A moment later his brother's eyebrows lifted, then slowly fell as he listened to whoever was on Dean's phone. "No, this is his brother Cord," he said and his eyes met Dean's. "Dean can't hold the phone right now, so I'll tell him. Shoot." The longer his brother listened, the more concerned Dean got.

"Who's on the damned phone, Cord?" Dean demanded, as he held his elbow to his chest.

"I see. So what now?" Cord asked and Dean's heart shot to this throat. If the attorney had told Cord what Dean wanted to hear, there would be excitement in his tone. Happiness. His brother's voice was too serious for it to be good news he was hearing.

"Tell me what he's saying!" Dean demanded. He let go of his arm to grab for the phone and pain shot through his collar bone and up to his ear. Dean moaned, sat back down and held it to his chest again. Cord disconnected the call and took a deep breath, while he stared at the woods. Definitely not good news. "Tell me what the fuck he said!" Dean shouted.

Cord finally looked at Dean, and his eyes were watery. "Jeremy isn't your son."

Dean suddenly didn't feel the pain in his shoulder anymore, the pain in his chest was more intense. "Did he say anything about custody?"

"Cindy's attorney has refiled the custody

petition, but your attorney has asked that the judge order Bobby Jones to have a paternity test too. He thinks Jeremy can stay here until they get those results back."

Dean looked down at the ground, trying to wrap his mind around Jeremy actually not being in his life anymore, but he just couldn't do it. A white card laying on the ground caught his attention, and he picked it up.

With everything on his mind, Dean had forgotten all about the woman he met in the elevator when he was in Dallas. He held the card up to Cord, and he took it.

"Call that woman. She wants to talk to you about a harassment suit against Laramie. I forgot to tell you." At least maybe one of their situations might work out okay.

Dean had a really bad feeling he had just lost his battle to keep his son. He needed to just start preparing himself to let him go.

***

Dean had been in bed four days. His shoulder had to be feeling better. His heart is what Tina was worried about. She had never seen a man hurting so badly. And he wouldn't talk to her or anyone else about it. He hadn't said two words to her since she'd picked him up from the field in the golf cart, even though she'd done everything she could to pry out of him how he felt. What he was thinking.

Cord had filled her in on what the attorney said, or else she wouldn't even know that much. Her new husband was a stubborn son-of-a-bitch when he was hurting or angry. Tina knew Dean was both right now, because Mr. Cranky Pants was back in the building again. If he wasn't tight-lipped he was a grumpy bastard to her and everyone else. Tina about had enough of it.

When she left Dallas, Tina had been worried about being bored and not having anything to do out here. Well, she had been terribly mistaken. She didn't have time to be bored, she had plenty to do. She was doing it all right now. Taking care of him, dealing with Jeremy and Laney, and keeping up with the house.

Mr. and Mrs. Dixon didn't want to leave, but they had to go to Dallas for his checkup with his doctor. The way Dean was acting, Tina had been half-tempted to load Laney up and go with them back to her apartment. The lease wasn't up until the end of the month, and all her stuff still hadn't been moved out to the ranch. But she couldn't leave Dean. Even as sour as he was to her right now, she knew it was because he was hurting.

Tina had no idea why, but she loved him. Laney loved him too. When he wasn't Mr. Cranky Pants, everyone loved him. They would get past this somehow.

If they just knew what was going on with both

of their custody suits, things would be a lot better. If their fricking attorney would return her calls to *tell* her what was going on. Tina had left three messages in the last three days for him, but so far he hadn't called. He was in court.

Well, if she had to drive to Dallas herself, she was going to get answers.

She balanced the tray of food on her hip, and opened the bedroom door. It was dark inside the room, so she reached in and flipped on the light switch and Dean groaned. "Get your ass up," she said she kneed the door open and walked inside. "Your food is here, Master."

He wanted to be grumpy? She could more than meet him grump for grump. Laney and Jeremy were at school, so Tina didn't have to worry about putting on a pretty face for them. She could deal with Dean just like he was dealing with her. Feeling sorry for him and coddling him hadn't gotten her anywhere. It was time for a little intervention.

"Not hungry," he said and rolled over toward the wall.

"Too damned bad, you're eating," Tina said as she sat the tray on the nightstand to turn the lamp on too.

"Cut the damn lights off and leave me alone. I said I'm not fucking hungry!"

"You want me to leave?" she asked softly, and his shoulders tensed.

"You won't leave." He said the words confidently, but Tina heard the worry too.

He needed to worry. "I'm thinking about it when your parents get back. If you can't talk to your wife, then I don't want to be married to you." It was true. Tina had married Dean Dixon under less than ideal circumstances, with a proposal that had to be the most unromantic proposal in history. She had cared about him then, but she loved him now.

She wasn't a martyr though. And if they were going to make a go of this marriage, he was going to stop feeling sorry for himself and start talking to her about how he was feeling. Caring about how she was feeling, because she was in the same boat with him, they were just paddling in different directions right now. She didn't have her legal situation solved either, which was her main reason for agreeing to marry him.

His voice was about as dark as she'd ever heard it when he said, "Leave then."

"Is that why Cindy left?" Tina asked knowing that would get a rise out of him. "Because you didn't care enough to ask her to stay?"

His whole body tensed, she heard a rumble that turned into a growl, as he spun over so fast the bed shook. His eyes when they met hers were so filled with hate Tina flinched. "No, the reason I let her leave was because she was a whoring bitch that couldn't give two flying shits about me or her son."

"You think that about me too? Is that why you

don't care if I leave?"

The anger left his eyes, and his eyebrows rose. "Hell no, I don't think that about you," he said then collapsed back against the mattress to throw his good arm over his eyes. "And of course I care if you leave. You're my wife."

"Then talk to me, because I *do* give two flying shits about you and *our* son," she said, sitting down on the edge of the bed. That's how Tina felt about Jeremy now. He was her kid as much as Laney was hers. More, because she was married to his father, and she loved Dean too.

Dean didn't respond for a while, but Tina was patient, because all she had was time. He finally swallowed then said, "If I lose him, I'll die."

"If you don't fight for him, you'll lose him," Tina volleyed, damned relieved that he had finally said something to her. It was a start.

"I fought and I lost," Dean said in a defeated tone. "I'm just waiting for the hammer to drop now."

"That hasn't happened yet, Dean. Jeremy is still here, and he needs you to be his daddy. You can't let him see you give up, or he'll get upset. I'm not letting Laney see that I'm worried either. The attorney still has that detective looking for my sister. The new school wants a copy of the guardianship papers and I can't produce those."

Tina's eyes landed on the congealed chicken and dumplings in the bowl on the night stand and her stomach lurched. She'd had a bowl of it last night and it hadn't made her sick, but just the sight of it disgusted her now. She damned well thought she might be getting an ulcer from all this. It definitely wasn't the flu she had, it had been going on too long, and she didn't have any other symptoms.

She took several deep breaths, swallowed then looked back at Dean. "You need to get up, get cleaned up and—" The rich buttery smell punched her in the stomach. Tina vaulted off of the bed and ran for the bathroom.

Dean heard Tina retching all the way down the hall. Worry shot through him as he shoved off the covers and walked toward the bathroom. He stopped beside her at the toilet to glare down at her. "What the hell is wrong with you?" Tina didn't look up at him, she just kept her head bowed and breathed. "This has been going on too long. You've been sick since we got married." Dean knew the stress they were both under was enough to make anyone sick, but this had to be something else. After his Daddy's close call with death last year, this scared him. It could be serious too. "We're going to the doctor *today* to find out what's wrong with you."

"I'll be fine," she assured him as she pushed up to stand.

"I know you will, because we're going to the doctor. I'll get Hope to watch for the kids when they get home. Get ready, we're going to the doctor." Dean walked down the hall to the bedroom, grabbed clean clothes and then went back to the bathroom. Tina still stood there. She had a strange look on her face, sort of shell-shocked. He didn't have time for her to dawdle. He wanted to know what the hell was wrong with her. "Now, Tina. Go get ready!" he said as he tried to squeeze between her and the door.

"I think I know what's wrong," she said in a trembling voice.

Dean stepped back outside to grab her shoulders. "What's wrong then?" he asked gruffly. Tina didn't respond, and she wouldn't look at him, so Dean tipped her chin up to him. "Tell me dammit!" Her eyes teared up, his heart shot up to his throat. "Fucking tell me, Tina, or we are going to the doctor right now," he growled.

"I'm pregnant," Tina said softly.

Shock rocked Dean, her words hung in the air, then echoed through his skull, before they registered on his brain. His chest tightened, his hand fell to his side and he staggered back from her. He shook his head in denial. "You can't be pregnant. How could you be pregnant?" he asked when he could breathe again.

Her eyebrows raised, and she crossed her arms over her chest, as if to say if you don't know I'm not telling you buddy.

"We used condoms." Every fucking time they had sex. Even though Dean wanted nothing more than to go bareback and feel her heat directly, he didn't want another kid. He had enough problems now. They both did.

He pushed past her into the bathroom, fumbled through the bottom drawer where he'd stashed what was left in the box he'd brought in from the truck. He found them and held them out to her. "I used almost this whole box." His hand shook as he pulled the single pack left in the box of thirty-six out and tossed it down onto the counter. "Explain to me how the hell you're pregnant!" A thought occurred to him, and a sense of déjà vu caused the hair on the back of his neck to stand on end. "Were you pregnant when I married you? When we had sex the first time? Were you trying to trap me like my ex-wife did?"

Tina's mouth dropped open, her arms fell to her sides, and her body practically vibrated. "Yeah, you're such a fucking prize as a husband, I decided I've got to have him," she said snidely then a nasty smile eased up the corners of her mouth. "You need to wake up asshole, before you run off everyone in your life who loves you. You just lost another one."

Dean watched her stomp down the hall. She stopped at the end and turned back to throw up her middle finger, before she walked around the corner. Dean picked up the condom box off of the counter, and held it close to his face to read the fine print there.

Ninety-eight percent effective. Two fucking percent didn't convince him she was pregnant with his kid. He kept reading and nothing else there did either. His eyes dropped to a narrow white box on the bottom right of the package. The print was a different font, and lighter than the rest so he held the box closer to the light until he saw it was a date.

A fucking expiration date. Two years past the current date. Dean sat down on the floor in the bathroom and crushed the box in his hand.

Tina couldn't hold back the angry tears that poured down her face as she walked across the yard to the bunkhouse. Her new home for now, because she could not live with Dean Dixon one more minute. And she couldn't leave him until Laney finished the school year. She was trapped at this ranch with him for now, but she didn't have to live with him. Or see him. Or care about him.

The tears came harder, as Tina just opened the door and walked in. Hope came out of the hallway looking sleepy. She must've been taking a nap, Tina figured, as she walked over to plop down on the sofa and hug herself.

"Hey," Hope said with a yawn as she rounded the sofa. She stopped and studied Tina. "What's wrong?" she asked as she sat beside Tina to put an arm around her shoulders.

Tina sucked in a shuddering breath and hugged herself tighter. "Later," she said and her throat felt raw. "Can I stay over here?"

"Of course you can. Did Dean pull something?" Hope asked with fire in her voice.

"I'm done," was all Tina could push past the knot of emotion in her throat.

"You want a drink?" Hope asked.

Tina shook her head, then her lips trembled as she said, "Oreos."

Hope nodded, got up off of the sofa and walked to the kitchen. God bless her soul, when Hope came back she had a huge glass of milk, a bag of Oreos, and various other junk food. She spread the bags out on the coffee table, and Tina grabbed the cookie bag and ripped it open.
Like a crack addict looking for a fix, she pulled a cookie out with trembling hands, then dunked it into the milk. The black cookie swirl on top of the milk made her smile. Drinking the milk after she'd eaten her fill of cookies was her favorite part.

Tina wasn't sure there were enough Oreos in Texas to take away the pain in her chest this time though. But dying of a cookie coma sure beat dying of a broken heart.

And that's how she felt. Like she was bleeding to death on the inside.

Hope picked up a cookie out of the bag, dunked it then shoved it into her mouth. Tina looked at her. They both smiled black cookie smiles. Tina ate her tenth cookie then grabbed the glass and downed the milk. She sat back against the sofa with a sigh, surveying the selection on the table.

Hope brushed the crumbs off of her hands and sat back too. Lacing her fingers together over her rounded belly, she said, "I'm pregnant so I have an excuse, but before we proceed with your pity pigfest tell me what the party is about."

"I have an excuse too," Tina said, sitting up to grab the bag of cherry gummy worms from under the bag of chips. More sweets first, then salt, she decided ripping the bag open.

Hope looked confused for a moment, then she gasped. She shot to her feet and squealed as she jumped up and down clapping her hands. She threw her arms wide, and Tina guessed her friend expected her to stand and get excited with her. Tina shoved two gummy worms into her mouth instead. Hope's face fell, as she sat on the edge of the sofa. "What's wrong?"

"I don't want to talk about it right now," Tina said around the wad of rubbery cherry deliciousness in her mouth. "Let's watch a movie."

"What's your flavor?" Hope asked getting up to walk to the television cabinet.

"Something funny." God knew she didn't want to cry anymore. She was done with that. Tina was going to stay here with Hope and Cord until Laney got out of school, but she wasn't going to just sit here. She was going to come up with a plan for the rest of her life that included her baby, but did not include

Dean Dixon. Apply for jobs and get something lined up, get the paperwork drawn up for a divorce. The last day of school would be the last day of her ill-fated marriage to him.

He better hope he had his ducks in a row where Jeremy was concerned by then. Tina had an idea on how he could fix that situation, planned on telling him about it, but after what he'd just said to her, she just didn't give a damn. She would pass her idea on to Cord, have him pass it on to his brother if he wanted to, but she was not getting involved.

From here on out, Dean Dixon was on his own.

Tina and Hope were curled up on the sofa laughing when Cord walked through the door of the bunkhouse. It was a little dim, because they had the lights off to watch the movie, but Tina saw the surprise on his face at seeing her there.

Hope shot to her feet. "Hey, honey," she said with a smile as she walked over to give him a long kiss. Tina dragged her eyes back to the movie, and opened the bag of pretzels. She shoved a couple in her mouth and chewed until they were dry dust in her mouth. She reached for the glass of milk and took a big swallow, but quickly found a new rule to add to her list of pigfest rules. Oreo milk did not mix well with pretzels.

Tina slammed down the glass and ran for the bathroom down the hall. When she finished tossing her cookies, she splashed her face, wondering when this would end. She remembered her sister was sick for the whole first three months she was pregnant. Tina figured she was probably a month or so along, so she had a long way to go.

Maybe she should lay off the junk food until then, she thought, as she weakly staggered back down the hall. When she made it to the living room she wanted to hurl again, but turned and headed back to the bathroom instead when she found Dean there talking to his brother. She heard him call her name, but Tina shut the bathroom door and locked it. He pounded, and she sat on the side of the tub and waited.

"Tina, open the damned door!" he shouted, and she crossed her arms over her chest. Everyone thought he was stubborn? They had never seen stubborn. He pounded and shouted until she heard the hoarseness in his voice. Finally, she heard his boot heels as he walked back to the living room. He was sorry? He was going to be sorrier very soon.

Dean would soon find out that sorry didn't fix some things. Tina's heart, what was left of it, shattered in a million more pieces. Like calling his wife who had done nothing but try to help him and his son a faithless whore like his ex-wife. Tears pushed up her throat again, but she refused to shed them. She held on until she thought Dean had left the bunkhouse, then opened the door and walked to the living room. Cord and Hope were sitting on the couch talking. She made sure Dean was nowhere in the bunkhouse, then joined them.

"Hey," she said forcing herself to smile.

Cord's sympathetic eyes met hers. "I'm sorry, Tina. My brother is an ass."

"That's not a news flash, Cord," Tina said as she sat down and curled her feet under her.

"No, but you being pregnant is," Cord said lightly then laughed. "I'm sure that shocked the crap out of him."

There it was. The first excuse from his family. That's why Dean acted the way he did toward everyone in his life. Because he could. "Don't make excuses for him, Cord. There's no excuse," Tina said, as she reached for the bag of chips, but changed her mind. She sat back to hug herself. Evidently Dean had filled them in on what happened.

"The condoms were expired," Cord said. Another excuse.

Tina shrugged. "Doesn't matter now. That's something he should have looked at before he said what he did to me. Once words like that are out, there's no taking them back."

"I agree, but—" Hope grabbed Cord's thigh, and he shut up.

"Just leave it, Cord," Hope said, and Tina sent her thanks with her eyes.

"I do have something you may want to tell him though," Tina said shortly.

She might as well get this over with so Dean

could get the ball rolling on fixing his situation before she left. "Tell Dean that his ex-wife has never really been a mother. Perhaps if she had a few visitations with Jeremy, she would change her mind about wanting to be one now. I hear children are very restrictive on a girl's social life."

That's what her sister said at any rate. When she whined about not being able to go out when Laney was a baby, Tina had offered to babysit because she loved Laney, and the kid wasn't any trouble at all. Those instances got more and more frequent, until she wound up being the child's mother. Tina realized now that just like Dean's family enabled him to be self-absorbed and treat them poorly by making excuses for him, she allowed her sister to be neglectful of her daughter by taking on the sole responsibility of caring for Laney.

What happened was her fault, but her sister had taken advantage of her too. Because Tina let her. Tina hoped that the detective the attorney hired would find Lori. She wanted to be able to tell her sister that. And give her the option of straightening up, being responsible for the child she had brought into the world, before she sought permanent custody of Laney.

It was the right thing to do.

Cord's face lit up, then his smile widened. "You're a smart woman, Tina Dixon."

Smart enough to know she didn't want to be Tina Dixon anymore.

Just Shoot Me

***

"Dean I need to talk to you." Cord walked up to Dean where he was loading hay bales in the back of his truck to carry out to the field for the broncos. He swiped the sweat from his face with his sleeve, and pulled off his gloves.

"Did you talk to Tina?" he asked the same question he'd asked his brother for a week.

"I'm talking to her tonight. Mama talked to her yesterday."

"She get anywhere?" Dean asked quickly. His brother's sympathetic eyes answered the question. Dean turned away to heft another hay bale. "I wish she'd talk to me," he grumbled as he swung it up and over the side of the truck. Damn, he forgot his gloves, and the wire cut his fingers. No more than he deserved.

"I wouldn't be surprised if she never talked to you again, Dean. If I said something like that to Hope, I'd probably be divorced before I could blink. We're trying for you, but don't expect too much. She's pretty set on moving back to Dallas once school is out."

Anger shot through Dean and he spun toward Cord and grabbed his collar. "She is not leaving." If he had to tie her up to keep her here, that's what he would do. Dean was getting just that desperate. She couldn't leave him. His heart took a dive in his chest and he rubbed it.

Dean bent to lift another hay bale, not even worrying about the sting of the wire on his hands. Maybe that would take away the incredible pain that had been in his chest since Tina had moved into the bunkhouse.

"She had an idea I think you should try," Cord said leaning against the truck.

Dean stood back up. He'd try anything Tina asked him to try to fix things between them. Whatever it took to do that. "What?"

"She suggested that you give Cindy a taste of what she's asking the court for. Call your attorney and suggest he get the judge to have Cindy be required to have mandatory weekend visitations with Jeremy. If he has to go live with her anyway, it couldn't hurt. He doesn't even know her. Might be a wakeup call for her and Daddy Bobby."

Dean thought about that for a second, and his spirits lifted a fraction of an inch. The more he thought about it, the better he liked it. "That sure would keep her out of the Cowboy, wouldn't it?"

"Why, yes it would."

"And I'm sure if I told Jeremy he could do any damned thing he pleases when he goes there to visit, as long as it isn't dangerous, he could come up with some pretty inventive things to do," Dean said with a laugh. Fully on board with the idea now, Dean added, "Hell, I might even buy him those markers and finger paints he wanted the last time we were in town." He couldn't help the grin that was plastered over his face. His wife was fucking brilliant.

"And horns and whistles," Cord added with a laugh.

"I want to be a fly on the wall. Maybe we could buy Jeremy one of those helmet cams, so he could record her face for us. Damn, I'd pay to see it," Dean said with excitement.

"What are you waiting for? Call your attorney and let's go to town."

On Friday night, Dean was nervous to let Jeremy go anywhere with Cindy, but he knew it was for a good cause. His attorney had thought the idea was a stroke of genius and the judge was more than happy to hear 'the parents' were working things out between them. Cindy's attorney waffled, because it was weekend visitation, but he couldn't convince the judge to schedule it at another time because she didn't have a damned excuse for not taking him for the weekend.

Cindy didn't work, never had. She had always lived off of the man she married. And that lucky bastard was Bobby Jones not him, thank God.

"Let's wait out on the porch for your mother, Jeremy." Dean couldn't make himself call her his son's Mama, because that would mean she actually was a mother. And Cindy Dixon Jones definitely was not.

"Daddy, do I call her Mama?" Jeremy asked as he sat in one of the rockers on the porch.

"You play that by ear, son. You call her whatever the heck you feel like calling her. Cindy is her name," Dean said gleefully as he sat down in the rocker beside him. She was raised in south Texas. The south. If Jeremy called her Cindy, she would shit a brick. But it was a helluva lot better than the other names he'd like to suggest his son to call her.

"Did you pack your finger paints and markers?" Dean asked.

"Yes sir, and my new whistles and horns!" Jeremy squealed. "Thank you for getting those for me. I love them. Laney does too. We play train."

"That sounds like fun."

"Maybe Ma-um, Cindy will play train with me," he said, looking at Dean uncertainly. Damn, he hated confusing his son. *This is going to help him though,* Dean reminded himself.

"Well if she doesn't, you can play by yourself."

"I'mma miss Laney," Jeremy said sadly. "Why can't she come with me?"

"Because Cindy isn't her mother," Dean explained patiently.

Cindy wasn't anyone's mother. Jeremy didn't understand that, because Dean's attorney had warned him about bad-mouthing Cindy to Jeremy. Dean knew he didn't have to say a word anyway. His son would understand it all on his own very shortly. And that was too damned bad, but Dean didn't have a choice here. If he did, his son would never be exposed to Cindy. If he didn't do this, Jeremy would probably end up living with her once the DNA results on Bobby came back.

"I wish Laney could come anyway," Jeremy persisted, but headlights at the end of the driveway told Dean the show had begun. He stood and handed Jeremy his backpack. "You'll have fun. Just play with your toys," Dean said, shoving him toward the steps.

And give that bitch hell, he added mentally.

On Sunday morning, bright and early, Dean was jarred awake by his cell phone ringing on the night stand. He patted around on the table until he found it, then answered. "Yeah?"

"Dean this is Cindy," she said angrily.

"Something wrong?" he asked innocently. He glanced at the alarm clock and saw it was just now six-thirty. Something had definitely happened.

"What the hell *hasn't* happened is a better question! I'm bringing Jeremy home on the way to the emergency room."

Dean sat up, and fear shot adrenaline through him. "Emergency room?"

"For *me*, not him!" she spat. "I slipped on his fucking marble, and I think I broke my ankle. Bobby is bringing me to the E.R. But we're bringing *him* home first!"

"Oh, I'm sorry you got hurt, darling,'" he drawled smoothly. "Hope everything is okay."

"It will be as soon as I bring him home," she grated through her teeth. "We'll be there shortly." As

Cindy was hanging up the phone, Dean heard her yell. *Jeremy get in the car! Now!*

Dean laid back in the bed and laugher rumbled in his chest, then spread to his stomach. Before long, he was on his side holding his stomach while he howled with laughter. Dean laughed so loudly that his mother came through his bedroom door in her pink chenille housecoat and fuzzy slippers, looking frantic.

"Dean, what happened? Is Jeremy okay?"

"He's fine," Dean said then laughed a little more. He was breathless when he said, "But Cindy's not. It worked, Mama!"

Barb Dixon grinned and put her hand on her hip. "That's my boy. Just as bad as his Daddy. I knew he could do it."

Dean sobered then. "He is just like me isn't he?"

"Worse. That nut didn't fall far from the tree for sure."

It was true. And damn he was proud of that boy. He just hoped that enough damage had been done that Cindy decided to drop the custody suit. That would be a huge relief, and he would owe Tina a huge debt. Not that he didn't already.

"Thank you for helping, Mama," Dean said, looking at her. She had talked to Tina twice, and even though it hadn't helped, at least she had tried. Dean wasn't giving up. He was going to keep fighting until she listened to him. He loved her, and she was going to listen to him. He only hoped she heard him, and believed what he said.

"I would do anything for my family, son. You know that."

And Dean would do anything to keep his family together. Anything.

The next day Dean got the call from his attorney around noon. He was out in the pasture, helping Cord move the bulls. Their lowing was so loud, Dean had to trot over to the tree line to hear the man. Dean's heart was beating a mile a minute, when he asked, "What happened?"

"Her attorney called. Cindy called him first thing this morning to tell him about what happened and her broken ankle. She and Bobby both agree that they want to drop the custody suit. She wants to give you full custody. No visitation even. Damn, you're good, boy. Better than me, even."

"No, Jeremy and Tina are good," Dean said as happiness like he hadn't felt in three years surged through him. He hung up the phone with the attorney he would no longer need and let out a loud whoop that echoed across the pasture.

The bulls split up, his father and brother cursed. Dean threw his head back and laughed.

It was a good day. The only thing that would make it better would be if his wife would talk to him. One problem at a time, he thought happily, as he kicked Blaze to go help the round up the cattle.

CHAPTER SEVENTEEN

One more month, Tina thought as she watched Laney catch the bus with Jeremy at the road through the window at the bunkhouse, then grabbed her purse and briefcase off the table by the door. "Hope, I'm leaving," she yelled and smoothed her hair. "Wish me luck!" Her hand shook as she twisted the doorknob, and excitement danced in her stomach.

"Good luck!" Hope yelled back from the bedroom.

She had her interview with Laramie Jeans today. Through the grapevine at his attorney's office, Cord had found out that Tonya Laramie had been fired by her father, so the position was open. Tina had the experience to get it, and she had a feeling she would.

She swung the door open, a cool gust of spring wind carried in delicious cologne mixed with pure Dean. He stepped around from the side of the door to block her exit. Damn, she had been able to dodge him for two weeks, but it looked like her luck had just run out. That didn't mean she was going to deal with this right now.

In her heels, Tina was tall enough to push his shoulder so she did, and tried to walk by him, but he grabbed her arm. "Let go of my arm," she grated.

"Don't leave," he said and his voice wobbled. "I'm sorry, buttercup, so damned sorry."

"I don't have time for this now, Dean," Tina

replied, hardening her heart.

"Where are you going?" he asked sharply.

"Dallas. I have an appointment." With Laramie, then with my attorney to file for divorce.

"Let me drive you," he said. "I don't want you…um, that's a long drive alone."

"No thank you. Now, let my arm go. You're going to make me late." And Tina definitely didn't want to be late.

"Jeremy is staying with Mama tonight. Have dinner with me so we can talk…please."

"No, thank you. I have Laney, and we really don't have anything to discuss. Now let me go," she said with a jerk of her arm. He turned her loose, but he didn't let her pass.

His stormy blue eyes held hers. "I will *never* let you go," Dean said through his teeth. "You want me to chase you? I love you, and that's not going to change. So I'll chase you as far as I have to, as long as I need to."

He loved her? *Too little, too late, cowboy.* A few weeks ago, those words would have meant everything to her. Now? They meant less than nothing. "Dean, I have to go. Please move." Tina pushed his shoulder again, but he didn't move.

His eyes fell to her hand. "Where's your ring?" he asked with anger in his voice.

Tina ran her thumb over her naked ring finger and guilt shot through her, even though she shouldn't feel a damned ounce of it. "I took it off."

She wasn't going to lie to him, and she wasn't going into this interview and have to explain her personal life when she suddenly became unmarried in a few months. Dean looked up at the ceiling of the porch, and his nostrils flared as he sucked in a deep breath. He finally looked back at her, and his eyes were so filled with emotion she thought he might cry. It would serve him right if he did, he'd done enough making her cry to last a lifetime.

His voice was raw and unsteady when he said, "I'm not letting you divorce me. That baby you're carrying is mine. You're mine."

"I'm not a possession for you to use and abuse, Dean. And I certainly don't want to *trap* you into anything. This baby is mine. You don't have to worry, you're off the hook this time. I don't need or want your help," Tina said snidely.

Dean looked down at the toes of his boots, reminding her so much of Jeremy her heart hurt. She was losing her son too when she left, but she had to leave. Tina took the opportunity to edge past him and head for her car.

He followed her, and she huffed out a frustrated breath when he wouldn't let her open the car door. "I'm sorry, Tina. I love you, and I want our baby. I want you."

"The damage is done, Dean. Sorries won't fix it. Nothing will," she said with emotion choking her.

"Now move, so I can go."

Why was Tina disappointed when he stepped back and opened the door for her? She looked at him for a second, before she slid into the driver's seat and pulled the door shut. Dean headed toward the barn with his head hung low, and Tina cranked the car, but she didn't pull out of the driveway until he walked inside. Her heart was heavy in her chest, but she put the car in reverse, backed up then turned and shot forward down the driveway.

"She's going," Dean said sadly as he met his brother in the office in the barn. He sat in the chair beside the desk, and pulled his hat off to toss it on the desk. He ran his hand over his face. "What the fuck am I going to do?" he asked, as if his brother had the answer to that question.

Dean had fucked up the best thing that had ever happened to him in his sorry ass life.

Sorries won't fix it. Nothing will.

Emotion shot up to his throat and it was all Dean could do to hold it back. He was going to lose her, lose his baby. Over the last two weeks, Dean had tried flowers, apologies, even a new engagement ring to go with her wedding band. All of it had been sent back to the house via Cord or Hope. He was running out of time and ideas.

"I'll have the money soon, if you want to buy her and the baby a house in Dallas. There should be plenty left after we pay off the settlement Hope made with Bridezilla."

As usual his brother had found the pot of gold at the end of the rainbow. Laramie was settling the lawsuit before their name got dragged through mud so deep they'd never see the light of day again. "She has a home here with me," Dean replied.

Cord sucked in a breath. "But she doesn't want it, Dean. The best you're going to be able to do, man, is take care of her and the baby."

"The best isn't good enough then."

"You can't make her stay here. Hope has talked to her, I've talked to her. Hell, Mama has talked to her twice. She's dead set on getting that job and moving back to Dallas when school is out. I'm so damned sorry."

You can't make her stay here.

Dean would just see about that, he thought, as he pushed up to his feet. There had to be a way to get her to listen to him. To forgive him. He decided he needed to take a trip out to the lake and think. "I'm out of here today. You're on your own."

"Take as much time as you need," Cord said as he walked out of the office.

Tina was worn out by the time she pulled into the driveway at the ranch. Today had been one of the most trying days of her life. Not only had the interview gone on way too long, because the HR woman was chatty, she had to interview with three other people up the food chain after that, all the way up to the owner, Cecil Laramie.

They said they wanted to make sure they practiced *due diligence* when hiring the next director of marketing for the company. Tina didn't let them know that she knew what that meant. What they were really doing was making sure they didn't hire someone like Cecil Laramie's daughter again, who had abused her position every chance she got. Like she had done with Cord. That had cost them a lot of money and credibility.

They had nothing to worry about there with her. Tina was probably off men for good now. Or at least for a very long time. She was going to have bigger things to worry about from here on out. They didn't offer her the job, but they'd come damned close.

She was asked about her salary requirements and availability. Cecil Laramie didn't even blink when she threw out a number twice the salary she made at Texas Tomboy. He also didn't have a problem waiting until the end of school, if they decided to hire her. Supposedly they were going to let her know by the end of next week. Tina knew in her heart she would be offered the job. She aced the interview.

But she had to cancel her appointment with the attorney. It was a little disappointing since she'd worked up a head of steam to do it, but she was kind of glad she had more time to think about it. She didn't want to let Dean's words this morning affect her decision, but they did. The sincerity she heard there, the abject misery in his voice, made her think maybe he had seen just how horrible what he'd done to her had been. Maybe he truly was sorry.

That didn't mean she'd forgive him. But she was thinking about at least letting him talk to her at some point in the next month. Before she made another appointment to file for divorce.

It was dark, so Tina pulled up under the light at the side of the front porch of the bunkhouse and shut off her car. She grabbed her purse and briefcase, then opened her door to swing her legs out of the car. When she stood a dark figure dashed from the darkened side of the bunkhouse. She dropped her purse and briefcase, preparing to run, but before she could a sack was thrown over her head and a rope was looped around her arms at the elbow.

Tina sucked in a deep breath, but before she could scream a hand clamped down over her mouth. She kicked out, and her high heel connected with something solid. She heard a grunt, but then she was swept off of her feet and carried. She squirmed and fought as much as she could, but stopped when a firm hand smacked her ass.

Hard enough to bring tears to her eyes.

Her breath came in short gasps, and her fear threatened to stop her heart. It was also damned hot inside the sack. Suddenly, she was tossed onto a seat of some kind. She felt around, and tried to push up, but a seat belt was looped around her, and she heard it click. Tina couldn't move now at all.

Good god, they were out in the country. Not in the city. What the hell was going on here? Surely some mountain man or hillbilly wasn't taking her up to his cabin to keep her as his forced bride. Did that happen in Texas? She'd heard about it in Kentucky or West Virginia. She supposed the same thing could happen here, and became even more afraid.

A powerful engine cranked, and she was jostled as the truck moved forward. Tina got her senses back and screamed as loud as she could. If this was a kidnapping, someone was going to know she was being kidnapped. Maybe Dean would hear her. God, please let him hear me, she prayed as she continued to scream until she was hoarse. A rush of wind blew in from the window beside her, and took her breath away. Tina sat there breathing, praying and hoping she would have a chance to get away from this madman.

Bide her time. That's what she needed to do. Wait for an opportunity, she thought, as she stayed still and quiet, while they drove over very bumpy ground for what seemed like forever. Suddenly the bumping stopped, and the truck engine was cut. A door opened and Tina's heart raced, wondering what her captor was going to do to her.

Who the hell was going to take care of Laney now, she thought and tears rushed to her eyes. What about her baby? More tears came, and rushed down her cheeks to slide down the V neck of her suit, before trickling between her breasts. The back door opened, and she couldn't be quiet any longer, "Please don't hurt me," she begged then sucked a gulping breath. "I'm pregnant and have a daughter and son who need me."

Someone leaned over her to unclick the seatbelt, then leaned close to her ear. "I need you too," a raspy, sexy voice said, before she was gently picked up off of the seat and heard the door shut. Tina sniffed again and caught a faint woodsy scent. It wasn't the natural woods. That was Dean's cologne, and Dean's voice! Dean had kidnapped her!

Tina struggled trying to break free, and his arms clamped around her tighter. "Be still," he said gruffly. Tina wasn't going to be still. Her own husband was kidnapping her!

"Dean put me down!" she said, fighting against his hold. His hand landed on her ass and she squealed, then a thrill raced up through her body.

What the hell was that about?

Dean walked a little further with her, then set her down on her feet. Tina was about to try to plant her heel in his shin again, but he stepped on her toe with his boot. "Kick me and I'll spank you good," he threatened.

A tremble worked through her, and moisture pooled between her legs. Dammit! This was scary, not exciting. Suddenly she felt herself flying again, then she was across his shoulder.

"Don't you dare move," he warned and she was jostled as he held her across his shoulder with one hand. Where the hell was he taking her?

Suddenly, she was set down on something soft. Tina scooted away, but Dean's hands followed her. She felt him yank the sack, and he pulled it over her head. He didn't untie her arms though. "Untie me!" Tina demanded shooting daggers at him with her eyes.

She had no idea if he could see her or not, because it was pitch black wherever they were.

"Dean, have you lost your mind?" she asked breathlessly. Sane men didn't do what this man was doing. Desperate men did though. A little fear snaked down her spine, but then she reminded herself that Dean had never hurt her. Not even close. But he might have snapped. She might have snapped him this morning. "We can get you some help, honey," she said smoothly, trying damned hard not to let him know she was afraid.

"The only help I need is right here in this deer stand with me. And yeah, I'm crazy…about you. But you won't listen to me."

So that's where he had taken her, the deer stand where they made love. Her heart kicked in her chest and Tina had a hard time hanging on to her anger.

"Just take me back to the bunkhouse, I'll listen. I promise." She had decided to do that anyway, just not this soon.

"You'll listen right here," he shot back, and she heard him sit down. There was rustling, he struck a match and suddenly the deer stand was filled with light. He put the cover back on the oil lantern then sat it to the side.

Tina's eyes moved around the deer stand and she was shocked speechless. Dean had little hearts made out of red construction paper taped to the walls. In each heart was a name. Hope, Cord, Barb, Silas, Jeremy and Laney. There was even one with a question mark, which she figured was for the baby.

"Where's my heart and your heart?" Tina asked meeting his eyes.

"Mine is right here," he said and put his hand to the center of her chest. Her heart did a dull thud in her chest then melted and dripped down her insides. "And I hope yours is here." Dean put his fist to his chest. "My whole family is head over heels in love with you. But none of them—nobody in the world—could *ever* love you more than I do."

"Dean—" she said, and he put his finger over her lips.

"Listen, buttercup, please." Tina nodded.

"I feel like a first class ass because of what I said to you. I deserve every moment of the misery I've been through for the last two weeks, every damn minute and then some. And I've got to tell you I've been one miserable son-of-a-bitch. I was wrong. No excuses. If you promise not to leave me, I'll spend every minute I have left on earth trying to make it up to you, baby. If you'll spend those minutes with me. Loving me, even though I'll never deserve it."

Dean Dixon was not romantic. But that was just about the most romantic thing any man had ever said to her. To hear him lay himself bare like that told her he really was sorry.

Stunned, Tina just sat there staring at him. She shook her head to make sure she was awake even. "Okay. Who are you and what the hell have you done with my husband?" she asked more than half-serious. "I'll pay whatever you want, because I love his grumpy ass."

"Oh he's around here somewhere, I promise," Dean growled and grabbed her shoulders to pull her onto his lap. "You haven't seen the last of him. But if he shows up, be sure to kick his ass okay?"

"You got it. Now untie me," she said looking into his eyes.

"Not yet." he replied with a secretive smile. "I have other plans I was going to use tonight to convince you. More for tomorrow if you still weren't convinced. I made plans to stay up here as long as it took to convince you to stay. Cord and Mama are on standby to deliver food when necessary."

Tina wanted to hear more about these plans of his. "Hmm…sounds like you were prepared. These plans sound interesting," she said smiling up at her handsome husband. "You could always tell them I resisted so we could stay up here longer."

"Baby, I love the way you think," Dean said as he lowered his mouth to hers.

EPILOGUE

It was dark as Tina pulled up under the light at the side of the front porch near the bunkhouse, and shut off her car. She stopped a moment, fiddled with her hair in the rearview mirror, and Dean watched from the side of the bunkhouse. He held his breath and curled his fingers into the rough burlap feed sack, as she opened the door and swung her legs outside the car. His heart rate kicked up a few notches as excitement filled him at the prospect of what he was about to do to her. What the mother of his brand new baby girl wanted him to do. A repeat of the night he kidnapped her to celebrate their first anniversary.

When she suggested it, Dean had gotten hard as a rock as memories of that desperate night and how it ended came back to him. Hell yeah, he'd do it again. And again. And again. And twice more in the morning, before they came back to the ranch house. If she was good, even if she was bad, he might tie Tina up and keep her up in that deer stand for a week.

Maybe for the rest of their lives.

Earlier today, his mother had made banana pudding, and it was damned good. He had some of that for later. His damn dick got harder and he adjusted himself to focus on timing his run toward her just right. She stepped into the light and he saw her ear-to-ear grin as she discreetly glanced at the dark side of the bunkhouse.

Dean's muscles bunched and he shot out across the yard toward her. Her gasp was comical as she turned and dropped her briefcase and purse then pretended to run. Dean jerked her back and yanked the sack down over her head, then wound the rope around her elbows. He felt her whole body quake, and a shiver of excitement passed through him too. He felt her chest expand, and he knew she was going to scream. He clamped his hand down over her mouth and grunted as he bent to sweep her up into this arms.

She squirmed and fought but not with much vigor. He smacked her ass pretty damned hard, she shivered in his arms and he smiled. Her breath came in short gasps, and Dean knew she was excited, his own heart was pounding in his ears as he opened the back door of the truck to deposit her on the seat. He leaned across her and snapped the seat belt in place. He wasn't about to let her get hurt, while they bounced over the uneven ground in the pasture.

He got into the front seat and cranked the truck, then drove across the field toward the lake. Tina must be playing this for all it was worth, he thought, as she let out the same blood-curdling scream she had that night. It was shrill, brain-piercing and Dean flinched. He let it go on and on so she could play her part, then he rolled down the window to let in the cool night air, and temper the volume of her scream.

Her voice was nearly hoarse when she finally stopped screaming, and Dean let out a sigh. Damned that woman had some determination. Enough to turn him, the man she called Mr. Cranky Pants, into a good husband and father. One who would do anything to keep her and their family safe. Tina, Jeremy and their new baby girl, Deanna, were his whole life. He didn't have a life before the pint-size woman came along. Dean, just hadn't known it at the time.

Tina Dixon saved him, and his son. If not for her, he would have lost Jeremy, and himself. And he wouldn't have Deanna, who, next to her mama, was the most beautiful woman in the world. Both of the women in his life looked at him like the sun and moon rose and set in his eyes. He would do everything in his power to make sure they always thought that.

He hoped his mother did okay tonight with Jeremy, Deanna and Laney. They were a handful, but she loved being their grandmother. And Jeremy would help her, he was sure. His son loved his baby sisters, and they loved him. Thank god, Tina's sister had the good sense to do what was right for her daughter by signing over custody to them when the detective finally found her. Tina was proud of her for doing that, Dean was just relieved. If they never saw that woman again, if his daughter Laney never saw her again, it would be too soon.

Tears came to his eyes, and he rolled them, then reminded himself it was over. His life was finally back on the right track again. And he had a mission to accomplish tonight. Dean stopped the truck outside the tree line, got out and opened the back door.

"Please don't hurt me," his wife begged then sucked a gulping breath. "I have two daughters, a son and a husband who love me."

Tina Dixon had no idea how much he loved her. How much he would always love her. But he was about to show her. Dean leaned over her, to unclick the seatbelt, then leaned close to her ear. "I love you too," he whispered roughly, as he slid his arms under her and picked her up.

He held her close, as he kneed the truck door shut. Tina playfully struggled trying to break free, and he clamped his arm around her tighter. "Be still," he said gruffly.

"Dean put me down!" she said, fighting against his hold. He knew what his kinky wife wanted, and was more than happy to give it to her. His hand arced, he brought it down on her firm round ass. She squealed and shivered again, and Dean smiled as he walked with her into the woods. At the steps to the tree stand, he sat her down on her feet. Her muscles bunched, and he figured out she was going to play this little charade to the hilt. He on her toe with his boot and growled, "Run and I'll spank you good."

Her little whimper sparked every nerve in his body. Dean bent and eased her over his shoulder, then grabbed the first rung on the ladder. She wiggled again, and he warned, "Don't you dare move." Getting up this ladder with her over his shoulder wasn't safe. That night a year ago, he'd had desperation, anger and adrenaline working to help him with the monumental feat. He hadn't even thought about the danger involved. Tonight, he was thinking about it, and realized what a fool he'd been to even try it. But she wanted it, so he was going to do everything he could to give Tina Dixon everything she wanted for the rest of his life.

He made it to the top of the ladder then sat her inside on the soft sleeping bag he'd put up there earlier. She scooted away toward the wall of the stand, and he climbed inside, then shut the door. He reached across the stand and yanked the sack over her head, but he didn't untie her arms, just like he'd done that night a year ago.

"Untie me!" Tina demanded, shooting playful daggers at him with her eyes. Her gorgeous blue eyes glittered in the moonlight shining through the opened flap of the stand. He crouched and scooted over to knock the prop out. The board flapped shut.

"Dean, have you lost your mind?" she asked breathlessly.

"The only help I need is right here in this deer stand with me. And yeah, I'm crazy, buttercup. Crazy about you. But you are one very bad girl lately, you just don't listen to me anymore."

"Just take me back to the bunkhouse, I'll listen. I promise."

"You'll listen right here," he shot back, as he

struck a match and lit the oil lantern he left up here since that night a year ago. He had brought his wife up here several times since then, until she got too pregnant and it wasn't safe.

Tina's eyes moved around the deer stand and she gave him a wobbly smile. He'd decorated the stand again, like he had before, but he added a heart for Deanna, his heart this time too.

"Where's my heart and your heart?" Tina asked meeting his eyes.

"Mine is right here," he said and put his hand to the center of her chest, and felt it kick against his hand like Deanna's foot had done in her stomach while she was pregnant. He swallowed hard and then added, "And I hope yours is here." Dean put his fist to his chest where his heart was beating like a drum. "My whole family is head over heels in love with you. But none of them—nobody in the world—could ever love you more than I do."

"Dean—" she said with a sigh, and he put his finger over her lips.

"Thank you for keeping faith in me, instead of just shooting me like I know you wanted to do many times." Tina nodded, and he continued, "If you promise not to never leave me, I'll spend every minute I have left on earth trying to make you happy, baby."

Tina just sat there staring at him. She shook her head, then smiled widely. "Okay. Who are you and what the hell have you done with my husband?" She laughed. "I'll pay whatever you want, because I love his grumpy ass." One side of her full mouth kicked up a little higher, then her face turned serious. "I'll always love you, Dean. I'm not going anywhere. You're stuck with me now, mister."

Mr. Cranky Pants. Dean still laughed at the nickname his spunky little wife had pinned on him. It fit how he used to be. Not so much now. He had too much to be happy about to be cranky anymore. "Oh, Mr. Cranky Pants is around here somewhere, I promise," Dean replied with a grin. "You haven't seen the last of him. But if he shows up, be sure to kick his ass okay?"

"You got it. Now untie me," she said looking into his eyes.

"Not yet. I have plans for you. More for tomorrow if you still aren't convinced that I love you. I have plans to stay up here as long as it takes to convince you. Cord and Mama are on standby to deliver food when necessary."

"Hmm…sounds like you are prepared," she said as a tremor shook her. One of her dark brows lifted, and she smiled. "You could always tell them I resisted so we could stay up here longer."

"Baby, I love the way you think," Dean said as he lowered his mouth to hers.

ABOUT THE AUTHOR

Becky McGraw is a married mother of three adult children, and a Southern girl by birth and the grace of God, ya'll. She resides in South Texas with her husband and dog Abby. A jack of many trades in her life, Becky has been an optician, a beautician, a legal secretary, a senior project manager for an aviation management consulting firm, which took her all over the United States, a real estate broker, and now a graphic artist, web designer and writer.

She knows just enough about a variety of topics to make her dangerous, and her romance novels interesting and varied. Being a graphic artist is a good thing for her, too, because she creates her own cover art, along with writing the novels.

Becky has been an avid reader of romance novels since she was a teenager, and has been known to read up to four novels of that genre a week, much to the dismay of her husband, and the delight of e-book sellers.

She has been writing fictional short stories and novels for fun, as well as technical copy for her jobs for many years. She was a member of the Writer's Guild on AOL during her last venture into writing romance, as well as a founding member and treasurer of the first online chapter of the Romance Writers of America, From the Heart Romance Writers. Currently, she is a member of both organizations.

You can contact Becky McGraw at
beckymcgrawbooks@gmail.com
Please 'Like' Becky on her Facebook fan page at www.facebook.com/beckymcgrawbooks and visit her website at www.beckymcgraw.com

Printed in Great Britain
by Amazon.co.uk, Ltd.,
Marston Gate.